JUSTIN FOWLES

A Novel by

James Jackson

Printed in Victoria, Canada

National Library of Canada Cataloguing in Publication Data

A cataloguing record for this book that includes the U.S. Library of Congress Classification number, the Library of Congress Call number and the Dewey Decimal cataloguing code is available from the National Library of Canada. The complete cataloguing record can be obtained from the National Library's online database at: www.nlc-bnc.ca/amicus/index-e.html

ISBN 1-4120-1454-9

TRAFFORD

This book was published on-demand in cooperation with Trafford Publishing.

On-demand publishing is a unique process and service of making a book available for retail sale to the public taking advantage of on-demand manufacturing and Internet marketing. On-demand publishing includes promotions, retail sales, manufacturing, order fulfilment, accounting and collecting royalties on behalf of the author.

Suite 6E, 2333 Government St., Victoria, B.C. V8T 4P4, CANADA
Phone 250-383-6864 Toll-free 1-888-232-4444 (Canada & US)
Fax 250-383-6804 E-mail sales@trafford.com
Web site www.trafford.com TRAFFORD PUBLISHING IS A DIVISION OF TRAFFORD HOLDINGS LTD.
Trafford Catalogue #03-1832 www.trafford.com/robots/03-1832.html
10 9 8 7 6 5 4 3 2

For Florence

1

Justin Fowles lay in the sun on the dry grass of the East Ridge. It was July, and the air was fresh from the ocean. In the distance seagulls shrieked. Three hundred feet below, a dinghy full of laughing children turned slow circles, its outboard a thin whine; it was from the smaller of two white yachts anchored down the inlet. The larger was a huge forty-five footer, *Liberty Belle,* flying the Stars and Stripes. Riordan Pollock said it had lain all yesterday off Ganges Beach, an unlikely anchorage for a luxury yacht, shoal-strewn and close off a deserted lee shore two miles west of the village. But it was—if one wanted to imagine conspiracies—the nearest sea approach to the Combat College, and invisible from the highway,

Justin lay on his belly behind a pine stump too small to justify his belief it concealed him. He hadn't examined the question of whether anyone would care to look. He suspected he was engaged in the ridiculous.

He moved his binoculars to view the village below, directly across the inlet. Through the summer foliage Justin could make out the top floor of Pollock's

Grocery, part of the flat black roof of the Starlight Coffee Shop, and the strident pink of his own Prospect Variety Store. At the turn of the century Prospect was a logging and then a mining centre, affording shelter for the ships linking the pioneer settlements along the south coast of Vancouver Island before the road came. All that stood now were seven aging stores and store-fronted houses, most built during a land-speculation fraud in the thirties, straggled along the broken asphalt of Kitchener Street.

But Justin's interest was not the village, and moving the binoculars he saw to the west and far beyond the forest that sheltered the village, the Stars and Stripes waving indolently above the Snuff Mercenary Combat College. Its camouflaged huts were barely distinguishable from the abandoned slash of the devastated mountainside, strewn with the dead ruin of the clearcut.

To the left of the village again, and the great shoulder of rock that thrust up from the inlet as high as the East Ridge on which he lay. The rock was patched with shrubs and bleached grass, with runs of evergreens up its declivities, and sparse groves of alders and maples in sheltered crevices. Beneath the afternoon sun, with the long inlet opening south toward the ocean, the clusters of pink-trunked arbutus trees suggested a heavy-leafed Mediterranean serenity.

Justin scanned the shoulder slowly, refocusing as the distance increased until, a good mile away, he saw a familiar configuration of tree-tops, a glimpse of Mogador the old Seymour bungalow, and yes, perhaps smoke rising as sly Mary Evens stoked her wood stove. Or perhaps not. Perhaps, and to be objective most certainly, no more than haze above the sun-warmed rock.

Justin rolled on his back and grimaced at the sky, uneasily aware of the absurdity of his actions. If he really meant to watch Mary Evens he should have continued on Fuck Trail, as the teenagers called it, along the ridge to the observation post overlooking the Strait of Juan de Fuca, built over a hundred years ago to watch for an invading Russian Fleet. He should have brought his spotting scope, packed a lunch, packed wine.

Today he'd acted on idiot impulse. He'd been idling down the highway when Mary had come absently to mind just before he saw the spray-painted hydro pole marking the turn off. He'd suddenly thought to catch her off guard, wrenched the truck across the shoulder throwing loose gravel and crashing through the bushes to find himself by pure luck on the track up to the ridge. With the impetuosity of a clumsy amateur. Justin Fowles, the too-perfect spy, certainly knew better.

But every newcomer to Prospect, and Mary Evens had arrived only three or four months ago, agitated him deeply. He had of course to act secretly, so that he would for instance enter Harold's Tonsure House or the Starlight Coffee Shop at their most crowded, enduring hours of fragmented gossip in the hopes of a brief mention of his suspect; or suffer the wandering monologues of Frank Mewhouse, the postmaster, while prying for a hint about the source or destination of a suspect's mail.

Justin's tensest moments, anticipated with thrilling dread, were those rare occasions when a suspect might come as a customer to his store. No one, he knew, would enter so uninviting a hovel unless duty compelled. The windows were scabbed with patches of peeling plastic, and anyone resolute enough to peer within would see the repulsive Scrofula, daughter of Idris, legendary cat-goddess of melancholy, exposing her sores to the filtered sun amidst the tortured shapes of undusted driftwood and Japanese glass fishing floats. If they ignored Scrofula they would be intimidated by forbidding walls of high-gloss mortuary grey, with rows of bleak shelves on which three or four tasteless pottery inventions squatted in smug isolation.

Justin lacked both retail skills and any desire to develop them. The legalistic terms of his banishment required him, as he recalled it, "to exhibit such vocational diligence as required to allay suspicion as to the source of his income". Bureaucracy gone bananas. He obeyed the letter but kept his commitment small. His window display was designed to discourage all but American tourists blind with lust for artifacts of the quaint local and actually non-existent culture, which Justin manufactured in his kitchen.

The anticipation of meeting one of his pursuers face-to-face recalled pursuits long past, so keenly indeed that he forgot he was now not the hunter but the prey. He prepared with professional thoroughness, buying a video camera in Victoria, rehearsing and revising a script of naive interrogation, testing the lighting, locating and relocating the camera. He went to Vancouver and bought an infra-red scope. After six months he realized that none of his suspects had entered the store. Justin's mind, accustomed to view the world through a prism of malice, refused to consider the possibility that no suspect existed.

But if his previous suspects were itinerants who drifted off before he could consider them seriously, he was sure Mary Evens was different. She had arrived unannounced, in a cab late at night, and had directed the driver unhesitatingly through the sleeping village to the vacant Seymour bungalow. The cab, its driver told Janice, the waitress at the Starlight, was so jammed with boxes he couldn't use his rear-view mirror.

Justin chuckled at such gauchely revealing behaviour. Someone who came at night to evade detection, on a mission urgent enough to justify cab-fare the eighty miles from Victoria, briefed well enough to find the long-abandoned Seymour place in the dark. She could have entered more discreetly with drums and bugles. He was sure that at long last the Ottawa brass had made their move, and he was on to them.

That afternoon he was picking up groceries at Pollock's when Riordan Pollock said, "You should've been here half an hour ago, Justin. You could've met our new neighbour up on the ridge. Knowing how curious you are about new faces in town."

"No more curious than anyone else," Justin said irritably, annoyed at the insinuation—of which Riordan wasn't the only source—that his serious purpose was less than secret. "So she's been down to the village already?"

"This once but not often, I reckon. She says it's too far and too steep, so she brought in two lists, one for Monday delivery and the other for Friday. She's a well-organized lady."

"Ha!" Justin said. "So she's thoroughly prepared to live like a hermit. She doesn't want to be observed. But she knew the way to the Seymour place in the dark of night! Did you know that?"

"Mighty suspicious," Riordan said sagely, but at that moment Maggie Sunflower his wife came by and said, "Justin don't let him tease you. The lady's name is Mary Evens and there's nothing suspicious about her. She knew the way to Mogador because she spent summers there. Years ago, when she was growing up. I don't remember her but she remembers playing with me and the other village kids. She was their niece and she's inherited the place. Mogador; that's what they used to call it, and—"

"But you say you don't remember her," Justin interrupted acutely.

"Well like I say it was a long time ago. But you better be careful Justin because she just bought a box of twelve-gauge shotgun shells."

Justin returned thoughtfully to his store. The report was plausible, although any agent would have a good cover. And it was demonically clever, to send an innocent-seeming little old lady to be respectably ensconced up in Mogador, the nearest thing locally for all its disrepair to a dynastic estate.

Much of his problem had been Annabel McKinley's impatience with his fears. For a long time—too long, he realized later— he'd been unable to tell her why they had him under surveillance, though Annabel was the only one in the village who knew anything of his secret past. She'd discovered it one morning early in their affair while rummaging naked in his closet for something to wear while she cooked breakfast, shrieking with delight at coming across the bespangled scarlet tunic of a commissioned officer of the RCMP. He felt a moment's terror of dreadful consequence, as if the tunic hid his lifetime sins now mercilessly to be exposed, which disappeared with her chuckling emergence from the closet, wrapped in the tunic which she threw open to exclaim, "How Canadian can you get, eh? A li'l beaver dressed like a Mountie? Justin honey, how would you like to mount me for a Musical Ride? Is this really you?"

"Of course," he admitted nervously, improvising wildly but without confidence: "My costume for my leading role in Rose Marie! An old musical, much before your time. Of course you don't know of my enthusiasm for amateur theatricals, do you?"

"I am always aware of your amateur theatricals," she said caustically. "This is real, isn't it?"

He saw there was no way out. "Okay. It's mine. Or was. There you have it, Chief Inspector Justin Fowles, before his existence was erased."

She'd agreed, reluctantly, not to tell. There were, he said, terrible problems if word got around. People he'd sent to jail, victims of people he hadn't sent to jail, resentful ex-subordinates, that kind of thing. He would face social ostracism; she would suffer by association; Canadians admired their national policemen but only in the image, etc., a run of eloquence which pleased him greatly and which he believed put the matter to rest.

Or believed at least within the bounds of his certainty about her. Even in their closest usually hilarious moments he wasn't completely free of doubts about the relationship. There was after all no convincingly good reason that an attractive and intelligent woman nearly half his age would enjoy his company, sleep with him rather soon after meeting him, and not try crawling into his head. She seemed to accept him with a warm but light-hearted indifference, which was reassuring in setting limits to their intimacy but perplexing whenever he felt faint tremors of need for a more substantial certitude.

They went to bed no more than twice a month, and met for coffee no more than once a week. These were constraints Annabel laid down, as she told him, "to define their commitment", but actually it reflected her need, in a time of personal uncertainty, to keep things in order. Whenever he questioned the arrangement she told him languorously that it satisfied her completely, that she'd be mad to give up so mature a man who was good in bed but not always drooling for it, and was literate and entertainingly complicated. She told him that for an ex-cop he was surprisingly generous and sane.

"You're disregarding a mountain of evidence," he had said resentfully. "My paranoia is rich and multi-faceted. You just shrug that off?"

"It doesn't turn you mean. It doesn't make you lock yourself in the john for hours, or sleep all day. I'm not belittling it, but even with all your problems, and I mean this compared to other men, you are a very sane man. It may even be, and here's a thought Justin, it may even be that your paranoia and all your less prominent neuroses actually prove your sanity, life being what it is."

But that was long ago and Justin, still on his back in the sunshine on the East Ridge and now savagely assailed by the need for food, knew the unmasking of Mary Evens was petering out, and was suddenly fearful of what that implied.

He struggled to his feet, conscious of his aching left knee, retrieved the spectacles from around his neck so that he could see where he had left the truck, and limped briskly toward it. The East Ridge ran south like a battlement to the sea, and he was parked on the rough track that followed the ridge to the lookout. Further along, the track was treacherously narrow above the precipice, and the underbrush remained penetrable only because of the spring traffic of screaming teenagers going out to Fuck Point.

Once before Justin's time Paul Ching, glancing southward one morning from his fishing boat by the government wharf, saw a jeep leap into the clear air a mile away above the inlet, shedding three small flailing silent bodies as it dropped. To everyone's astonishment Paul hadn't mentioned it to anyone until the next day and Justin, hearing the story, recalled Auden's Icarus, where everyone was too busy to notice "something amazing" —if he had it right— a boy falling into the sea.

He returned to Prospect, driving slowly, burdened of mind. It was perhaps the folly of going up to the ridge that darkened his mood. He was committed, as he often told himself, to a life of reasonable activity but of an emotional tranquility appropriate to his age and, damn it, thoroughly deserved, and he had been admirably successful in suppressing the more voracious monsters of his past. But things were becoming unhinged. Annabel was a joy and a blessing but unsettling. The possibility Mrs. Evens posed no threat was unsettling. Then there was Mandril Gulag, commander of the Snuff Mercenary Combat College, a pig-headed exhibitionist menace to society and the nation, or perhaps at least a reminder of Justin's own triumphs and failures amidst the international threats and conspiracies which occupied much of his career. And then there was the mundane but distracting fact that last night with Annabel, and not for the first time, he had remained limp.

When he got to his room behind the store it was not yet noon, but he opened a can of spaghetti and ate it cold with beer, and fell asleep on the unmade bed. He had no idea how soon he woke, hearing a noise. He opened one eye cautiously, to see Annabel at his kitchen table, holding a coffee mug and rummaging through her usual bundle of overstuffed manila envelopes. Annabel owned the local newspaper, and carried much of her office with her. Her presence shocked him awake; he hoped she didn't intend a post-mortem on last night. He mumbled guardedly, "Well, a pleasant surprise!"

Annabel chose not to look up. She was not at all sure that her visit was a good idea. She had copy to prepare and a meeting to attend and she didn't have the time, especially as she'd have to practically break

Justin's arm to get the straight answer she wanted. She needed to judge his mood. She said, "Are you all right, Justin?"

He said warily, "I am fighting fit. Or will be when fully awake. I wasn't expecting you."

"I just thought I'd drop by and see how things were going."

"Most unusual," he muttered, sure now of the worst, grasping for a diverting topic indicative of mental vigour. "As it happens you're just in time for an important announcement. I've decided I must restock the store. It's early in the season and there are already two fat boats in port laden with Yankee dollars. I've decided it will be a big year for Prospect and I must throw my energies into merchandising. Moreover last winter I manufactured at least fifty genuine arrowheads, flensing blades, scalping knives and soapstone carvings. Not to mention a magnificent feathered headdress—"

"Of local aboriginal origin, of course," said Annabel.

"A diverse culture. Yes. So similar in many ways to our own multicultural society here in Canada, ma'am. And different from your great melting pot. Hah! In three cardboard boxes, somewhere in this mess. I must overcome sloth. Laziness. A natural inclination to do bugger all. It's a defect of character and the first halting step toward senescence. I must fight it."

"Oh dear," said Annabel cynically. "A change of lifestyle. For one so young." His ability to evade an issue always amazed her, but she held back, not being all that confident about what she had to say.

"No dear girl, not a change; a reversion. To the hyperactive person you never knew. And put your mind at rest; this isn't another manic syndrome. I've made a rational decision—" Justin saw Annabel as a person of thoughtful, somewhat judgmental calm, so that whenever he indulged his imagination he felt she tested each sentence for imprecision and hyperbole. He added somewhat deflated, "I am capable of rational decision, you know."

"Of course you are, Justin," she said quietly. "But I was worried about you. If you'd buy a phone I could have phoned without bothering you."

"My God, woman, don't ever worry about me. I have the constitution of a grizzly and the spiritual strength of the Pope. I may be somewhat dogged by guilt, but as you've said yourself, I am extraordinarily sane, and I—"

She said, "Cut the horseshit, Justin. What were you doing this morning?"

"I was in the store this morning," he said with forced vivacity. "I even opened today, Sunday, in the expectation of tourists. But my magnificent sign should be down by the wharf. It's useless on the lower road. I must petition the regional Committee of Condemnations and Rectitude to reconsider—"

"Oh come on," she said, thoroughly out of patience. "Late this morning."

"Well," he said, and paused. This was not her usual lightness of spirit. "I intended to breakfast at the hotel, perchance with the Fabled Jazz Hall Lady, but everything was closed. And then I intended to drive down to Port Renfrew." He hesitated. "Or up to Sooke."

Annabel shouted, "Stop evading the issue, asshole! You intended this and you intended that but what did you do?" She put her hand to her face, closing her eyes in annoyance at having let go, and added contritely, "I'm sorry. I can hardly accuse you of being evasive when I'm being indirect. I was bugged last night by your Mary Evens fixation. This thing is out of control."

"Ha!" he shouted, striking the air for emphasis, as if he had to convince himself as well as her. "She seems so innocuous that she demands suspicion! A master of disguise and mannerism! An agent of the utmost cunning patience; three months and she has yet to make a move!"

She stared at him balefully. He saw he had pressed her too far, but the relief of not having to discuss his impotence filled him with affection. He rose from the bed, almost tripped on a pile of books, turned back to retrieve his glasses, shuffled across the linoleum and stopped behind her, put his hands on her shoulders and his face in her hair, and then went over to the stove. He said, "More coffee?"

"Okay," she said, still unsure whether she had made her point. "I mean thanks. I really hate to bug you like this. It breeches our understanding."

Justin was groggy from the nap and still confused by her unexpected presence, but alert enough to realize he had to give way. He took a deep breath. "As to what I did, I ended up this morning on the East Ridge, watching the Seymour place. So now you know. Ah, how confession cleanses the soul!" He paused, expecting her reply, then added, "I'm sure now she's not RCMP. She may be CSIS, but if so she's inept and I can ignore her. That collection of mutes and pass BAs."

He brought the coffee and sat down across from her. She knew it would be pleasant to share coffee with him and chat, but now she had opened the question she had to take it as far as she could. She said, "You haven't even met her! A couple of weeks ago the kids and I had tea up at her place, and what a hoot it was! The kids, bless them, behaved like angels. Mary Evens may be a nut case, but she's harmless."

"You actually had tea with her? And you didn't tell me?"

"There was nothing to tell."

"In the world of intelligence, even negative reports are precious." He was astonished at her guilelessness.

"I'm not in the world of intelligence, and I'm not running to you every time I meet someone."

"You may have given me away to her."

"For Christ's sake, Justin," Annabel said incredulously, "To tell someone you have a store and you're my friend is breaking a confidence?"

"You could have saved me days of painful uncertainty."

"My poor, poor baby," she said mockingly. "That's entirely your own problem, dear heart. What I want to know, what I really want to know is how long does this idiocy go on?"

He couldn't bring himself to admit that the conspiracy Mary Evens represented was crumbling around him. He said, "That's the question, isn't it".

She looked up at him in astonishment. "Do you know what you're saying?"

"I'm saying that's the question. Yes."

"Oh no— Justin!" She was gripping the edge of the table, glaring at him in frustration. "You're pushing me too far. Everyone has their pet obsessions, and you project yours with imagination and civility. Maybe I'm too permissive but I'm not much disturbed by a retired policeman who thinks the police are watching him. It's sort of a cozy domestic illusion. But now you're conceding it can go on forever. Don't you realize? This thing has already made you a village eccentric."

"My methods are invulnerably secret!"

"Oh face reality, Justin! Susan came home crying a week ago. One of her little friends told her I was screwing a nut case."

"That's a bloody slander!"

"It's beside the point. Village gossip is village gossip and it doesn't rule my life. And I'm sorry about this; we agreed to keep this relationship light. But personally, for me, your thing about Mary has gone too far." She was losing control, and cursed herself inwardly. "It's beginning to bug the hell out of me. You've—you've got to promise me to quit tailing that poor woman."

He reached across the table and gripped her hand, because it was the first time he had seen tears in her eyes and it made him afraid. He said, "I didn't mean to do this to you. I'm terribly sorry. But yes, okay. Yes I'll promise." He was confused not just by her outburst, but by the depth of feeling it revealed, a jarring departure from their usual relaxed banter. It was quite new between them, a moment of emotional truth in which he suddenly realized, with an instant's jolt of panic, that there was no way out of a full confession. He said uneasily, "I— I maybe sometime perhaps implied this isn't all in the theatre of self-indulgence. No. The truth of the matter is. Well. It's not fair to keep you in the dark." The unfairness was obvious; what he was less conscious of was the hope confession would bring her closer. "The truth is I was in Security, the Security Service. It was great fun, and I was very good at it, and it was trendy. The elite. Plain clothes, expense accounts, work your own hours, everything. Fast promotions. I liked to operate with irreverence and style. I had a very low tolerance for routine, pennants and horses, spurs, and standing at attention to salute politicians. Ah, I—it could be said I was undisciplined and insubordinate."

"This is giving me a very strange sensation about you," said Annabel, who had never imagined Justin at work as anything but uniformed and stalwart.

"Well I don't know about strange," said Justin. "But things sometimes got a little out of hand."

"You're talking about Quebec," said Annabel.

"Oui, mon pays. Mostly Quebec. All of which led up to the McDonald Commission, which was before your time but which investigated our so-called misbehaviour. I mean undercover work can be pretty raunchy, and the brass were shit-scared of our bad image. The RCMP image occupies a good deal of their time in Ottawa. In fact oh God can you imagine it—so obsessed with image they handed it to Disney for safekeeping?"

He took some coffee and calmed down. "You see I'd been in it too long; I knew too much. Also they knew bloody well if I got on the stand I wouldn't toe the party line. So there was a quick secret disciplinary board that found quote a long record of disobedience and questionable judgment unquote, followed by the swift purge of everything with my name on it. For my pension they made a deal with the Department of Veterans Affairs to list me as a human vegetable, a totally disabled survivor of Dieppe. Reflecting their fondest hopes, the records say I have no face, no tongue, and no balls at all."

Annabel was sitting back in her chair, her eyes wide open. "Well," she said. And then, "Of course I never know if I can believe you. You started out so solemnly that I thought you'd done naughty things with the horses." She paused. "I'm glad you were a rebel; I find that appealing. I just hope you weren't inhumane."

"Counter-espionage is not gentle. I didn't say I was gentle—"

"I mean if you'd killed or tortured people. Like in South America. The Disappeared."

"Oh come on," he said, irritated that she would confuse him with the CIA's animals.

"I'm sorry. I'm not a very good citizen; I don't remember the RCMP scandals, whatever they were. If you say you were shafted, I'll believe you. But I still don't see why they'd keep you under surveillance."

He said darkly, "Because I was, I am, a political menace. I know where the bodies are. I also know the Paris and Washington connections. The separatistes are demagogues. They were—they are—leading the Quebecois down the garden path."

She chuckled, surprised. "Oh come on, Justin. Not political conviction, not from you!"

He was offended. "Well my indignation may be highly entertaining but I don't think it's hypersensitive to react with heat—hell with righteous rage, eh?—against politicians trying to take Quebec away."

"But if it's a legitimate political desire."

"No!" he shouted. "There's nothing legitimate about destroying a country."

"There are hundreds of thousands of people in Quebec who want to create a new country—"

"The Quebecois are being betrayed! I know those people. I lived with them for years. They are beautiful people. I love them."

"While you were spying on them."

"While I was keeping traitors and terrorists under control!"

"You don't even speak the language!"

"That has nothing do with professional competence!" He could see she wasn't to be persuaded.

She was surprised at the strength of his feeling, although with Justin one never knew how much was act. She shrugged skeptically. "Well I don't know, Justin. How far are we from Quebec? Maybe there's reason enough to watch your every move so far away. If you say so."

"The devious know no bounds."

She said, a little too placatingly, "Oh sure." And then, suddenly seeing the absurdity of Justin under anyone's orders, she leaned across the table and put her hand on his arm: "Would you have been happy, staying in? Do you think after this McDonald thing there'd be any place for a prima donna?"

No one had asked him the question before. The injustice had been so outrageous as to put the whole matter beyond examination. He growled irritably, "That's not the point. That's not the point at all."

"It could just be, Justin," she said, "That it was the best thing that could have happened to you. It could just be that life would be a lot better for you if you admitted they did you a favour. Perhaps all that anger you cultivate should be gratitude."

She had gone too far. "Cultivated anger? Gratitude?" he said, standing up abruptly. The room was too small for him to make leonine strides, and after several paces that resembled a disintegrating pirouette he sat down on the bed. "I should be grateful for banishment? A Chief, ah, Inspector of the Force? I'm not constitutionally equipped to relish shit. I am entitled to my anger! In Ottawa I enjoyed a fifteenth storey apartment on The Driveway, a Mercedes 450SL, clothes from Holt Renfrew, a smash of Chivas Regal regularly at bedtime, and I'm reduced to this; one all-purpose room ingeniously compressed behind a store, a toilet concealed by a threadbare curtain, and a decrepit four-wheel drive. There's moss growing in that truck, did you know that? In Prospect, the anus of the continent, moss grows on steel!" He pulled the sheet over his head to escape the heartless amusement of her smile.

"Justin darling," she said rather too impishly, "It was just a suggestion."

He heard the sound of paper being moved and threw off the bed sheet to see her standing up, stuffing yellow typescript into a folder. "You're not going?" he asked, alarmed. It was so typical of women, he thought, to be untouched by great worldly events, the ruination of careers and bureaucratic betrayal and all the relevant heroic emotions, and yet to be transfixed by some passage of sniveling sentimentality. "What is it to be this week? How tiny blonde Moonglow Robinson carries peonies to her granny in the nursing home?"

"I'm way behind having this ready for the printers. And right now I'm late for a meeting."

"I don't see how you can smash half the furniture in my well-ordered head and go blithely off to edit copy."

"I've just stumbled on a new theory about you, Justin." She opened the door and looked back. "You're an exhibitionist and you needed the Force because it was such a good contrasting medium. You really loved being an anarchist. You relished being thrown out so dramatically. And it fits, you see, how much you like that awful Franz Kafka. You miss that bureaucratic dread. It's not being fired that drives you mad, dear, it's the intolerable freedom of life in Prospect." She added, edging backward, throwing him a kiss, "I have the tenderest feelings for you, Justin. Even more so after last night! Thank you for the coffee. Goodbye!"

He jumped up and made a step after her, shouting. "You said you came here out of deep concern for me. You throw me into a state of extreme agitation and then exit. Some bloody concern!"

He heard her start the clattering Volkswagen engine, but when he got to the window she had gone. He stared out disconsolately at the left-overs from his various jobs; rusting oil drums, a few rolls of wire fencing, piles of old lumber, bricks, paving stones. And his rusting Ford pickup, the door lettered with one of his less successful jokes: J. FOWLES INC - PROSPECTOR - (what else, he'd ask, do you call someone who lives in Prospect?) MAINTENANCE AND REPAIRS.

He stood alone in the room, trouserless, his bare feet on the bare linoleum. The phrase fitted perfectly: smashing the furniture in my head. Bitterness welled in his heart, miserably conscious of betrayal and pervasive, borderless doubt. She had roused fears that normally plagued him perhaps once in several months and only at night, waking him in the small hours to a disordered parade of his failures. He was gripped by melancholy rage and shouted, "Trudeau congratulated me, eh? Personally? We could have kept Quebec! Could anyone else have caught that CIA bastard G. Myron Resnick? We were the only ones fighting and they screwed us!"

To cry out helped the anger, but the evidence was strong; May Evens was not here to spy on him. He was not under surveillance. (And yet he was sure there'd been a watcher in Saskatoon twelve years ago . . . and his mail had been opened when he was in Prince George . . . although Prince George was seven, eight years past.) So that actually, no, he couldn't swear to any contact since a clerk had handed him forty thousand dollars in old bills and demanded his uniform, which he said he had burned. And now they had decided he was no longer worth keeping track of.

He struggled with the conclusion, in the midst of which Annabel's visit came to him with a vague promise of tenderness. She had shown concern for him, perhaps an ambiguous concern, perhaps mainly for her reputation in the village, but she had been near to tears. It wasn't their usual banter of male initiative and female rejection in which there was much more fun than feeling. But her asking for reassurance or whatever it was put things in a new light. It caught him off guard. He was the dispossessed, the exiled, and he was used to that. He was absurdly too old for anything closer with her. His two marriages had been disasters of his own making.

He stared at the far edge of the table, the mug of cold neglected coffee in his hands. For the first time, he needed her comfort, solace perhaps, but he had no idea what he could give in return.

2

Provincial Highway 14 runs southwest down the coast from Victoria to Port Renfrew, passing Prospect about half a mile inland. Annabel's meeting was at the Far Pacific Hotel, which was on the highway a hundred yards east of where the road came up from Prospect. She drove more heedlessly than usual, troubled by Justin, by her behaviour to him, by her indecision. She liked clear arrangements; disarray bothered her and the whole damn thing with Justin was going that way. She was not even being honest with him.

The meeting ahead was no more promising. The message on her answering machine from Dirk Plantagenet was as clumsy as a teenager asking for a first date. He was either calling a press conference, or giving a speech, or inviting her and Mandril Gulag and the hotel's owner, the Jazz Hall Lady Jane, to lunch, to discuss " . . . like, powerful initiatives for the sun-drenched south coast of the island, eh Annie?" She could imagine no more irritating lunch companions than Dirk Plantagenet and Mandril Gulag, and was really attending only because she might have time alone with the Lady Jane.

Dirk owned the Sensuous Rendezvous Resort, about a mile east on the highway from the hotel. She hadn't at first believed the name—Sensuous Rendezvous—it offended her personal taste and professional judgment; surely to God it was only on the edge of nowhere that people could take such a name seriously. She had met Dirk only twice before; he was a self-proclaimed entrepreneur and bon-vivant or, as Justin called him, the local agent of the Victoria sleaze industry.

Dirk's ancient phalliform Jaguar convertible was already in the hotel parking lot, and Annabel went directly through the lobby to the stairs down to the Rib'n'Rye Room. The Lady Jane had a mahogany office on the main floor with Laura Ashley powder-room ensuite, but the Rib'n'Rye Room below was her habitat. The restaurant upstairs was clean and light, but she was never there; her domain was in the downstairs gloom in a niche behind the end of the bar, with two telephones in front of her and a green-shaded lamp on a brass bracket by her right shoulder.

Annabel had once adored the Lady Jane intemperately, as if finding a lost mother of longed-for warmth and sympathy. That was a couple of years ago, before she found that the Fabled Lady was less mother than mother spirit, an ageless abstraction embodying warmth and sympathy in abundance, but in a puzzlingly unreachable form.

She remembered being exasperated at the Rib'n'Rye Room's darkness and the stench of stale beer that made her dizzy. The Jazz Hall Lady had exclaimed, "But darling this is where humanity began! Yes I know we were all once hunters or gatherers but there's absolutely no humanity in hunting and gathering. That didn't begin until people started drinking. Alcohol was the first mind-altering drug, and people didn't realize they had minds until they tried altering them. That's why Dionysus is the true god of humanity."

Annabel, feeling that day in particular need of a good party, said, "Perhaps he could lay on a small orgy," and the Lady Jane said, "Just come around any Friday night. Don't wear anything you don't want torn off."

"I meant a little private orgy, dear, not a mass swill."

"You're so pernickety! A party's a party. A Prospect party's maybe a little more physical than what you're used to Toronto or Philly, but don't sneer at it. Just remember, now we're civilized we have cocktail lounges and art galleries but in the beginning was the cave. There was just the cave—" The Lady Jane opened her arms to the dark ceiling above: "—and the tribe gathered to talk and draw on the walls and get drunk and plan how to trap mastodons. And fuck! Have you ever noticed how the tables in a beer hall are just the right height for a man to take you from behind? Oh how we fucked!"

And now Annabel, near the bottom of the stairs and frowning into the sweetly tainted gloom, could make out only Hermes, the bartender, polishing glasses in a little lighted cubicle far away. The Lady Jane called, somewhere beyond the tables, and Annabel found her in a booth with Dirk. When he smiled, his mouth stretched to the sides of his face to reveal large stained teeth. Annabel guessed he was about forty-five. He breathed expansively, half rising, "Well Annie, it's sure good of you to come."

Annabel grinned, sat down. "How's the Fabled Jazz Hall Lady? I heard you were with flu."

"Always in the lowest spirits, sweet child," said the Lady Jane. "The forenoon is disaster for me."

The Fabled Jazz Hall Lady Jane was possibly in her late fifties, the unchallenged sex-symbol of Prospect and all points east and west. She seldom appeared in daylight, but when she minced peremptorily across Kitchener Street at high noon, her hips moved left and right with the authority of barked commands. She dressed to display a splendidly lubricious figure but her taste was ambiguous; she mixed Wal-Mart and Holt-Renfrew and cheerfully called the result "my very own Whorehouse Vogue, darling".

Her secret—the only secret she admitted—was a creamy unblemished skin and elegant facial structure. On Saturday nights the Rib'n'Rye Room was crammed with horny celebrants from Esquimalt to Port Henley, and the Lady Jane moved through the room like a sexual dynamo emanating invisible light, inaudible sound, a power pulsing with each twitch of her buttocks, hard high heels impacting the floor like bullets, a glance, tossed hair, flick of a bare arm, and every tank-topped sweating hairy male steamed with pent lust and uttered not a single syllable of his coarse desire.

"It's just the skin and the bones, darling," she explained to Justin one night, inclining her head to one side. "See? Patrician features; a universal language. And out of an Olduvian slum. I'd be dead ten times over it weren't for my skin and bones. No one beats the shit out of a lady."

Arranging herself in the booth, Annabel said, "Dear Lady Jane, you always look, hm-m, so exquisite."

"Oh sweet child of youth, you lie, you lie!"

Dirk Plantagenet sniggered and said, "She's a reporter, eh?" He nudged Annabel infuriatingly with his elbow. "That's part of the training, eh Annie?" He seemed to caress the masculine timbre of his own voice. She disliked Annie almost as much as she disliked jocular nudging, but restrained herself. She edged away from Dirk and said, "So is this a press conference, or what? Dirk your message was garbled but was there something about a press conference?"

"I guess you could call it that. Sure." He placed his fingers together and affected magisterial presence.

"Some of us were thinking we should have a little talk with you. About your paper. You see, we think you have a real feel for this part of the world, Annie."

Annabel wasn't sure if he were being sarcastic or was simply clumsy with language. She said, "Some of whom?"

Dirk said inconclusively, "Yeah. Well." He conveyed discomfort, as if wishing the Lady Jane would rescue him. "The Jazz Hall Lady here. And me. You see there's some of us see a great future for this area. An unlimited future! Oh yeah, and Mandril Gulag. You know Mandril?"

"The nazi down the road?"

"Well that's a little unfair, now," Dirk chuckled indulgently. "You've never met Mandril eh?"

"Never set eyes on him," Annabel lied, provoked by Dirk's condescending tone. She had even written an editorial once, protesting Mandril's proposal to use the village to practice house-to-house combat. "I heard he lives in the clearcut."

Dirk grinned at her and winked toward the Lady Jane. "Well that's the objective media, eh? Call a man a nazi and never seen him?"

"I also damn well resent Herr Gulag giving my son a paintball gun. Can you imagine that, giving a nine-year old a weapon?"

Dirk chuckled again. "Like cigarettes, eh? Get 'em hooked early. He's a real entrepreneur!"

Annabel seethed silently. Food arrived. She wondered how she'd not noticed what a prick he was. She'd heard he claimed Henry VIII as an ancestor, apparently unaware of the distinction between Plantagenet and Tudor. At their first chance meeting—it was at a garage sale —he'd broken in on a conversation she was having with Jill Ymenko, the RCMP officer's truly gorgeous wife, obviously trying to come on to Jill. He'd apparently taken Annabel, then newly separated and at her most sexually inert, as the local librarian, and had asked her about the library before turning his charm toward Jill. Jill reported later how swiftly he'd retreated when her husband appeared, coming off duty in uniform.

But now, after ignoring Dirk's crudity for harmony's sake, Annabel saw he was persisting, saying something about " . . . never looked like a nazi to me". She said angrily, holding him square in the eye, "I didn't know nazism was appearance. I thought it was a matter of ideas, and Mr. Gulag's ideas are clear enough in the pamphlets he leaves round the village. Possibly imported from Alabama. Mr. Gulag seems to be an obsessive pamphleteer; he averages a pamphlet a month. Have you read any of his pamphlets, Dirk?"

Dirk looked away and grimaced toward the kitchen, opening and closing his hand nervously. He tried apologetically; "Look Annie—"

"I really appreciate Annabel," said Annabel. "It's not so Little Orphan."

"Okay. Okay. I guess I got off on the wrong foot. Annabel. Yeah. Not so Little Orphan—hey that's right on—" He guffawed, but with effort. The Lady Jane smiled faintly into the distance.

Annabel persisted, "You've read Mr. Gulag's pamphlets?"

"Oh sure," Dirk began, and then as if aware of some higher accountability in Annabel's glare, "Okay, no I haven't. But shit that stuff is just advertising. I mean he draws a pretty tough crowd, eh? They go for the white supremacy stuff. It's business eh? He has to give 'em what they want."

The Fabled Jazz Hall Lady Jane said quietly, "Annabel my precious bounty, pay no attention to the poor beast. And Dirk, butt out. I have seldom seen anyone screw up so thoroughly so fast. It's like watching a man go into court for a parking ticket and walk out to be hanged. Annabel dear, this is pure and simple business lobbying. All Dirk really wants is to ask you to give local business more space in your paper."

"Well," Annabel said, "You have my rate card. All you have to do is give me copy. And money." And then she remembered—"But Gulag; is he part of this? Is it you want me to accept his ads?"

"You mean Mandril doesn't advertise in the Clarion?" said Dirk. "What a jerk. There's loyalty to local media for you!" As if from something he'd read, he recited, "You gotta understand, when you talk media, that begins with local media. Local business needs local media! It's essential for the businessman to include media in their community concept, in the vision, in the business plan! Media is the life-blood of local free enterprise! I'm gonna have to talk to Mandril about this."

Annabel, startled at so earnest a flight of rhetorical cliché, said, "I won't accept his ads. He tried a couple and I refused them. They were offensive crap."

Dirk looked astonished. "But hey that's not freedom of speech, hon— Annabel. That's restraint of trade. That violates the first amendment. You can't do that."

"Oh God!" sighed the Lady Jane. "Dear Dirk, the first amendment is—"

Dirk waved his hands, "Okay. Okay. American. A detail, eh?"

Annabel said impatiently, "The last one he sent me was headed *HONE YOUR KILL-SKILLS AGAINST THE MUSLIM TIDE.* I mean, come on!"

The Lady Jane said, "It's not Mandril's ads, and Dirkie-boy doesn't want to buy more space. He just thought it would be nice if you could write about local businesses. Occasionally. Maybe even an insert."

"Yeah," said Dirk. "I don't think you give us a fair shake. The Far Pacific Hotel is big business in these parts. The Sensuous Rendezvous Resort is big business. Even if you don't like his politics, the important thing is the Combat College brings lots of money into the community. You can't mix up business and politics."

Annabel said, "None of your businesses affects Prospect at all. The Far Pacific is the best trough west of Colwood so it attracts the rutting set from all over. I don't imagine a single one of my readers has stayed at the Rendezvous since it began. As for Murder College, sure they come into the village, for coffee or a head-shave or just to hang out along Kitchener, but mainly they stay on the base."

"Oh shit," Dirk said. "I'm not talking about the village. They just play at business, those people in the village. They don't understand business is serious— Hell, who's that asshole—" He gave a contemptuous laugh. "That truck eh? Justin Fowles, Prospector! I know for a fact he's not a prospector. It's too, it's too—"

"Frivolous," the Lady Jane suggested.

"Yeah! Frivolous. Serious business doesn't kid around like that. Serious postulates a commitment to the community."

The Lady Jane giggled, and Annabel, keeping a straight face, asked, "What else would you call someone who lived in Prospect?"

Dirk looked mystified, as if suspecting he'd missed something, and then laughed in sudden relief, "Oh! Oh yeah! Ha. Prospector! Yeah but it's still not serious, eh?"

Annabel said, "Look; my readers are not your customers. There are small farmers, seniors, bed-and-breakfast people, a lot of commuters with families who work in Esquimalt and Victoria. They're not interested in Saturday-night drinking and screwing and shooting people."

"Okay, okay," said Dirk, nodding profoundly. "I'll give you an example. Last month I announced a million-dollar expansion at the Rendezvous. A million dollars! I sent you a press kit. It made the Victoria papers. It made CFAX radio. It made TV. But where was the Prospect Drum and Bugle or what you call it? Nowhere, eh?"

"Last month it was the Clarion and Diversifier," muttered the Lady Jane.

Annabel said, "So where's the expansion?"

Dirk said, "There's a financing challenge, but I'll tell you what! Here's the vision, eh? I can see a special edition, the South Coast Business Edition, featuring small business success stories from Esquimalt west, eh? I'll let you in on something, this is off the record, eh? Mandril's just signed a contract with the Oregon Christian Crusade! The Snuff Mercenary Combat College is licensed to produce Soldiers for Christ! It's a franchise, eh? The business that man is going to bring in! The American bucks! You got to stop ignoring us, lady!"

Annabel said angrily: "You should be damn grateful I do. If you'd dropped by the Starlight Cafe about the time of that million dollar caper you'd know how it was going over with the locals. You came just *that* close to having to fight it through every zoning committee and planning board in the region. If I'd done just one editorial, they'd have been all over you. Fortunately for you, the story bored me."

Dirk stared at Annabel. "That was big news. Don't you print news? What kinda business you in, lady?"

"I just print what I like. In the long run I think one tries to capture whatever creates place and meaning. To give us a local habitation and a name, as someone said. If nothing about Prospect were ever recorded, nothing would remain. That's the west coast; everything decays."

The Lady Jane threw one arm around Annabel and cried, "Oh I love this woman! Oh you add a dimension, you do!" And then, anticipating Dirk's predictable put-down, she added, "Dirk, I'll say it again; bug out!"

"Oh fuck off!" said Dirk angrily. "Maybe I shouldn't advertise in the paper. I've got major plans for this area, see, and no one better stand in my way. I don't get mad, remember; I get even!"

Annabel was repelled, but the Lady Jane smiled calmly and said, "Dirk, don't try intimidation. It won't work, and it makes you look cheap. Urinal cheap. Just be glad she ignores us. She doesn't report how many people throw up in my parking lot or how many drunks Ymenko catches on the highway every Saturday night. She doesn't report you employ whores—"

"That is a goddam slander! That is a lie—"

"Be calm, ambitious lad, and remember, you and I know damn well our ads don't bring in a single customer. We advertise for good will, and we'll go on advertising because the locals don't really like my beer trough or your Lust Motel, and that little bit of goodwill helps keep them off our backs."

Dirk was moving to leave. He said, "Yeah. Yeah. Goodwill." He looked grateful, as if the Lady Jane had at last come to his rescue. As he stood up he said with forced heartiness, "Hey, Annabel! I'll tell you what; when did you last visit the Sensuous Rendezvous?"

"Good grief," said Annabel, "Does a woman of virtue dare admit visiting the Sensuous Rendezvous?" Dirk looked mystified, and Annabel added, "I'm sorry Dirk, I've never been. By the way, didn't you say your Gruppenfuhrer friend was going to be here?"

The Lady Jane said, "Mandril's chronically unreliable. He's probably searching for one of his clients. They get lost in the forest, or get splattered with that oily blood stuff and lose their nerves. "

"Hey!" Dirk repeated. "Annabel, I'll tell you. You come on over next weekend with your friend. Ah? What's—"

"Justin. Justin Fowles."

"Yeah, Justin. I'll reserve— Oh my God! The truck—"

Annabel and the Lady Jane both screamed delightedly. Dirk's face went crimson. He stared at the table, shaking his head. When the laughter subsided he kept mumbling, "I'm sorry, ladies. Annabel I'm sorry. I'm really sorry." And then, recovering, "But I really mean the offer, eh? The Pussy Cat Suite for you both. A weekend on the house. It's an erotic delight. There's a heart shaped bed, and a whirlpool bath like you wouldn't believe." Dirk chuckled hideously, leaning over with his hands on the table to confide quietly, "It's so erotic anyone checking into the Pussy Cat who's over fifty-five, we get them to sign a waiver!"

Annabel exhibited elaborate alarm. "Oh heavens. Justin's way over sixty-five. I think he's nudging eighty."

The Lady Jane shrieked again and Dirk, even more bewildered, grimaced as if in gastric agony, muttering, "Oh God I've done it again. I'm sorry."

Annabel patted Dirk's arm, surprised at how conciliatory she felt, and thanked him, but said conscience insisted she devote the weekends to her children, which was true, and how busy Justin was, which was altogether questionable. As soon as Dirk had gone, she said, "Good Lord I never imagined! What on earth was that all about?"

"It was basically about, well, Dirk. Dirk has his dreams. One of his problems is that he only learns by doing. He's unteachable. He has to screw up before he gets anything right."

Dirk Plantagenet had in fact gone from each failure to something grander. He started young, driving a truck, eventually buying into a gravel pit, and made money until he took a contract that was too big and went broke. He was possessed of great energy but was weak at sums. He started an excavating business in Nanaimo, which he claimed gave him his first million, until he went broke again, but came out of it with a share of a desolate shopping mall outside Duncan and several acres of forest near Prospect. He became a builder, doing small projects around Nanaimo and Parksville, but by the time that work got too scarce he'd finished a dozen motel units on the Prospect property, which he began operating as the Sensuous Rendezvous Resort.

"Unteachable," Annabel echoed. "How inspiring."

"It's your yuppie urban values, sweet Annabel. You want your men to emerge fully formed from graduate school, pin-striped, acne-free, programmed to fill conversational pauses, cool as cologne and worth six figures per. A hundred years ago when the west was young, Dirk would've given you the liquid hots."

"I find Justin quite comfortable."

"I wouldn't dream of arguing with you," said the Lady Jane. "I'm sure there are few more comfortable relationships than between a woman in her thirties and a man deep into his seventies. The tribe wouldn't countenance your arrangement with Justin, but they wouldn't have to intervene, because the cave would see to that. The wine and the dancing would get rid of that elitist poker up your ass and bring you back into the world."

Annabel chanted merrily, "The girls along the highway say, The Rib'n'Rye for a real hot lay."

The Lady Jane grimaced. "Well no dear. You can do better than that."

"But I really am too busy. Oh, and I wanted to tell you. Cliff has sent me another assignment." Clifford Osborne was a partner in the agency she'd worked for, Smith Lang Osborne in Philadelphia. When she left he'd implored her to stay in touch, and had already sent her a job that would pay off her mortgage. "It's to outline a campaign for a new drug for—don't laugh—constipation. Aimed at doctors."

"Constipated doctors."

"Ah—"

"You really are getting back into it, aren't you."

Annabel was drawing circles on the table in some spilled tea. "My subscribers like me being here. Justin likes my being here." She was still a little confused by the encounter with Dirk, but suddenly saw the absurdity of implying any certainty in Justin: "No. No I know what you're saying, dear. I do know I've got to make a decision."

"Would you go back to Toronto?"

"Oh no. Philly is where the action is for me. I love the States. I mean it sickened me after we split, and in many ways it's a shitty place to live, but the people are wonderful and there are such opportunities! It's not the money, in itself I mean. But with that money I can avoid a lot of the shit. I can send the kids to good schools."

"So what are you waiting for?"

"I really don't know. There's no more scar tissue. I'm not sure I'm ready to go back, but there doesn't seem to be any reason to stay any longer."

"So then you have decided. Which shows you're ready!"

"Yeah. I guess. Maybe."

"But what will become of Justin?"

"Justin. Yeah. I dropped by this morning. We had this ridiculous set-to about his Mary Evens thing. You know how much it bugs me. And this really knocked me out: I asked him how long it was going on, and you know what he said?" She flicked her hand as if swatting an insect. "Oh to hell with going into it all. No. But I did get him to promise to stop."

"Do you really think he seriously believes she— ?"

"Your guess is as good as mine. So much of the time he's civilized and irreverent and fun to be with. He's almost contemporary! And then he goes off on these crazy tangents. He reverts. This morning he was Corporal Canada again. How he saved us from Rene Levesque. I say look Justin it's a different world, Levesque is dead. Read the papers, watch TV. Sometimes I think he's truly bananas. Do you think it's senility? God, that's more than I bargained for!"

They parted, and Annabel went back to the ten by ten room on Palgrave Street she called her office. She had met Justin soon after he arrived in Prospect, when he was moving into the store vacated months earlier by the Keating brothers, who had been busted for selling marijuana over the counter. He said he was from Kelowna, which she learned later was a lie. He said he was opening Exquisitely Petite Leathers, Inc., a tannery for small rodents, maintaining that the market in Singapore for vole-fur penis-shields was unlimited. When she reported the newcomer's plans at the Starlight there was an uproar; Tim Flegg maintained a tannery smelt worse than a pulp mill. Justin thought it a huge joke. "Have you ever seen a vole? It would be like tanning a postage stamp."

"You bugger," she said. "It was all a bloody act!"

"I am skilled in deceit, madam. It is my life!"

She found his personality intriguingly fragmented. He was by turns fractious and accommodating, accessible and secretive, possessed of manic energy and extended torpor. He railed with grunting reactionary venom against the moral sloth of installing condom machines in schools, but praised Henry Morganthaler as a saint and martyr. He would slip straight-faced into antic fantasies, for instance that of the Seven Priestly Eunuchs of San Francisco, rulers of secret societies more terrible than the Tongs, who miraculously caused the San Francisco earthquake of 1906, and engineered the downfall of the Hawaiian monarchy in 1898. It was they who had financed the world's first nuclear manufactory, which through miscalculation blew up in 1883, consuming all traces of its origin—scientists, laboratories, several four-masted ore carriers, and a sizeable seaport—to be reported to the world, history's greatest cover-up, as the eruption of Krakatoa.

Annabel's feelings toward Justin were short of romantic, but hardly casual. She had arrived in Prospect filled with such icy sexual disdain that the merest passing smile from a man left her tongue-tied. By the time she encountered Justin it had been months since she had even fifteen minutes' conversation with a man; Justin had wit and imagination, and his age was reassuring. He was literate and informed; she felt comfortable with him. They shared a sense of the grotesque which made their forty years' difference in age a source of amusement, so that they were finally drawn to bed not so much by desire as by curiosity, an ironic sense of mutual adventure sharpened by the suspense of not knowing what might come next. "I'm not exactly sure it's fair," as Annabel had said, "It really depends so much on you, doesn't it. To perform. So far past your prime and all."

She had left Philadelphia because she'd come home early one afternoon to find her husband mounting his squealing secretary on the kitchen floor. She sent the children to Marlene, her sister in Toronto, while she tried for three months to understand the stranger she found herself married to, and knew she was going mad. When she fled to Toronto, Marlene told her to get her spoilt, smart-assed brats out of the house before she strangled one of them. Annabel left Toronto in shock without a destination in mind; all she knew was she had to get away from the whole Philadelphia-Toronto horror, to keep going west until she found sanctuary, and Prospect was about as far as she could go.

She knew the worst thing for Susan and Marc was for her to collapse, so as soon as she found a house she searched for work. She noticed the local newspaper was moribund, with few ads and sparse local coverage. She was sure she could revive it, bought it for nearly nothing from its dying alcoholic owner, and found she loved being reporter, manager, bookkeeper and publisher. Justin entered her life unexpectedly; she had come here to recuperate, to re-establish herself because she wasn't immediately sure who she had become. It was definitely not to accommodate herself to a life with Justin Fowles.

Fortunately the children weren't enthusiastic about Justin. They thought him dismissive, eccentric, and too hairy. Annabel took up with Justin as a comfortable diversion, a confidant up to a point, a companion perhaps but with clear emotional limits. That was why the sudden upsurge of concern she'd felt for him last night was troubling; Her affection for him was sincere, but any greater involvement was out of the question. Her conversation with the Lady Jane was reassuring; it affirmed her readiness to go.

When she got home that evening she sensed something was up. Susan and Marc were sitting too solemnly on the front steps, and before she could apologize for being late Susan presented her with an oblong cardboard box, bent in the middle and tied loosely with gold ribbon.

"It's something for you," Susan said. "It was by the door when we got home. It's from a gentleman admirer, as they say in old books."

Marc added, "We don't think he's exactly a gentleman."

Annabel said, "You opened it! Children that's awful! I've told you, you must never open other people's mail."

"We didn't think this was mail. We discussed it."

"Stop hiding behind the literal! Mail, parcels, packages, come on!"

"I'm trying to tell you," said Susan, "It was already open. It was all over the front porch."

"As if hurled in rage," Mark said.

The box bore a label which caused her to cringe. It featured a string of tiny Union Jacks around the words "British Tweed - The Elite of Victoria Florists - Serving a Distinguished Clientele in Oak Bay and Uplands from 1967". Inside the box were a dozen red roses on long broken stems. "Wow!" she exclaimed, holding them up joyfully, bringing them to her face and smelling them. "Oh how gorgeous! And all the way from Victoria!"

"There's a note," said Marc, with noticeable restraint.

Annabel tried to recall her birthday, an anniversary, anything that would have inspired dear Justin to such thoughtful generosity. A gesture of reconciliation, perhaps, after his silliness this morning; it warmed her heart. She opened the card, which showed a cartoon, garishly coloured. There was a rowboat flying an enormous Union Jack and containing a fat leering man, one of whose hands gripped a tumescent fishing rod between his legs, the other thrust between the two huge breasts of a woman whose upturned skirts revealed spotted bloomers and crimson garters. A balloon from the fat man's mouth proclaimed "GOT MYSELF A COUPLE OF WHOPPERS!"

Annabel stared at the cartoon, unbelieving. It wasn't Justin's style. She opened the card gingerly. Inside was scrawled:

To a truly arousing luncheon guest.
Whoop de doo, I lust for you!   Dirk.

She felt hit in the face. She breathed, "Bastard! Slimy coarse crude filthy little bastard!" —and remembering the children, "I'm sorry, I was misquoted. You misheard. I—"

"We tried to warn you."

Enraged, she marched to the phone, shouting, "Out! Out! Both of you! Down to the bottom of the garden. Anywhere out of earshot! Your mother is about to utter profanities that are not for small ears! Go!"

The children were out of the house before she found his number in the phone book. As soon as Dirk answered she shouted, "I am phoning to tell you just don't ever try that kind of fucking trick again. Don't ever! Keep your goddamned erections to yourself, or go beat yourself off in the washroom." She put down the phone and called a cab to take the box to Plantagenet's office. As soon as she finished that call, Dirk was on the line again, "Annie, I don't— "

She slammed down the phone, and then took it off the hook. She poured herself a glass of wine, swallowed a large part of it and went to the door and called, "Children dear! Children come! Come tell your mother about your lovely day of high achievement."

3

Several days later, Justin sat in his empty store beside the cash register, staring out morosely at the rain-drenched afternoon. His morning's energetic optimism had gone, leaving him uneasy and fretful, a mood which made the Combat College commandos loitering along Kitchener Street strangely menacing.

The morning had been productive. He'd found the cultural artifacts he'd made last winter, twenty-seven pieces—rattles, spoons, small bowls crudely inlaid with bits of sea shell, and a cradle, all of cedar—perhaps less colorful than he'd once described them to Annabel, but marketable with a little work. In fact some of the stylized wolves and orcas and salmon were, yes, quite splendid.

By the time he'd sanded off some rough patches and rubbed on a little earth in dark varnish for authenticity he was imagining a retail triumph, a victory over Annabel's skepticism and the lethargic antagonism of his merchant colleagues. He worked till noon, and made himself lunch of a grilled cheese sandwich and a tin of Pepsi. By then he was a little weary, and so took fully clothed to the unmade bed, grappling with an old Globe and Mail crossword until he slept.

He got up and shoved a mug of the morning's coffee into the microwave, feeling groggy because he had napped too long. He needed to apply himself to something, anything, and he went into the store to perhaps count the petty cash or study the indecipherable manual on the provincial sales tax, and found Barbara Tuchman's book about the World War I mystery of the Zimmerman telegram on the counter. He'd been reading it a couple of days ago, or was it three weeks ago, and he was about to pick it up when he noticed the commandos. Two of them were sheltered from the rain under the sagging canopy of the abandoned service station across the street. They wore the Combat College uniform; dark camouflage coveralls with a small American flag as a shoulder patch. They stared down at the puddled street, immobile, sullen. Justin recalled patrolling downtown Montreal during the October Crisis of 1970.

A vacant lot separated the service station from the two-storey building farther away, on the corner. The building had a frail wooden stairway up to a second floor balcony, from which a clothes line drooped under rain-soaked children's clothes and men's jeans and workshirts. Every few days there were shouts from the second floor apartment, after which either a man or a woman would emerge to sit half way down the stairs, even in rain as heavy as today, glumly smoking a cigarette. The present occupants were from Drumheller in Alberta. Before that there was a family with five kids under ten from Newfoundland. The dispossessed, with whom at his more self-pitying he felt a fierce reluctant kinship.

The building was old, its stucco walls cracked, patched, stained with rust. Its owner, in a nursing home in Victoria, hadn't raised the rent since 1976, and often forgot to collect it. The ground floor had large storefront windows, but was vacant. The windows were papered over inside, making visible the graffiti spray-painted on the glass. *Shit on Dykes. VandalZam - Political Ham. HOMOES UNITE!* A third commando was standing motionless in the rain, staring at the graffiti. Justin could see a corner of Pollock's Grocery another block away across the intersection, in front of which a fourth commando, maybe a woman, was sitting on the curb with her feet in the ditch.

This presence of sentinels in the streets was a recent development. When they came into town off-duty they were in groups, usually loud and often destructive, but this was different. They must be under orders, for what but orders would keep anyone in the joyless streets of Prospect in drenching rain? It might even be that Major Gulag was about to stage street-fighting as he'd threatened months ago during Justin's confrontation with him in his office. Justin imagined crawling through the slash and broken timber of the clearcut on a day like this, the kind of thing he'd done in the Force decades ago when he was tough and horny.

The female commando had now risen from the ditch and was slouching off toward the Starlight, while the commando from the storefront window was moving toward the intersection she had left, his post having in turn been taken by one of the commandos from the gas station. It was obviously choreographed. One commando remained at the service station across the street, as if briefed to watch Justin's store.

Briefed to watch—what had Gulag called him—a *designated hostile*? His distrust of Mandril Gulag had grown since their violent meeting in the first weeks of his arrival in Prospect. He should press Ymenko to question the College's legality, or write his member of parliament or the Department of National Defence; another of those many resolves that seemed to slip away under the pressure of events or into the void of procrastination.

It wasn't turning out a good day. It was dark, which created shadows and uncertainties. It was one thing to be harassed by the past, but the present too had become less than tranquil since the row with Annabel—was it as much as a week ago?—before her purported meeting at the Far Pacific Hotel. And since then his unease had fixed itself on her connection with Plantagenet, starting that afternoon when the jangle of the storefront bells had broken his siesta to send him staggering across the all-purpose room to fetch up heavily against the doorway to the store.

Someone called, "British Tweed Florists!"

"No this is the Prospect Variety Store," he grumbled, struggling to assume his retail charm, groggily observing a weedy young man in jeans and sweater holding a large oblong box tied in gold ribbon.

"No I'm the one from British Tweed Florists," said the impudent boy. "In Oak Bay, in Victoria. Are you Fowles?"

Justin said icily, "My name is Fowles. Mr.—" he paused magisterially, "Justin Fowles."

"This is for a Ms. McKinley at 3303 Mercator Street, but there's no answer and a note on the door says to contact you in an emergency. I figured not being able to deliver our premium long-stemmed roses after bringing them all the way from Victoria was an emergency, eh?"

"Good thinking," said Justin acidly.

"You know this Ms. McKinley? She your daughter? You'll get this to her? I mean they'll chew my ass if they aren't delivered. It's more'n two hours' drive out here, y'know. That's big money. This Plantagenet, he has the hots for this chick, eh?"

"The seething hots—" barked Justin, "—it would seem. Surely you want to leave that here and immediately resume your hectic schedule?"

"I'm supposed to say the directions for enjoying the cherished sentiment of your British Tweed Fresh-Kut®

Roses for many happy weeks are inside the container. Your personalized British Tweed Fresh-Kut® Roses should be placed gently in lukewarm water mixed with the enclosed Vitality Salts™ as soon as possible after receipt goodbye sir and have a good day."

Justin remained beside the cash register, fuming. Plantagenet, with his supply of chambermaid lovelies and American playmates was hardly in dire physical need of Annabel, and was certainly too stupid to appreciate her. Or so Justin told himself. On the other hand it was always possible that his overworked oleaginous charm hid rare discrimination, and that approaching forty or so he was casting about for a companion with an intelligence to match his heavy-lidded entrepreneurial guile. Or so Justin told himself, advancing slowly on the decorated box. He laid the box on the kitchen table and opened it. The card inside was inscribed in a thin clerical hand: "To a truly delightful luncheon guest. From your admiring Dirk Plantagenet."

Justin contemplated the decoration on the box and snorted. Plantagenet was evidently ignorant of Annabel's distaste for commercial Britishness. Then, suddenly inspired, he took off rapidly down Kitchener to the post office. Frank Mewhouse had been to Britain last year and had brought back some examples of boisterous Brit vulgarity; one card had struck Justin as an ultimate offense to Annabel's sensitivities, and it was still there. Triumphantly, he composed a new message, substituted his card for Plantagenet's, and drove immediately to drop the box off at her house before the kids returned from school. For a woman of taste and restraint, who moreover thought her breasts too small, nothing could be more destructive of the despised Plantagenet's evil purpose!

When he'd heard nothing from her twenty-four hours later, he began to wonder if it was as hilarious as he'd thought. He'd expected her to tell him of the incident immediately, furious at the card he'd found. But as the days went by her silence became puzzling and then, in suggesting Plantagenet as a rival, disturbing.

Staring out into the rain and the grey street, he recalled the long forgotten doubts that he'd not given enough—of his time, of love, of tender attention—to Maggie his first wife (whom he called Magus after the novel by the distant and probably unrelated relative) or to his adored Stephanie so sadly gone from this earth and him. His failure with them, the impossibility of knowing why, added another uncertainty to Annabel's silence.

Agitated, he put aside Tuchman and went back into the all-purpose room, unusually aware of his poor housekeeping. Laundry, books in boxes, piles of old newspapers. The two women he had lived with tidied so automatically he thought it an instinct of gender, but Annabel ignored the mess, only once snorting something about his living in shit.

Shortly after his arrival he had planned a great bookshelf project, to help order his life and to cover the cracked plaster and peeling wallpaper of the general purpose room with a book-lined veneer of style. He had more than enough books; in the Sixties he'd gone underground for a year as a student at Dalhousie to monitor campus unrest, and after that he'd added courses at five or six universities on his postings across the country and always kept the books. So he had cut the shelves, and then become diverted to something else, and the shelves were somewhere on the workbench by the back door, under several months of detritus; discarded newspapers, shopping bags, soft-drink tins, cereal boxes. Carpentry promised greater relief than reading or brooding about Annabel's behaviour or the other hazards of dismal afternoons. He levered a shelf out from under the debris, and looked for the measuring tape.

His last go at carpentry—apart from some odd jobs for J. Fowles Inc.—was his magnificent sign, his defiant answer to the community's skepticism about his mercantile resolve, proclaiming:

PROSPECT VARIETY &
HERITAGE MUSEUM
BUSINESS CENTRE --->

His colleagues in trade had called it an abomination on the landscape and persuaded some piddling regional authority to have him move it from beside the government wharf to a deserted tract of the Lower Road. More rankling was Annabel's newspaper report, which made him a public fool. The incident had revealed hidden erotic truths, because she'd come through the back door that evening shouting, "It's done, it's done!" discarding her sweater and brassiere, turning off lights, grabbing his belt and gasping, "Oh God Justin why does a new issue turn me on like this? Come on, come on, get hard darling!"

Annabel was indeed feeling buoyant, but actually driven less by passion than by exhausted relief, because finding advertising for this issue had been hell, and in the final stages the printers had mislaid two pages of copy. It had been irritating, and she needed his company and the relief of some quick sex. But Justin was quite unprepared for her spirited attack on his crotch. He had been comfortably on the bed, fully clothed, reading *The Merck Manual* because his damaged hand had been unusually painful. He blurted, "Hey—you're being much too energetic. Arousal is best done with sensuous deftness. You are very close to flagellation, which only works for a closet minority. Besides my head is still full of hyperuricemia and metacarpophalangeal joints, none of which I fully understand."

Annabel ignored him and gasped, "Oh Justin darling, I do truly love you," not because he was showing promising signs of tumescence but because even when she was hot enough to proposition some sweating drunk from the Rib'n'Rye (which despite the Lady Jane's encouragement she'd never done) Justin's articulate civility made the most unconstrained passion seem human and affectionate.

The Merck Manual was quickly replaced in Justin's mind by a welling of sensual pleasure, including the sight of her shadowy body above him and the sound of her little cries of delight, slowly gathering into a single mutual overwhelming pelvic urgency which soon compelled her to collapse onto him, and then him to roll over onto her, and both some time later giggling and slippery with sweat to slide asymmetrically onto the floor where amidst a fervent exchange of libidinous entreaties Annabel reached her third climax and Justin, as befitted his age, his hard-earned maximum of one.

It was after this, after they regained the bed and held each other tenderly to doze a little in each other's arms, after Annabel had showered and while they were sitting together with coffee and the new issue of the Prospect Clarion and Metaphor (Annabel fully-dressed, cursing typo errors, and Justin wrapped in a blanket), that he came upon what she had done to him:

Mr. Fowles has operated the Prospect Variety Store for some time, and indeed although his storefront bears that name, a prominent billboard by the Government Wharf now proclaims a new entity, the Prospect Variety and Heritage Museum. "Heritage Museum" is common and self-explanatory if a little tautological, but a Variety Museum is something new and strange. What does Mr. Fowles have in mind? We had thought of museums as places of collection and preservation, and will be intrigued to see how variety is to be so treated. Mr. Fowles' interpretation of variety will be worth watching, particularly as his store has not been noted for vivacity and flair.

He leapt to his feet, holding the page at arm's length, and shouted, "You bitch! You bloody post-coital bitch!"

Annabel sighed sadly. She said, "Oh Justin sweet, don't go into a silly snit. *Please!* I'm feeling so good."

"Are you crazy? Well I *was* feeling good too. Sated and lovingly disposed to you. This is slander!"

"I wish you would try to understand what I'm doing—"

"What you are doing is called rape. Now I know why you were horny when you walked in: because you'd made a public nerd of me. Hey look everyone—Justin Fowles, the guy who makes ungrammatical signs and runs the dullest store in town! Do you know what turns you on, lady? It's power. It's power to make people look idiotic!"

She had been quietly aglow, her defences melted and the stress of the last two weeks dissolved, and he had shattered everything. He refused to listen to explanation. She hurled the coffee across the room and screamed, "Stop acting like a paranoid child! Are you so fucking insecure that a little fantasy sends you up? The store's been a public joke for years!"

Incensed, he began mopping up the coffee. "You really need to study your motives. You get in heat from scoring off me. Your definition of foreplay is to flail it alive. But it fits, eh? It's called sadism. The female variant is called ballcrushing."

She gave a sarcastic laugh. "Oh poor wee defenceless hundred and seventy pound ex-Mountie. Don't make me throw up."

It wasn't one of their best moments, but they eventually apologized for shouting and agreed the publicity might help the store. Justin was in fact half-hearted about the store. He was a man of action, not a shopkeeper, and was most himself as J. Fowles Inc., driving his truck to deliver parcels, cleaning eaves troughs and power-washing roofs and repairing broken windows and lawn mowers. Even if such missions were remarkably rare, and that many degenerated into the comradely sharing of a few beer with his clients.

It was also true that recently he was afflicted by fragmented dreams which contained sequential episodes that bridged interruptions of sleep, often lay dormant for several days, and even occurred if he dozed at the kitchen table or lay in the sunshine down at the beach at Semaphore Bay. He had become cast in episodes of the RCMP's famous Musical Ride, to which to his great relief he'd never in reality been assigned, to perform the famous charge again and again—as the director ordered retakes—across a stubble field before a bank of cameras from Walt Disney Enterprises, all the while watching the corporal on his left who was, he knew intuitively, never to be trusted.

This was the notoriously accident-prone Corporal Milton Milton, who had once been banished from the real Musical Ride for gelding a colleague's horse with his lance, and whose pilot's license had been revoked for contesting a landing at Edmonton International with Max Ward's huge Boeing 747 coming in the other way.

There was another dream-sequence that appealed to Justin for its heroic overtones, recalling those hopes of his earlier years in the Force. The cameras had gone and the stubble field had become the prairie stretching miles before him and Justin, mounted and in scarlet, was holding a huge waving pennant. In the distance the rising sun illuminated two white grain elevators toward which he was now galloping, his mind fully committed to a purpose which though undefined he knew to be high.

And who should appear miraculously beside him, riding what was undoubtedly a swaybacked reject from the Regina stables, but none other than Corporal Milton Milton again, waving a broken beach umbrella and shouting supportively, "I am with you sir! On! On! Gallant 41st Acadians!"

The reference to Cervantes' knight of doleful countenance was clear enough, but Justin knew the knight to be half-mad and there was nothing half-mad about knowing his country to be threatened. The jingoism south of the border repelled him, but his own humanistic patriotism, as he called it ironically, was no less strong. For all his phobia about ceremonial, he kept somewhere in his papers—more proudly than he'd admit—an eight-by-ten colour print of the young Constable Justin Fowles of the immortal Mounted, with glistening boots and slightly-bowed legs at attention, saluting the Maple Leaf forever in full glorious scarlet against tumbling flags and banners, in Ottawa the Nation's Capital on Canada Day or was it then Dominion Day, so many years ago.

And many years before his banishment, which—adjusting the table saw to cut the three shelves he had now measured—he was not sure even Annabel completely understood. He could however turn freely to the Fabled Jazz Hall Lady Jane. She was ageless wisdom and infinite patience, of such startling omniscience that to keep anything back seemed coy. She had said, "If you run a bar you get confidences; if you spill confidences the bar goes broke," and he had told her his secret past even before Annabel found the tunic. She was indeed a woman out of time, possibly not a woman at all but a being passing through the present, some quantum thing immune to the processes of decay. A time-carrier, in the same way that Scrofula, scion of Idris, was a carrier, crammed with a lexicon of fatal feline diseases but immune to them all.

"But immortality has its cost," she said one day, grasping his wrist, shocking him because her touch was ice. She said, "I'm one dimensional, darling. I have little feeling and no passion. My metabolism is cold fusion. What you see is much less than what you'd get."

He would visit her in the late afternoon, a time when three or four beers bestowed a tranquil nobility on his thoughts, so that he felt mellow even toward himself. When he was with her serene visions shimmered on the dark plywood walls of the Rib'n'Rye Room, a scattering of nymphs and carefree fauns across a pastoral Attic hillside, shading trees, perhaps a distant temple in the Doric mode, and the Fabled One reclining on a divan beside him, her robe fallen carelessly open to reveal, as she poured ambrosia into his silver goblet, a tit of porcelain perfection, a nipple of sugar candy dusted with starlight.

If he went on too much about the great injustices and heroic failures of his life, of his future victories, she reacted with kindly exasperation. "Justin dear, you have a right to sit back. To withdraw with honour from the field. Look at all your white-haired peers doddering happily into the sunset, tranquilized by warm illusions of self-fulfillment. Justin, are you listening?"

But typically, wrapped in himself, he would say, "Only the grandmothers, enjoying the post-menstrual amnesia which hides the futility of their domesticity. The men are long dead of guilt and remorse."

He was at his best, he believed, in political monologue, which bored Annabel because she thought politics superficial and Justin's politics archaic. As he'd said to the Lady Jane, "She lacks mature perspective. She doesn't understand I served high national purpose. No small-town work, eh? No traffic tickets. No heavy-booted criminal investigations for me." (He took her raised eyebrow as a tribute to his eloquence.) "This was the grand design, eh? Le grand pays? Un nation? A nation with borders, despite Gulag's nonsense. It was still possible then and I thought, I believed intensely, *I am guarding the country's borders! I am keeping this country together!*"

"Come on Justin! It's still together."

"Ha! Le grand seigneur got bored and retired to Mount Royal, leaving us with that little slippery newt-like thing with the small sucking mouth-parts. The branch-plant foreman, selling us off to Wall Street. But I must tell you about my dealings with Trudeau, the androgynous prophet of our times. Trudeau and Levesque, what a pair! But I was you see distressed with Levesque. He was so small, so tanned in nicotine. He was always hunched over a burning cigarette, as if celebrating ritual suicide. When he pulled himself upright his face was alarm and outrage, as if interrupted in an act of self-destruction."

"But Levesque surely was your enemy."

"He commanded respect; he was sincere! He had so much hate. Hate of les Anglais, hate of himself. They used him, you see, the political pros. One of the biggest was even on our payroll. But no one used Pierre Elliot. He was a realist. And tough. He told Nadon—Nadon was Comissioner then—to get him an officer and two men, his 'three vestals' he called us, to be without detectable sin. He told me, 'I can't admit to spying on France because Cabinet thinks it would infuriate fucking Paris. *Realpolitik* makes them squirm. And it's heresy to suspect the CIA. But Washington and Paris have something going with Quebec, and that's what you must find out.' That's what he said. His exact words. We were E Specials and we were assigned as—what the hell was it?—oh yeah, 'PM Private Household'!"

The Lady Jane said, "You were obviously the best in your field."

"Hah!" he barked ironically; "My field was opportunity lost."

The sweet fetid depths of the Rib'n'Rye made so much agreeable. Annabel was sweet but self-centred and her interest had limits; crossing them provoked her instant boredom, but The Fabled One was always amenable. Long ago when he apologized for talking too much about his first wife Maggie, she said, "I gave up on issues centuries ago, dear lad. The important things are human, and for those my capacity is limitless. So I can handle your awful domestic failures."

Maggie's activism for prison reform and against the Indian Act bugged him. "I had the classic mind-set, eh?

A wife must not have a mind of her own. But it was the beginning of my deconstruction. I could take down a drunk Cree quick as anyone. I believed in jails. I hunted Commies. The irony was she was a lawyer and so she knew what I was into. And she was from Alberta, where Mounties can do no wrong. And yet we went in opposite directions. By the time I was seeing things differently, Maggie was gone."

"So then you married Stephanie to make up to the native people."

"That's unfair. Stephanie was a sweet woman. She deserved more care than I gave her. There was just so much about her I never knew till it was too late."

"In contrast to Maggie," the Lady Jane chuckled. "When you didn't know about yourself until it was too late."

"I guess," he said, but unresponsively. Mention of Stephanie chilled his heart. There were things he couldn't even bring to the Fabled One, and the distracting mood returned him to the present, the image of Stephanie persisting so damnably he turned off the table saw, knowing a moment's inattention could lose him a finger.

When the saw whined down he could hear the rain again. It was a calming sound, but he was too agitated to be calmed. "Bugger it all!" he shouted, not to the Fabled Jazz Hall Lady but to the rain on the roof, to the sombre interior of the all-purpose room. "Yes, bugger all of you!" And to Scrofula, who now crashed through her small springed entry in the back door, soaking wet and bawling discontent, "Stop complaining! Your food's been by the stove all morning. Where the hell have you been?"

He thought the outdoors might clear his head. To breathe fresh air. To drop by the Starlight Cafe. He put up the *back in ten minutes* sign, and left the store. The commandos had gone. Perhaps he had imagined them.

4

Justin had noticed uniformed men in the village a few days after arriving in Prospect, and was puzzled because there was no military base near by. The waitress at the Starlight said, "They're commandos. They're from the Combat College, but they don't come here much. I think they're CB, you know, confined? It's a sort of army camp over in the clearcut."

But it wasn't military, and it bothered him that no one knew its legal status. He'd asked Annabel but she ignored the question and showed him a racist pamphlet from the College and said the place disgusted her too much to talk about. She said Mandril Gulag had told her it was just a business. Constable Ymenko said, "I think it's got Department of National Defence approval," something Justin had never heard of.

Justin's only close and as it turned out violent contact with the College was shortly after he'd set up J. Fowles Inc. The company's first project was to find weathered cedar fence rails for a retired couple who wanted to enhance the rustic ambience of a house they were building down the highway toward Port Renfrew. He'd heard of an old snake fence in the woods west of Prospect, on the long-abandoned Mason property between the village and the clearcut, and was out one morning to see if it was worth salvaging.

It was unpleasant going, because the air was damp and cold and the undergrowth wet from the previous night's rain. It didn't help his mood to find the fence too far gone to save. Most of it was on the ground; he had followed it for a hundred feet or so, hoping it would improve, but eventually the remnants disappeared under the fallen leaves and moss. He had stood up from examining the final visible rail when a sudden impact on his chest knocked his breath away and spun him so that he slipped and fell. His first thought was of a heart attack, and then that a branch had fallen on him. Then he was sure he was shot because there was blood on his hands and over his Cowichan sweater. But then—scrambling to sit up— he saw it wasn't blood but some kind of cold gelatinous fluid and he realized he'd been hit by a paintball.

A distant voice shouted triumphantly, "I got ya right'n'ass!" followed by the sound of someone crashing clumsily through the forest. Justin, slightly stunned, hadn't quite recovered himself before he was confronted by a short robot-like figure wearing camouflage coveralls and heavy black boots. A shiny black box-like helmet encased its head, with the face concealed by a mirrored rectangular eyepiece and a latticed snout. It carried a large paintball pistol and said irritably, in a shrill female voice that seemed to come from an echo-chamber, "Shit, you're not Charlie company."

"You are absolutely correct," Justin said emphatically, "I am not Charlie company. And who, may I ask, are you?"

The masked woman stared at him for several seconds and then shrilled metallically. "You know the rules. Captor anonymity. But immediate voluntary captive self-identification is mandatory. Come on. Name, rank, serial number. Let's have it!"

"What the hell are you talking about?" The situation was bizarre; he was becoming furious. He tried to get up, but his damn left knee stabbed him with pain and the masked woman jerked the pistol toward him.

"I said identify yourself!" she squealed, "Do you want another load of this shit right in your face? You must be as stupid as you are scruffy-looking. You live in the woods, eh? One of the local bums?"

"Put that damn thing away before you get into more trouble." Justin shouted. "You've already committed an assault and if you keep pointing that thing at me I might add forcible confinement."

He tried again getting to his feet but the masked woman screeched, "Sit down! You stay sat down, d'y'hear?" She was tugging a length of yellow nylon rope from her knapsack. "You're a goddam terrist! You haven't got name rank and serial number because you're a goddam terrist! Well you're a POW now, man, and you're coming with me." The woman threw the rope around Justin's neck. "Come on! Chop chop!"

Justin submitted, fuming. The situation was ridiculous; he could toss the bitch for a fall in a moment, but she was probably trained to counter a quick move. She held the gun steadily and he didn't want to be hit again.

"I'm tying you to this tree until I find an umpire. We get extra points for terrists."

"It'll get you two years in the slammer for illegal restraint or maybe kidnapping."

The woman waved the gun in his face. "Don't try intimidating me, buster. You're paid to be captured. I'm reporting you to the commandant."

"For Christ's sake," Justin shouted furiously, "Come out of your dream world, lady. This is not Nintendo time!"

She squawked, "Shut up! I told you shut up."

She was good with the rope, catching him even when he held his breath or tensed himself to leave slack for working free. When she finished she removed her helmet, which opened on hinges, and he saw that she was young, maybe in her twenties, with the pinched features of the emotionally deprived. Her hair was fluorescent orange and her skin pale, except for an infected patch around a glass stud in her left nostril.

She came close and put a hand on his crotch, rubbing him. "Maybe to make this realistic I should rape you. Isn't that what male grunts do to women?"

She stood back, grinning. "I get the feeling. Power. Yeah. But I don't know how I can fuck you standing up when you're trussed like a turkey. And you're bloody old; maybe I check if it gets hard."

She made one step toward him when something dark and the size of large book flew out of the trees and exploded in her face in a shower of rotted cedar. She gasped and dropped to her knees clawing at her face as a young boy leapt from the bushes and snatched up the paintball gun.

Justin astonished, confused, heard a young voice shout, "Keep her covered, Marc!" and a thin young girl stepped out from behind him. She said, "I bet you're Mr. Fowles. Mummy told us about you. Annabel McKinley? She said she'd seen you in the village, although you look more bedraggled than she reported. I'm Susan, by the way, and this is my brother Marc. I'm eleven but he's only eight."

"Eleven," repeated Justin, utterly bewildered. "Eight. Well now."

Marc shouted "Good morning, sir. Do you know anything about the Geneva Convention? Would it let me let shoot the prisoner? At close range?"

"I imagine the Conventions—" Justin tried lamely—

"Oh Marc, don't be ridiculous, of course not," said Susan, kneeling to untie Justin.

But the commando, tugging at a lanyard around her neck, produced a chrome whistle from a breast pocket and managed to blow a long shrill blast before Marc yanked it from her mouth.

Susan said, "Don't get too close to her or she'll grab you."

"I'm not *stupid*." Marc said. "But she was calling for help. I'm taking the course some day, but Mummy says I can't go yet because I'm too young."

Susan said, "Mummy says a lot of people come up from the States to learn to shoot blacks and drug dealers. Americans have a constitutional duty to carry guns, so it's a good idea for them to learn how to use them."

The woman looked up defiantly. "You can laugh all you like about the College, but you'll be on your knees in gratitude on The Day. When Armageddon cometh, and the nations are powerless against evil in the streets and from the skies. The College teaches the skills for us to triumph on those glorious killing fields."

"Exactly who were you thinking of killing?" asked Justin.

The woman laughed with forced irony. "There's something about North Americans that makes me want to cry. We're all so *out of it!* Islam can take our oil, the pisshead niggers can burn our cities and government can take our sacred rights, and we don't give a damn."

Marc asked, "Which Canadian city did you say?"

"I'm saying we must drink the blood of the hosts of Satan to gaze into the white light of Jesus' blessed face."

Justin said, "How did Jesus come into this?"

"Oh that dazzling cynical wit! It lets you avoid the truth, eh? Well I'm not ashamed of believing! What I'm ashamed of is my country's cowardice, in hiding behind America in World War Two and Korea and Viet Nam and South America. Everywhere the forces of evil have risen and we've been absent."

Justin, disgusted, wondered if she were as confused as she sounded. He said, "You'd better clear off. You'd better go. Go on, lady."

"I'll have my sidearm and emergency whistle back."

"Heck no!" said Marc. "It's legitimate booty. The spoils of war!"

"I said *Go!*" Justin barked, waving her off.

She stood up, scowling. "You'll hear from the Commandant about this. He knows how to handle employees like you. As for you kids, leave this evil man. He has power to corrupt you!" She turned away and stumbled back into the forest.

Justin said, "Well this is extraordinary! You are amazing! I'm glad you arrived, believe me. And thank you for the rescue; that was brilliant. That bloody woman hit me with a paintball, as you can see. But aren't you supposed to be in school?"

"This is Saturday."

"Ah. Of course. I must still be in shock. But yes, you were marvelous."

Susan said, "We were making too much noise for Mummy to work so she told us to go for a walk. A long walk. She is a single mother and therefore tends to be highly strung. Marc and I think she would be less tense if she had a man. For the usual purposes. But there's no one around who would really do."

"And I think you are probably too old," Marc added.

"Oh much too old," said Justin, amazed at their precocity.

"Hush!" said Marc in a loud urgent whisper. "Someone's coming! Reinforcements! Mr. Gulag I bet, the mad major, to claim my captured arms! Come on Susan! Goodbye sir!"

The children, mouthing goodbyes, scurried into the underbrush in the direction of the village. Justin stood transfixed; they were charmed, gifted with such vitality as to seem another species, perhaps another evolutionary step in human development. But he was still enraged at the paintball attack and decided to follow the commando and have it out with whomever she was running to. He heard her blowing her whistle again somewhere ahead, and once caught a glimpse of her through the trees. He intended to follow from a distance but came suddenly to the edge of the clearcut to see her standing beside a jeep in a turnaround at the end of a rough logging road, talking animatedly to two men. When he came out of the forest she shouted, "There's the bastard. Yeah, that's him!"

The men, in highly polished boots and wearing red armbands bearing the letter S in white, turned toward Justin with outstretched arms. One of them shouted, "Hey, you can't come further. This is private property!"

Justin assumed the S stood for Staff. They were in their late twenties, over six feet tall and enough overweight to give an impression of power. When Justin kept walking toward them the second instructor shouted, "You heard what the man said. What's it about private property you don't understand?'

They barred his way, frowning, their fists clenched, and Justin thought, *bloody thugs.* It had never occurred to him that age might diminish his skill at close and dirty combat. He had subdued three-hundred-pound loggers in picket-line scuffles and taken down countless raging drunks in darkened bars from Halifax to Prince Rupert. The two thugs' intimidating glare did not impress him. He said, "Horse shit. You can get me to your commander or whatever you call him. Or you can get out of my way. But fast."

The instructors stood their ground but were clearly confused. Justin was too angry to calculate his chances against them. He pushed them aside impetuously, climbed into the jeep, and barked, "Cut the crap. Just drive me to his office. Now!"

One of the instructors, frowning sullenly, drove him up the logging road, which climbed steeply before running across a slope from which Justin caught glimpses of the whole College encampment half a mile away. His immediate thought was of a concentration camp built after a nuclear blast. Four or five watchtowers joined by sections of high fence rose from the sun-bleached detritus of the clearcut. Directly inside the fence were several areas half the size of a football field scattered with the trenches and barriers of obstacle courses, which surrounded some half-dozen one-storey barrack-like buildings painted in camouflage. The road turned down toward the camp and ran beside the fence, which was topped with barbed wire. They passed a watch tower, from which a man waved down. There were searchlights on the tower. A sentry at the gate saluted as they entered and Justin noticed a truck being serviced on a ramp, a fire hydrant, a small shed with a red cross symbol on the door. And then they were driving around a small parade ground to stop in front of a low, windowed building. A sign in front of it said *COLLEGE HEADQUARTERS.*

The instructor said, "I'll see if I can make an appointment."

Justin slid out of the jeep. He said, "Don't bother," and marched into the building. He marched across an entrance hallway to a door holding a plastic sign announcing *Major Mandril Gulag, Commandant,* rapped once with a clenched fist, and marched in.

Mandril Gulag, seated behind a large desk, was unlike anyone Justin had ever seen. Gulag's domed head emerged bald and neckless from broad shoulders like a giant lizard, and the planes of his reconstructed face were greenish chitinous plates forming a huge beaked nose and armoured eyes. As Justin entered he turned from the window behind him and growled, "What the fuck?" and then glaring, rising from his chair, "What the fuck is this?"

Justin wiped his hand through the muck on his sweater. There was a file holding papers open on the desk and Justin said, "The fuck, seeing you ask, is this!" He slapped the hand palm down on the papers so that the gel splattered across the table. "Some goddamn woman in your fancy College costume hit me with this crap. I was not, as one of your goons will no doubt insist, on College property, whatever that is. This idiot woman of yours knocked me off my feet with a paintball and tied me to a tree."

Gulag stood up. He was about five foot ten, and powerful. He had evidently already been briefed. He said dismissively, "It was an honest mistake. She mistook you for an opponent. You live in the woods, old fella? You're taking a few risks, eh?" Gulag came around the desk and lowered his voice. "But I'll tell you something. Folks around here don't like transients." He produced a roll of bills and pulled off two twenties. "You head on back to Victoria. Find a dry cleaner. Have a drink or two while you wait, eh?"

"What the hell are you talking about?" shouted Justin, thoroughly aroused. "I happen to live in Prospect. I am the resident owner of an established maintenance service and will soon be opening a vital retail estab—"

"Shit!" said Gulag with a burst of laughter. "You must be new in town, eh? I'll be goddamn!"

"What you can give me right now is a reason I shouldn't charge you and your student for assault and unlawful confinement."

"Oh fuck me gently, man. So you came onto her in the woods. She defended herself from your sexual advances. Maybe with your fly open, yeah, with your fly open! Her word against yours?"

"She defended herself by tying me up? I've got witnesses."

"Yeah, I heard. Two little kids. Unreliable testimony. But you go ahead. I'll meet you in court any time." Gulag bounced on his toes, grinning as he held up his fists. His moves were tautly athletic. "Fuck, even if you won we'd make you look like an asshole."

Justin hated conceding the law's impotence but Gulag, damn him, was right. He said, "Don't count on it" but it lacked the defiance he intended.

"Shit," Gulag said. "It's a little thing eh? Put it in perspective. This girl gets too keen. She makes a hit. She ties you up. She's trained, eh? But in fact she goofed, so I'll apologize." He went behind the desk, reaching for the intercom. "A written apology."

"Don't bother."

"You're from the village and I want to be on good terms. They misunderstand me. You know the woman who does the local tabloid. Macsomething? An alarmist for shit's sake!"

"McKinley. I haven't met her yet."

"She wrote a piece saying I planned house-to-house combat in her fucking village. I'd never thought of it, eh? But why not? Is there a bylaw against it? Does Prospect have borders? Does it exist? Are there borders in the global village? This is a new age; boundaries are obsolete."

Justin was vaguely prepared for the physical threat that Gulag's athletic moves conveyed, but the remark caught him off guard. It was too close to his heart, to his self-proclaimed sacred cause and mission, and he barked, "Bloody nonsense, man! Borders define nations. Borders define cultures and there is nothing more important today than maintaining our culture."

"Cultures? Shit! Borders don't stop trade or travel. They don't stop terrorism. Governments set boundaries but governments mean fuck-all. That's why this business is booming. Because civilizations are crumbling and people want to know how to use intelligent force to keep order. That's the College's motto, eh? *To Use Intelligent Force!* Our waiting list is eight months long!"

Justin had come to protest a paintball attack but Gulag was too irritating and absurd to ignore. He glanced over the office. There were three large portraits behind the desk, Napoleon Bonaparte, Ho Chi Min and Omar Bin Laden. Gulag said, "You notice them eh?

Bony the master of yesterday, Ho Chi Min the prophet of the new age, Bin Laden precursor of tomorrow."

There was a map occupying most of the wall to his left, but as Justin turned to it he caught for an instant the first four words listed on a board to the right of the desk—

Airport security
Anti-terrorism
Assassination
Attrition —

The map was about ten feet wide and six feet high—beige land and blue sea—and he recognized the shape of Prospect's inlet in the centre. There were four red circles, one labeled *Combat College* to the west and one labelled *Rendezvous* to the east, with *Prospect* near the centre. The roads were coloured blue, and there was a network of dotted blue lines which he assumed were trails. There was a dotted green line going south from the College to a green square on the coast labelled *Beachhead,* from which a white dotted line fell south, presumably toward Washington below the map's lower edge. There was a broad black arrow pointing to *Rendezvous,* and the the arrow held a scarlet "A" and some text, and Justin was feeling for his glasses to read the text when Gulag danced across and pulled a curtain across the map, exclaiming merrily, "Hey! Highly classified, eh? For my eyes only! A military camp gotta have military secrets, eh?"

"You have a connection with the Rendezvous? It's a motel, isn't it?"

Gulag posed solemnly with feet wide apart and hands on hips. He was wearing riding breeches and polished riding boots, at which Justin had to check a smile. Gulag said, "It's a whorehouse. It's off limits. I catch a cadet near that place and he's out. No refund, no certificate. Dishonourable discharge. You haven't met the whoremaster Plantagenet."

"Not yet. He's giving you trouble?"

"Me? Fuck he tries troubling me and I'll show him what trouble is. He runs Sodom and Gomorrah in our midst, for fuck's sake. Poisoning the countryside!"

Justin had no idea what the Rendezvous represented but Gulag's pompous self-righteousness made him irritated and combative and he said, "Poisoning a virtually unpopulated rural coastline? Poisoning a village full of seniors? Are you kidding?"

"Plantagenet? The Rendezvous? Put it in perspective. Okay it's chicken-shit corruption. Small but symptomatic. But look at the globe. The social order is crumbling. Simple charity is controlled by racketeers. Healers are befouled by greed. Politicians live and breathe corruption. Governments are impotent. You show me a government that isn't on the—"

"Hold on! Hold on—" The man's volubility surprised him but he disliked being ranted at. "That is hyperbolic and absurd, man. You're overstating—"

"Overstating? How about the disgusting Clinton? How about the Moscow Mafia selling drugs and pimping pre-pubescent boys and girls around the globe? The FBI killing and burning across the Disunited States? Genocide and sexual disease in Africa? Rwanda, South East Asia, Timor. This disgusting female circumcision. The terrorist humiliation of gallant American forces?"

"Tell me, is it worse than the eighteenth century, is it worse than from say 1850 to 1919?" The man was going round in circles but there was venom in him. Justin said anrily, "I don't follow you. I don't see where you're coming from. Or are you just a general shit-disturber? What side are you—?"

"There are no fucking sides! I tell you there's chaos! Nations like the Stupified States are spending billions on over-sophisticated weapons deployed according to 1914 concepts. Nations are irrelevant, and hi-tech weaponry's no security in the new age!"

"Bull shit," Justin said. "National identity has never been more important. It has never been more important for this country."

"Borders again!" cried Gulag. "The era of territory is gone, man! The new deployment is terrorism and it knows no borders! It uses hijacking and car bombs and suicidal force. Uniformed troops in regiments and squadrons are powerless against it! So our strength now is in men and women dedicated individually to the ideals we hold sacred, alert always to treacherous attack at any time of the day or night. People must train to survive the final collapse. People want to know how to preserve our civility, to strike down evil! I say to them, we must be pro-active against evil!"

"So when does this all take place?"

"How can we know the when of future? The future is now."

"As in vigilante? As in pre-emptive attack?"

"If we don't, who will?"

"You'll end up in the bloody slammer."

Mandril bent in a crouch, grinning, his hands open by his shoulders. He said, "For instance, are you ready?"

"What do you mean? I sure wasn't ready to be lectured at."

"I mean personal physical readiness. I mean can you survive sneak attack? It is every man for himself. That is what I teach."

"That damn woman of yours certainly knew about sneak—"

Suddenly Mandril leapt at Justin, who instinctively grabbed Mandril's right forearm, dropping to his knees and yanking down hard. Justin somehow didn't get it right because Mandril failed to fly over him to crash against the wall, but ended up pinned face down beneath him, struggling ineffectually to escape and grunting. "I'll be fucked. I'll be fucked."

Justin released him and got up, shaking his head in disbelief. Mandril scrambled to his feet and was bent over, breathing heavily just as the door flew open and the receptionist cried out, "Is there something wrong, Major? I thought I heard—"

"Nothing," Justin said. "The Major was just showing me some of the finer points of assault and battery." He gestured to her to leave. "The Major would like you to bring round a jeep to drive me back to the village." When the door closed he turned to Mandril. "What the hell was that for? Of all the damn fool things—"

"I'll be royally fucked," Mandril said, rubbing the back of his head. "Where the shit you learn that?"

"With the gallant 41st Acadians, Field Marshal Alexander's favourite storm troops in the bloody assault on Monte Cassino. Before you Americans were even in the war. One of those ineffectual regiments you were mentioning. And before your time, I think."

"Yeah well I'm a Canadian and I've been in combat, eh?" The major sounded defensive. "I was proud to volunteer for Nam beside my American brothers while fucking Canada slept."

"Proud of what? So we weren't in it, which makes you a mercenary, killing for money. But you haven't answered my question; what the hell are you trying to prove by coming on to me like that?

"My fucking foot slipped or I would have—."

"Horseshit," said Fowles. He evidently wasn't going to get an answer. "You move without thinking, like the way you talk. The rant is colourful, Major, but I don't have time to argue with such garbage. Your idiot cadet, commando, whatever she is interrupted a job I was on. The building of a fence. A menial task in your grand perspective no doubt, but I must get back to it."

"Well fuck you too, whoever you are."

"The name is Fowles. I thought you'd never ask." He opened the door to leave. "And just make damn sure your troops look before they shoot."

"You keep your fucking head down from now on. You're a hostile, eh? I'm designating you a hostile."

Justin said nothing on the drive back to Prospect. The driver was a young commando who announced he was from Texas, but Justin was too full of his own thoughts to ask questions about the College's training. The accidental victory in taking down Gulag had been something of a catharsis; it had deflated not only his outrage over the paintball attack but also his subsequent astonished anger at Gulag's ideas. He was left in a kind of contemplative confusion from which gradually emerged a cool hostility to the man, to his blatant bullshit and opportunism, to his militaristic presence as a wannabe George S. Patton complete with cavalry breeks just ten minutes' drive from his home.

Small doubts also arose and subsided about what had gone wrong taking the bugger down. Even if he'd ended up on top, it was a technical flop. Some neglected skills had evidently rusted, and he should perhaps enquire about martial arts night courses in Victoria. Although realistically the idea of an hour's drive each way, and two hours working out, was too exhausting to contemplate.

Back at the store he lay down on his bed, weary and not a little bewildered. The ranting, the sudden attack, were incomprehensible. The man was bloody well mad. He was so bloody mad he couldn't be true, and that was a relief because otherwise he'd be a boundless menace. Justin fell into his afternoon nap wondering vaguely about the wall map, about the arrow pointing to the Rendezvous motel, and the dotted line leading south across the Strait of Juan da Fuca to Washington.

In the following weeks he tried with little success to find out more about the College. It was obviously much more than the usual paintball club where friends fired gobs of paint at each other. It was all too substantial; he'd seen offices, barracks, a mess hall, and classrooms, and there were large practice areas outside the fence. There were trucks and jeeps and a front-end loader. There was also an old BC Hydro cherry-picker used to hoist linemen up to the hydro lines, from which Mandril was said to supervise hand-to-hand combat. Somewhere as well there was a firing range, although Ymenko had been skeptical of that.

Justin said, "Look man, they fire machine guns. I've heard them. I don't mean Isuzus; I mean heavy point-five calibre stuff. I think they have a mortar."

Ymenko said, "Well that would be illegal. I haven't had any report like that. I haven't heard any small arms fire. You're sure, eh?"

Ymenko's tone was definitely indulgent, which made Justin bristle. "I didn't fight six months in Normandy without learning what machine guns and mortars sound like for Christ's sake."

Which, setting aside the fact that Justin had never been closer to Normandy than Halifax, was as far as the matter went. He came across Combat College ads torn from Montana and Texas papers for "guerilla training" reading FREE AMERICA FROM BIG GOVERNMENT and CRUSH THE TERRORISTS". He had seen a milder ad—one Annabel had refused— in a Canadian magazine extolling the virtues of outdoor challenge and team-building, whatever the terms meant, but the curriculum never appeared in print. A commando he met one day in the village said it was a word-of-mouth thing; his gang back home knew there was weapons handling, hand-to-hand combat and anti-insurgency work. "The real thing," as the commando said. "They don't bugger around, eh?"

"The students," Justin said. "I heard the CIA sponsors some students."

The commando grinned. "We're sworn to secrecy on all internal matters, sir."

Justin distrusted militarism, parade ground drill, and certainly an armed encampment flying the American flag in Prospect's back yard. Perhaps they were prevailing after all, and his brilliant outfoxing of C. Myron Resnick of the CIA had been wasted. That file had probably gone to CSIS and been closed, because CSIS would crumble in the bureaucratic infighting with External, where as some pale junior diplomat had once told him, they sought "accommodation rather than confrontation." He had spent too much of his career trying to outguess people amidst the tangled interplay of espionage and counter-espionage and diplomacy, which was perhaps why Tuchman's book attracted him, the secret history of the secret telegram that brought American into World War I.

But money was often the clue, and one day he sat down to figure if the College was viable financially. A forensic audit, as they used to say. He gathered from talk at the Starlight that each courses had 24 students and there were always three courses in progress, which meant there would always be 72 students in camp. Fees were advertised at $700, to put the total daily income was around $3,700.

There were said to be seven instructors, four cooks, four or five maintenance people, and the two women he'd seen in Mandril's office. Including Mandril the daily payroll must be at least $4,000. Which didn't start to cover food service, hydro, laundry, ammunition, insurance, advertising, administration, and vehicle maintenance, nor the capital costs for vehicles and buildings, concrete firing range, fencing, and everything else. The figures were rough, but they didn't add up. There had to be a very fat subsidy from somewhere.

Justin heard dimly from afar the call of distant duty. To defend again the undefended border. But God it was an impossible task, and he was too old. And somewhere he had taken an oath to stay out of all that on pain of spending the rest of his legless, armless eunuch life in an RCMP dungeon.

5

Annabel's tea with Mary Evens that had so provoked Justin's alarm wasn't her first meeting with the old woman. Annabel had run into Mary shortly after she had arrived, but only briefly, on the street outside Pollock's, and found her lively and warm-hearted. The tea party was several weeks later, and by then word of Mary's secluded habits had got around and the children had created a mythology for her, of an old witch who saw her way in the woods at night, who rose before dawn to collect salamanders and frogs and baby raccoons, and who sat hunched for hours by the seaside, waiting—according to one of Marc's friends—for drowned little children, to suck their blood as refreshing as ice-cold Diet Pepsi.

The meeting came about by chance, during a hike Annabel inflicted on the children one Saturday morning to ease her guilt. Her fear that she was maternally inept drove her to do more for them even while suspecting she was doing too much, a conflict that typically asserted itself in erratic behaviour. She was kneading dough, having had the sudden notion that children should have memories of homemade bread, when the saccharine voice of an American female shill reached her from the living room extolling a confectionized breakfast cereal. The final sprightly chorus, "Just reach for more, just tip and pour—" so affronted her sweating efforts that she slammed down the dough, marched into the living room and shouted, "Turn off that shit! It's ten o'clock and you're still in your PJs. We're going hiking. We're going down to the ocean! You must experience the real world!"

She led them briskly to the end of Mercator, the gravel road that passed the house and became the trail down to Semaphore Bay. They were half way down the trail and well into the forest when a voice above them trilled, "Ah, three lost children in the woods! Surely your mother has not left you untended?"

Annabel shouted hello, and introduced the children. Mary said jovially, "Annabel! I do apologize! You look so young my dear! And Susan! How lovely you are! You must come for tea. I think I have chocolate chip cookies, and Coke. If you're allowed Coke—"

Annabel hesitated, but Susan made a pleading face and Marc who had gone off on a detour broke cover shouting, "Wow, Coke and goodies!" and she relented.

Mary led the way upward, calling back to the children, "How would you like to live in the forest? We could find a great hemlock with drooping branches, like that one, soft and encompassing, with the lovely carpet of old needles to sit on, and just listen to the forest. Listen!"

Everyone stopped. Annabel heard the wind's roar in the upper branches and gulls calling harshly from the ocean. There was the crack of a falling snag far off in the forest, and a bird singing furtively nearby. To Annabel, for all Mary's enthusiasm, the sounds were ominous, reminding her how out of place she was in the forest, perhaps in the country.

Marc and Susan had run ahead, and Mary said, "They are lovely children, Annabel. Susan looks so like you! I look forward to meeting their father."

"That would be a little difficult. He lives in Edmonton. The kids are visiting him this summer. We're divorced"

"Oh splendid!" Mary grinned over her shoulder. "I am sure it was the right decision. I think Marc probably has some of his features."

"He does resemble him slightly, yes."

"It's the weak chin, isn't it? And the lower part of his face is unmistakably common. But those features can suggest an attractive sensitivity, later on. The trouble with you young women today is you mate with no thought to breeding. You should know the stock before you invite impregnation; it's entirely up to the female. If you permit yourself to be impregnated by a male with a limp mouth or shifty eyes what can you expect? He was more a cad than a bounder, was he dear?"

"I think—" Annabel managed breathlessly, too pressed by Mary's leaping pace and too surprised by her opinions to discuss genetics, let alone to discriminate between caddishness and bounderism.

"But bad seed need not be dominant. One simply has to watch carefully, and instruct, and I can see your influence with them both is decisive, decisive. Susan is an utterly charming girl, with great style, and Marc will have a pale romantic allure! That is one of the great benefits of divorce; it removes children from the influence of fathers."

Annabel, amusement replacing her uneasiness, said jokingly, "It doesn't help with the dishes."

"Housekeeping is immaterial. The loss of fathers is invariably beneficial, because the mother's influence becomes undivided. What we really need is a humane substitute for war, because children are brought up best when the men are away fighting and if possible getting killed. Society has given the male all these family responsibilities which of course he is completely incapable of fulfilling. Quite out of his depth, poor thing. Not designed for it. The male's sole natural responsibility is to service the female, whose sole responsibility is to bear and rear her children. Bear and rear: fight and fornicate. It's really so simple."

The children, above them, suddenly squealed with pleasure and when Annabel reached where they had been she was looking down, a hundred yards away, at an old sprawling bungalow, low-lying, with a cedar shake roof over shingled walls. It stood in a gothic thicket of conifers and arbutus, and its sagging eaves trailed an entanglement of vines. There were leaded lattice windows and thick moss on the roof, and a deep verandah. One window was covered in plywood, and a piece of faded blue tarpaulin was tied over a corner of the verandah roof. This was Mogador. It was in terrible disrepair.

The devastated garden began a few yards away, where the dismembered skeleton of a gate lay on the dry grass, and the vines off to her right had mounted a stand of trees carrying up pieces of fencing like flotsam in a surf. There were unrestrained patches of honeysuckle and lilac amidst which she glimpsed, mossy and eroded, the small stone figure of a grieving angel.

"Ah!" Mary sighed rapturously. "How magnificent it was in the thirties, Annabel! A Mediterranean villa! I spent so many summers here. It was an enchanted place for a little girl. Croquet and badminton on the green lawns, and roses and wide-brimmed hats!" She raised her arms, as if welcoming a remembered dawn. "It's fairyland, absolute fairyland."

The children were examining an old concrete bird bath and Annabel thought how marvelous it was for them to discover such a decaying magic place. Listening to Mary, she tried to imagine manicured avenues of lawn and paths of raked gravel beside trellises draped with pale pink roses. Despite what Mary said, there didn't seem much room for lawns.

Mogador had been built in the early twenties by an English officer retired from the Indian Army, who decided that the Gulf Islands, to which so many of his colleagues had retired, were too sheltered to provide the bracing discomfort essential for manly vigour. He was Brigadier Ralph Chester Coulthurst, a military engineer, and he and his wife Etheldred and their decrepit butler Blenkinsop lived there for twenty years.

Etheldred dreamed of a sunlit English garden, and oversaw the sturdy lads of the village laying it out, but the garden was beset by high winds and drought, and did not thrive. The main reason however was neglect, for after four decades of Imperial service the Brigadier's priorities were not easily altered. Once he had dutifully provided Etheldred a house, he turned to surveying the property, mapping four sites along the beach for machine gun emplacements, and a flattish area to the north where artillery could be deployed. He discovered the cave in the south face of the rock, which he called the Cinnamon Cave and in which he installed a robust hand-operated winch. There was a period when several tons of broken rock appeared on the forest floor directly beneath the cave, and the villagers speculated the Brigadier was creating a local Gibraltar.

In his later years he took to oriental religion, and went blind staring into the rising sun. He was well into his eighties at the time of Pearl Harbour, and one night, soon after a Japanese submarine shelled the Estevan Point lighthouse far up the coast, he decided the Japanese were landing on his property. He pulled from the closet the moth-eaten scarlet tunic of his full dress uniform, and was feeling his way down the stairway down the cliff when he slipped, smashed through the rotted railing, and died on the rocky scree below.

The Seymours, Partland and Millicent, acquired Mogador in 1943 from the Brigadier's widow, whom they found a lean woman of impeccable mannered coolness. Her last words to the Seymours, spoken without emotion, were, "I hope you can make it what it might have been."

But, in fact, the Seymours did not. They were genteel and exhausted, and bought Mogador with their last savings to escape a terrifying world. They ignored the garden and couldn't afford to repair the house. Thus Mogador now wasn't all that different from the Mogador Etheldred Coulthurst had left, and Mary's romantic recollections were of another world, that never was.

It wasn't until Annabel entered the house that she realized its appalling state. She came suddenly out of the sunlight into virtual darkness in which she could barely make out high dark wood-paneling, dark passages and archways, water-stained ceilings, worn oriental carpets of ochre rich as the dried blood of Empire. The air was heavy with dampness, old wood, mold. "There!" Mary exclaimed, waving an arm toward a doorway through which Annabel saw a soot-stained granite fireplace below a large framed engraving of eighteenth century naval battle, ships of the line with shot-torn sails and broken masts closing amidst smoke, and above the frame two crossed naval cutlasses bracketed to the cracked wall.

"The first thing I saw that night I returned! I remembered it so well! The Battle of the Nile, the swords! Partland's mother was a Brandley and Sir Joseph Brandley was one of Nelson's captains. An Admiral of the Blue, although he certainly didn't have much money, poor Sir Joe."

"Partland Seymour," said Annabel hopefully, trying to bring the conversation within her range. "Your cousin?"

"Oh no my uncle, my dear, my uncle! And the general's nephew. Such a dreadfully ineffectual man. When I heard Partland had driven into the Fraser Canyon it didn't surprise me at all. The most abstracted man you'd every hope to meet. Oh it was quite awful." Mary was fishing cups and saucers out of an enameled basin filled with a cold grey-green scum. The kitchen seemed coated with grime. Mary's fingers were thin and blue, like plucked turkey wings.

"I took the bus from Calgary and stopped at Boston Bar. In the canyon. The car was at Harrington's garage, which has been there for centuries; it was squashed absolutely flat! Absolutely flat! It was no more than eighteen inches off the ground. You see it fell right to the edge of the river, ricocheting off the side of the canyon all the way!"

"How terrible," Annabel said, puzzled at Mary's evident delight.

"They were both still in the car when it was found," Mary went on, pottering between the drying rack and the plate cupboard. "Their bodies had been torn open by sharp metal and their internal organs had been expressed disgustingly by the enormous pressures. Aunt Millie had been decapitated, and her head was never—"

"I think the kettle's boiling," Annabel interjected decisively, to avoid further horrors.

Annabel was prepared for tea to be a disaster. All there was for the children were a near-empty bottle of obviously flat Coca Cola and the promised chocolate chip cookies, crumbling with age. The drinking glasses for the coke were smeared in visible grease.

The children however revealed unsuspected resources of social charm. They nibbled bravely on the cookies, and avoided any crisis over the flat coke and dirty glasses by asking sweetly if they could have tea. They excused a lack of appetite by lying so convincingly about the huge breakfast their mother had served that Annabel wondered if she could ever trust their word again.

She watched them now in the far corner of the room, beside a glass cabinet with Mary beside them saying, "They do not teach you about the Empire these days, so I will have to tell you! Marc you will find this very interesting. Long before you were born, a famous general lived here. He was my great uncle; Lieutenant General Wellington Coulthurst! And here is a pistol he wore during the great Indian Mutiny. It is a flintlock; you see you had to pour the powder into the barrel and tamp it down with this little rod. And the flints were kept . . . "

It was comforting, Annabel thought, for the children to have grandmotherly attention. It might help civilize them. Distantly, by the far windows, Susan was listening attentively to Mary who was now holding a fierce African spear. Marc was making machine-gun noises with the pistol; his leaping moves dusted the shafts of sunlight with sparkling gold. She was warmed by the scene until it struck her the talk was about war and weapons that she implacably prohibited at home.

Annabel looked about uneasily at the escritoire by the far wall, the delicate antique chairs, the great marble-topped sideboard. Mahogany, scuffed and aged. Dust-covered Victoriana. And the memento mori; the brass shellcase umbrella rack in the front hall, the terrible cutlasses above her head, the two disintegrating heads—a leopard and some kind of antelope, an impala she thought—on the far wall. It was the contrast that struck her; the vivid contrast between this dark heaviness and the light and vivacity of her children.

She thought Mary refreshing. She had an intimidating precision of mind, even if it was difficult to sense her centre. Her conversation went off in strange directions, and sometimes disappeared completely. Annabel was unsure; she must give things time. Amidst which thoughts she became aware that Mary was sitting beside her, saying " . . the children wanted to explore the garden. We must take a little time—you must tell me about yourself, my dear. My delivery boy tells me you publish the local paper. You call it the *Pacific Reporter*."

"Well not exactly. That was last month. Originally it was the Prospect Advertiser but that seemed so blah, and there are such beautiful newspaper names. The *Examiner!* The *Advocate!* So now I switch whenever something new really appeals to me."

"Oh splendid! But it must be hard work."

"Getting advertising is usually hell, but I've just found a girl Sandy Kelvin to help. As for content, around here there are lots of letter-writers, bless them."

"But you're competing for news with the bigger papers, the *Times Colonist* in Victoria and the Sooke paper, what is it—?"

"The *Mirror* in Sooke, yes. But I decided I wasn't going to bother with that kind of news, and I guess *Reporter* was misleading. I mean I can't possibly *report.* You see my background is advertising and I've always believed you don't try to sell reality. I mean who really gives a damn for the reality of a sanitary napkin? You try to draw your customer into a fantasy in which the napkin is effortless and trendy. You create a fable, and draw the people into the fable! So that's what I do; I take things that happen and create fables that express my own way of seeing, which is really all any writer can do."

"But Mrs. Pollock says some people are very angry with you."

"Oh I know, and that includes my friend Justin. They don't understand it's not literally *them* in the fables. And the fables are so important to me."

Mary exclaimed, "I must subscribe to your newspaper. You are obviously a clever young woman." And then briskly, as if turning to the next item on an agenda, "But you are a lusty young woman Annabel, and attractive. What do you do for sex? I am not confident of this Justin Fowles. Mrs. Pollock mentioned him. A shopkeeper who keeps an empty shop, I think she said. I saw him once and took him for the village layabout. Quite unkempt. But does he communicate with clarity? That is so important, to communicate with clarity."

Annabel laughed. "Really he's very open. Often much too open! No, he's articulate and thoughtful and makes me laugh. Apart from the possibility that's he's certifiably insane, he's a good deal. Oh he's a mass of susceptibilities. But yes, we get along."

"I am not sure that simply getting along is adequate for you, Annabel. Too many women take that route."

"Perhaps, but—" Annabel thought Mary oddly aggressive, as if she were conducting a cross-examination, and Annabel had no intention of saying more about herself. But there was a cry from outside, and Mary started dramatically, holding up her hand—

"Hark; what was that?"

The cry turned to laughter. Annabel said, "Oh, they're okay. It was nice of you to show them—what did you say?—your artifacts."

"Well, it is all gone, you see, it is all gone. The history, and what history gives us; the sense of belonging together, in continuity." She shrugged. "Showing them a few trinkets is not going to imbue them with a sense of their history; I suppose I do it without thinking. It is foolish of me. But oh!" She jerked up her hand again, finger extended. "Oh I don't mean it as a narrow family thing. It is essence. It is that of which I am part; the context in which I exist."

Annabel had lost the thread somewhere and Mary, suddenly animated as if appealing to her, gestured around the room: "I was so fortunate to have this context bequeathed to me. In which I could create something my own and yet of those who went before. The continuity. It is so necessary as the end draws near, to create context."

"But you have that, Mary. And you have children, don't you?"

Mary grasped the arm of the divan, just a little too quickly, almost a grab. "But I told you it is all gone. It is a rage of discontinuity. Yes, I have a dear daughter a good deal older than you and I have not heard from her for twenty-five years. A brilliant lawyer. She lives in Ottawa. I write to her constantly and she never replies. A rage of discontinuity. I am terribly bitter."

Annabel said, a little perplexed, "I'm sorry to hear that."

"I was a perfect mother," said Mary resentfully. "She was my only child and I doted on her. A child naturally rebels, against the pain but the grown child learns the pain was caused not by malice but the parents' weakness and error. That is why reconciliation is so magical. It is one of those basic human acts that has to be done. Just as one must see and touch the dead body of a loved one. The parent and child must embrace in reconciliation. It is all a part of context. There must be context."

Annabel thought it time to leave. Mary had moved off into space and she wasn't up to the effort of pulling her back. She stood up, saying something about the children's homework.

"But you need something for yourself," Mary said. "Perhaps you need to think more seriously about your Mr. Fowles."

Annabel made an ironic chuckle. "To provide context? Justin is totally a man without a country. He was born in Vancouver, but he has no home."

"Oh come, my dear," Mary said in alarm. "That's impossible. Everyone has a home. Everyone must make a home. Is he educated?"

"He's lived everywhere in Canada, He's picked up courses wherever there was a university. I think when he retired was the first time in his life he'd faced himself. As a person and not as a piece of bureaucracy. It was some kind of government job. He thought coming back west would be coming home. But it wasn't."

"Men are so unaware of such things," Mary said. "I am completely at home here; what can he possibly find strange?"

"He's appalled at how much the west is anti-Ottawa, anti-Quebec, anti the First Nations."

"First Nations indeed. Quebec and the Indians?" Mary said dismissively. "Well as a westerner I've never given them a charitable thought, I can tell you. And I'm as native as anyone who lives on a reserve on Indian Affairs handouts."

Annabel hesitated, tempted to argue, but Justin had taught her the futility of fighting geriatric politics. Just as they parted Mary gripped Annabel's arm and said with surprising intensity "But I must see more of your lovely children. Oh I must! I shall entice them here!"

Mary had presented Susan and Marc each with a farewell cookie, and as soon as they were out of sight of the bungalow the children lofted the cookies into the trees, and bent over in suppressed giggles, bounding down the slope. When she finally caught up with them she shouted, "You were both absolutely wonderful! You were a mother's joy! I never realized I'd taught you such behaviour!"

"You didn't," said Susan bluntly, and Marc added, "We learnt our manners from TV. It isn't always the evil you think it is."

"Not the commercial shit," added Susan. "It was PBS. There was this big old house with a huge conservatory, and servants—"

"A butler," said Marc.

"—yeah and a butler, and they were having afternoon tea. The tea was bigger than dinner, and so Marc and I watched and practiced it. After that Mrs. Evens was easy."

"Clever children," Annabel said. "Did you like Mrs. Evens?"

Marc called back, "She's spooky."

Annabel cried out, "How can you call such a dear old lady spooky, who showed you all those wonderful things?"

"It was like a museum," said Marc. "Or maybe a mausoleum."

"You don't understand, mummy dear," said Susan. "Mrs. Evens is a woman of mystery and loathing."

"A legend in her own time," added Marc.

"Stop interrupting," shouted Susan. "Our friends will totally freak when we say we've met her. We can't admit she'd just an old woman who serves stale cookies."

The children ran off noisily ahead and Annabel followed, reflectively, remembering the forbidding atmosphere of the living room and Mary's gruesome account of the Seymours' death, and it rose from nowhere into her mind as she said it aloud, "Grandmother Death!"

It was hyperbole, but the visit had left her unsettled. Mary's final words of invitation made her uneasy at the thought of the children being at Mogador alone. She would have to get that across to the little prodigies, who were angels of obedience to logical requests but tended to petulance and argument for anything less. She thought too of the flintlock pistol, which brought dimly to mind cinematic images of witless blonde English subalterns firing revolvers into heathen hordes hurling themselves against the outposts of Empire.

She realized suddenly that something didn't fit. She would have to look it up to be sure, but the Indian Mutiny happened when native troops refused to bite into cow-fat on their cartridges. Cartridges. So if the British Raj had cartridges, Mary's pistol would have been obsolete years before. The general—whom Maggie Riordon called a brigadier and Mary Evens has promoted a couple of levels to lieutenant general—would have used a revolver.

But perhaps a little invention was excusable; Mary was after all just trying to entertain the children. Except that Mary had presented it as context, the bond—not that Annabel was certain what she was getting at—the bond of a common history, which surely demanded accuracy. She pulled a shaft of bracken fern from the side of the trail, broke off its top, and launched it like a spear as Justin had taught her, as Justin remembered using them as a child. And suddenly the reason for her uneasiness came to her. She had no use for the past. Whatever the past had been, it was now a lie. Mary Evens had been trying to draw her children back into a past that only reinforced the lie.

Annabel called out, and ran to catch up.

6

Annabel had thrown Dirk Plantagenet's roses as far as possible out the kitchen door. Three days later any thought of him provoked a chill fury, but tempered now by an ambiguous warmth whenever she saw, through the kitchen window, the roses in a straggling row where Susan had stuck them into the vegetable plot in the back yard.

Dirk himself had dropped from her mind. The newspaper kept her busy but for once preparations for the next issue were running smoothly, which left her evenings free for the work she was doing for Cliff Lang, much of it by email with her portable computer set up on the kitchen table. Everything was going so well that she decided one day to indulge herself with a quiet lunch at the restaurant at the Far Pacific. The restaurant had tablecloths and high windows which gave a magical view of the inlet, with the steep East Ridge running south to her left and the forest to the right sloping away southward past glimpses of farmland until, a mile or so away, it ended at the rock of Mary Even's Mogador. The restaurant was isolated even on a Saturday night from the lust and thunder of the Rib'n'Rye below, and the view gave no hint, beyond an occasional drift of smoke, of the village's existence.

The place was never crowded and Annabel loved its tranquility. It attracted city people in suits and dresses having business lunches, and couples who touched hands and glanced up nervously at newcomers. There was muted conversation and measured laughter, and not a local face in sight. It was a touch of the urban life she missed.

But suddenly, just as she sat down and picked up the menu, Dirk Plantagent slumped into the chair opposite. He exuded inner torment, and started to speak with desperate solemnity without even a quick hello. "Look, Annabel, I don't get this. I don't get that crack about masturbation. So I send a nice thank you note for you turning up for lunch along with nice roses and is that bad? Most attractive women go for nice roses, eh? This thing is really getting to me."

She smiled a thin cool smile. She felt more guarded than angry; he seemed sincere. She had put the card in her purse, not wanting to leave it around the house, and she handed it to him. "So this is a nice thank you note?"

He stared at it, lifted his eyes to stare open-mouthed at her for a moment, and then got up and dashed from the room. Annabel stared at the doorway he'd left by, irritated and embarrassed. She'd recovered enough to sip some coffee when he returned, handing her back the card. "I'm sorry," he said. "No I am really sorry. That was a terrible shock to me. I should not have left you like that but it was impulse. There's a copier out there and I had to have a copy. Let me buy you your lunch to make up for my bad manners."

"Of course not, Dirk. It's no big deal."

"Some bastard was getting at me, and I'm going to get him, believe me."

His intensity was embarrassing but affecting. She said lightly, "Oh Dirk, come on! You've seen those things before. Someone is having us on, that's all. It's a joke, man. Let's forget it."

He stared at her, glowering, before saying, "It is unforgivable. It is a terrible insult to us both."

Obviously he hadn't sent the card, but she was uneasy at his anger. And the question remained of how the card got in the box, and by whom—

The mystery moved uneasily in her mind, but only for a moment, and then suddenly it was clear! She clenched her fists beneath the table, suppressing a shriek of delight. The courier had read the note on her door giving Justin's address. The poor courier had innocently presented the subversive roses to the Master Spy himself! Annabel had an instant's vivid picture of Justin leering treacherously through his beard as he forged the card with practiced hand, drove past her house probably without stopping as he hurled the package in fury onto her front porch. And she had faithlessly doubted her dear children's truthful report of the state they had found it in.

"This is amusing?" he asked anxiously.

"Oh no. No not at all. I just thought of the card. I mean it's crude it's funny. Quite hilarious."

"I don't see it that way," he said sternly. "I'm getting to the bottom of this. I'll hire detectives. This makes a fool of me, eh? And it insults your honour.""

"Dirk, for Christ's sake!" It was appalling. He was so naively gauche and so sincere, so opposite to Justin. She said in a rush, horrified that Justin could be exposed: "No you can't do that. Hasn't anyone ever played a practical joke on you? It was just some social vandal. Yes I think that's a very good term for him. Or her, of course. Social vandalism. And by the way don't trouble your mind about my honour—" She was becoming angry, perhaps at his ignorance, perhaps at finding herself protecting Justin just as their relationship had become onerous. "—My honour is my own bloody business, and I God damn well resent your interest. Your idea of female honour is the market value of female sexual inexperience, and you can take a flying fuck at yourself, mister."

He retreated, apologized, pleaded he was misunderstood, and promised to call off the detectives. She was ready for a good fight, but it wasn't the place and Dirk's concern, obnoxious as it was, implied a protective intent which was comforting. And if being cherished alarmed her, it also conferred power, which buoyed her confidence.

The lunch marked a change in her opinion of Dirk. He was still half-shaven, and sweated if anything more heavily than she remembered, but he was becoming more a stumbling admirer than an oafish boor. His teeth weren't nearly as bad as she'd remembered them. His restless energy attracted her.

About a week later she had her scheduled morning coffee with Justin. She decided not to mention the card; he would only deny knowing anything about it and it would be entertaining to see how long he could keep it to himself. That afternoon she was just leaving for home, closing the door of her office on Palgrave, when Dirk walked by. She said she was surprised to see him in the village.

He said, "Perhaps you have caught me in an act." He hesitated. "I would like to show you something. Do you think I can trust you?"

"Well you can only try."

He touched her arm, inviting her down the street. "I would like to. I would very much like to. The Lady Jane says I can trust you." They reached a one-storey building which Annabel had thought was vacant and Dirk unlocked the door. "And I am a gentleman, so you may trust me." He led the way down a passage lined with office doors, their glass panels still bearing the names of forgotten enterprises. "I appreciate this time you're giving me. You see I'd like to be at ease with you, like a friend. I'd like to confide in you like a trusted friend."

She had no idea where this was leading but she laughed, amused by his ingenuousness and his elaborate respect. "If you want me for a trusted friend—okay. Let's be trusting friends!"

He opened the last door at the end of the corridor, turned on the lights and waved her in. The room was windowless and about twenty feet square, harshly lit by banks of florescent tubes on the low ceiling. There were several plywood tables, a large tilted drafting table, and in one corner a cot next to a desk holding a computer. There were rolls and sheets of charts and blueprints on the tables and on the floor, and in the middle of the room a large square table draped in blue cloth over an unevenly mounded surface. He said, "This is my secret headquarters. I have it here because there is nowhere secure at the Rendezvous." He held out his arms expansively. "Welcome to Prospect Palisades, the Plantagenet development of the future!"

He said land around Victoria was filling up, and the only path of expansion was to go south west, toward Prospect. He had in mind retired people with money, who wanted good sized residential properties, out of town but within easy driving distance. He spread a crudely-drawn map across the nearest table. "West and south-west of Prospect," he said enthusiastically, "There's Crown land in there, and some old farm allotments. Really old. I'm doing some digging to clear up the titles. To assemble it all."

She was astonished at this new dimension to Dirks's personality. His enthusiasm grew as he led her from table to table showing her blueprints of lot lines, road allowances, the water and sewer system, plans for hydro access.

"It's terrific, eh? If I can get a good landscape guy in there I can give every home a view that'll blow your mind! I figure I can get a hundred and fifty estates, average selling price maybe half a million. I'm talking real quality stuff, eh? No short cuts, nothing trashy. Big substantial homes. The carriage trade. How about that? Plus a great plaza. This guy in Seattle he's designing me what he calls a country club plaza. It's open plan, eh? With covered walkways. Very upscale."

She wasn't too clear about the size of the project but was carried along by his energy. His words didn't come smoothly, but tumbled out with a conviction that intrigued her. She'd managed hugely complex million-dollar marketing projects, but nothing this tangible, nothing that involved roads, bridges, mansions and a shopping plaza. She wasn't unaware that he was describing nothing less than re-inventing Prospect and flattening farms and forest around it, but the scale of the enterprise and its unexpectedness, and above all Dirk's enthusiasm filled her with amused delight.

He paused, staring at her suspiciously. "This is big business, you know. You seem to think this is a big laugh."

"Oh for Christ's sake Dirk, I'm not laughing! If I'm smiling it's because I'm enjoying your, well, commitment. This is fascinating, it really is. If we're going to be trusted friends we'd better have some trust."

He seemed reassured, and led her to the desk and they sat down. She said, "You're talking millions of development money, up front. Can you find that kind of backing? How much do you need before you send in the bulldozers?"

"Oh no, lady, not so fast! This is very complex business. This is very long range. The first big money isn't for bulldozers. It's for lawyers and surveyors and PR jerks to grease the plan through the bloody bureaucracy. A hundred and twenty layers of bureaucracy. To get the permits, the approvals. I'll be lucky if the bulldozers are rolling in two years."

She said, "I'm not trying to put you down. But you're a resort owner and you've been bankrupt, and the first thing you've got to do is to hire a bunch of lawyers and surveyors—for *two years?* That's expensive talent."

He smiled complacently, almost condescendingly. "I got enough in the bank already to go for six months, once I finish the plan. And I've got some properties up island I'm off-loading. The big problem is I got to increase my cash flow from the Rendezvous by three point two percent. That's key. Three point two percent! So that's another thing I'm working on." He chuckled to himself, watching her. "It's going to be wild! But I can't tell you about that! You'll be surprised! What a piece of marketing!"

"You need marketing advice?"

"Naw. Me and Mandril, we're pros, eh? We got it all worked out."

"Mandril *Gulag?* Are you kidding?" She restrained herself. He probably had no idea of her background; he had never asked her anything about it. She said, "You've got to understand, I'm having a hard time with this. It's very exciting and I'm impressed by, well, all your homework. But I've always been against buying up old houses and cutting down old trees and—"

Dirk interrupted solemnly; "These will be well-treed estates, arranged in unique venues. In the residential quadrant twenty-seven percent of the present forestation will be retained, plus extensive plantings of seventeen varieties of domestic and exotic decorative and flowering species."

"Ah, very enlightened of you," she said playfully. "I've got to admit I'm changing my opinion about you, Dirk."

"Hey!" he exclaimed, "You mean there might be some hope for me?"

"Mm-m. If you play your cards right and don't deal too fast." She was thankful he could drop his grim earnestness; it was fun to flirt.

He stood up and took her arm gently, which she found pleasant, and led her to the covered table in the centre of the room. "You have seen the detail stuff, but here's the big picture."

He pulled back the blue cloth to reveal a topographical model extending from east of the Sensuous Rendezvous to well beyond what she took to be the Combat College in the west, and as far inland as the highway. Everything was in colour, and buildings—even her own house—were represented by tiny painted boxes. The clearcut to the east had become a lush forest surrounding a huge ordered encampment leading down to the sea. When she bent toward it, Dirk said excitedly, "Mandril's plans for the Combat College! I'm giving him a complete extreme-recreation complex! It'll be fabulous! Cliff scaling, survival skills, mountain biking, advanced kayaking. See the towers? They're for parachute training."

Annabel frowned. The blueprints were fragments but the model brought it all together and it shocked her. A golf course occupied the farm-land north and west of Prospect. Worse—she stared at the expanse of asphalt and roofing in disbelief—a shopping plaza obliterated the whole village. The planned residential area started on the west shore of the inlet and spread across Mary Even's property and on into the clearcut leaving no sign of her bungalow. Dirk said, "Quite a layout, eh?"

"You didn't tell me this included Mogador," she said coolly.

"What's Mogador?"

"Dirk!"

"I don't know this Mogador. Honest! What's Mogador?"

He wasn't pretending. Of course there was no reason he should know of Mogador. Mary never came to the village, and Dirk only came to lock himself in this office. Her initial anger had been spontaneous, out of a loyalty gone dead.

He had started to work his computer, and in a couple of minutes he said, "Mary Messalina Evens, who purchased the property from Millicent and Partland Seymour, who purchased—"

"Purchased? Did you say purchased? Not inherited?"

"Purchased," Dirk said emphatically. "The only inheritance is to Etheldred Coulthurst from Ralph G. C. Coulthurst, Brigadier (retired) Royal Engineers, who acquired it as a grant of Crown land. That's registry office records."

She was baffled. "And you're sure, not bequeathed from Seymours to Mary Evens?"

"I don't know if that would show, but it says here purchase, fee simple, no record of mortgage."

That bloody old woman, with her nonsense about consanguinity and heritage. Mogador wasn't a family estate or context, whatever that meant; it was a junk museum.

"This Evens property," Dirk was saying, "Is key to the concept. It gives a prospect—hey, joke eh?—of the ocean or along the coast or the Olympics. Without that property it's just a subdivision in a valley, eh? But if I go up that bloody rock the whole project climbs the sky!"

"So what are you going to do about Mary Evens?"

"Hell, buy her," he said offhandedly, moving away.

She said, "I don't think that'll work."

He was over the other side of the room, putting some papers in a file folder. He laughed, "Oh sure! Someone who don't like money! Take it from me, Annabel, in business money always talks. Don't you give it a thought." He went on sorting the papers, as if her allotted time was up.

"I don't think you understand," she said, straining to remain tactful. "Mary Evens is maybe different from the people you're used to dealing with." He had apparently dismissed her, moving briskly to a filing cabinet further away. As if she'd had her ration of his time. She stood up and yelled, "Will you listen to me, Plantagenet?"

He turned to her with a perplexed stare. "What—?"

She shouted, "I am a little touchy about being ignored. I was saying something about Mary Evens. I was saying it for your benefit."

Dirk moved his head uncomprehendingly, fixed where he stood. "I said I can handle her."

The tone of quiet final male authority infuriated her. "For a moment I thought you said I shouldn't bother my pretty head. Maybe you should have announced you were turning to serious men's work so I could get on with my embroidery. Just get it into your thick sexist skull that Mary Evens is the biggest problem you've got. The only thing you're right about—" she swept her arm dramatically across the room — "is that Mogador's the key to this whole lousy exploitative plot. But you won't get Mogador because Mogador is Mary Evens' existence; it has nothing to do with money. Go up there and offer money and she'll see you off with a twelve gauge. Prospect Palisades will die on the drawing board. And forget this shit trying to impress me how much you can afford. I'm not totally unfamiliar with major financing. This plan's got margins so thin they're microscopic. Even a woman can see that."

She pushed through the tables to the door and marched down the corridor and out onto Palgrave Street, wondering where she'd left the Volkswagen.

7

Very early one morning in late July, Justin gave up trying to sleep and half fell, half rolled from his bed onto his clothes, into which he struggled in the dark, finally regaining the bed in a sitting position to lace his worn runners, not unconscious of the smell of feet, crotch and armpit, and shuffled across the curling linoleum and through the kitchen area into the store itself, no more populated before dawn, it occurred to him wryly, than at the height of any business day. Empty. Darkly shadowed. Smelling of mold.

"Indeed," he said loudly, the sound of his voice sending a host of tiny demons scurrying away into the darkness, clearing his head remarkably. "Indeed a promising day for the retail trade. Can I interest you in this teapot, madam, with a genuine scene of Captain Cook converting the local Christians to cannibalism?"

A brisk morning walk, of course! He peered through a clean patch on the front window to be sure the street was deserted. He didn't want to talk, and some of the more gregarious villagers kept insanely early hours. It was still quite dark, but he imagined something bundled by the door of the abandoned service station across the street, a transient youth no doubt, a city dweller reluctant to leave the security of hard pavement for the luxury of the forest floor. Or one of Mandril's thugs detailed to watch—what were his words—a *designated hostile?*

He opened the front door, moving it carefully to avoid jangling the bells, and was arrested by Scrofula's low protesting growl, demanding admittance.

"Be off," he said, "Your door is at the back. Let me by!" He stooped, feeling around to push her out of the way, wherever she was, and her blunt teeth clamped angrily onto his hand. "Bitch!" he muttered, shaking her off and squeezing through the doorway. Scrofula, unrelenting, growled defiance from the shadows.

He crossed Kitchener to the road down to the bay, the Lower Road, a hard gravel track bordered by impenetrable razor-thorned blackberry bushes which had consumed here a fallen gate, there a caved-in shingle roof, an upturned moss-covered clinker hull, or twenty paces further on a leaning sign pocked with old bullet holes, its flaking blue letters announcing 300 YARDS TO BELL'S OCEAN MARENA - FISHING - BOATS FOR HIRE. The blackberries had long ago covered not only Bell's Ocean Marina but also—so legend had it— an hotel, two saloons, a funeral parlour, and several bordellos.

The sky above the east ridge was touched with palest peach and against it the firs and cedars rose black out of the morning mist. Justin walked sedately, controlling the urge to move faster, or to stop so suddenly that whatever watched or followed might betray itself by a footstep, an exhalation from among the branches. If he were to take the next trail off the road into the dripping underbrush, reducing his pace, moving stealthily into the cedars he might in a few seconds suddenly leap out to catch it standing there, of towering height perhaps, grotesquely deformed and yet obscured in the mist and darkness from which only a face of indescribable horror might peer down—

"Indeed," Justin exclaimed by way of exorcism, kicking the gravel. "I was walking this morning," he added offhandedly, picturing Annabel listening, or Andy Flegg or perhaps a rare customer in The Prospect Variety Store, "Along the Lower Road. I felt I was being followed by my past. When I at last confronted it, it was far more unnerving than I imagined. I had always thought old age brought reconciliation."

There was an exhilarating catharsis in sounding off against those who had done him wrong, but his own sins and errors seemed —and this was something new—to be organizing subversively in his subconscious. He would of course resist, remain active, strive. He had come to terms with the past. He had done appropriate penance. He wished he were sure of it.

"Crap!" he announced, and started to march briskly, arms swinging at shoulder height, head erect, chin in, eyes unwaveringly to the front, resplendent in glorious gold and scarlet, a Chief Inspector of the Mounted which—and it took no more than ten bracing paces before the resentment welled up—had banished him. The obliterated man. L'Etranger. Although this morning he wasn't tempted to wallow in sweet martyrdom, it being more prominently in his thoughts that even to be found marching briskly along a rain-soaked forest road by the old lady of the rock, for instance, even with stained beard and tartan shirt over jeans hiding at least in this pre-morning grey the scarlet tunic and cavalry boots that could compromise him—

"I never thought of you as a military man, Mr. Fowles," he heard her say.

"Only in my youth, Mrs. Evens. As a mere private in an obscure Nova Scotia regiment of foot." Obscure but glorious, as he was tempted to go on, the glorious 41st Acadians—

"Hardly with such an arrogant air, Mr. Fowles. You are not candid today. Why for instance are you wearing those enormous ceremonial spurs, and carrying a riding crop, and smelling distinctly of the stable?"

"Nonsense," commanded Justin, noticing for the first time looming above him the immense bare shoulder of rock on which Mrs. Evens lived, silhouetted against the dawn's first pale light.

"You don't understand," he said to no one in particular. "Hiding is a common experience. Criminals hide to escape prosecution. Husbands hide to avoid supporting their children. I am not hiding. I have been hidden!"

The road came out of the forest and ran along a cleared embankment which afforded an unobstructed view of the bay. It ended at the government wharf, half a mile away. He felt less threatened in the open; when he spun about to check behind him there was nowhere anyone could hide.

There was as well the comfort of the familiar, for in a few minutes he was in sight of his magnificent sign, five feet wide by three, on six-foot posts, banished from its prominence down by the government wharf and now, as he saw peering closer, sadly defaced:

PROSPECT VARIETY &
AGE MUSE
BUS   CENTRE -->

It had been a thing of rare beauty with its dark brown lettering on a pale cream background, the sole redeeming feature of a virtually abandoned roadside littered with old mattresses, piles of broken lath and mortar and rusting tin cans and ruptured green and orange garbage bags. He turned away from the sign, resigned to the vandalism but wishing it had at least shown wit.

There was a suggestion of fog at the mouth of the inlet to the south, but around him the air was so clear that he was inspired to run, and although this lapsed quickly into a lumbering jog, by the time he reached the wharf he was out of breath. Half way down the car ramp he stopped to lean against the railing, panting, staring down at the boats at the jetty below; fishing boats, runabouts, a couple of small sailboats, Mel Trotter's old twenty-five-foot Chris-Craft under its orange tarpaulin. Nothing new. But when he looked down the inlet, to the dark eastern slope with the dawn lightening behind it, he stopped, alert at what seemed a trace of paleness on the water.

There were always sticks floating, logs, bottles, boat fenders, but this seemed different. It was no more than an indistinct ribbon of a lighter shade, but it intrigued him. He marched down the ramp to the wharf to get closer, cursing at having left his glasses at home, but the thing became no clearer. There was no one around who might help. He was always uneasy on the water, but his curiosity soon led him to commandeer Paul Ching's rowboat, which would be quiet and wouldn't involve trying to start one of the outboards.

It was about this time, as Justin stroked laboriously onto open water, that Mary Evens emerged from the underbrush at the shoreline some six hundred yards to the south, intent on locating the floating shape she'd seen from high on the rock. She had been sitting sleepless on her verandah, bundled in a quilt waiting for the dawn, and on a whim she had taken the path through the garden to the edge of the precipice. When she looked down into the black inlet she'd seen something indistinct and pale on the black water. She thought romantically it was a swan, a lone swan drifting across a stygian sea. She fetched the Brigadier's powerful night glasses from the study, and was disconcerted to see it was surely a man, impudently nude, swimming toward the base of her rock. But eventually his remorseless immobility convinced her he was dead, and the inlet became a dark canyon of doom, through which the corpse in its slow drifting would run its ceremonial course majestically on the tide down the solemn unpopulated fiord past Schooner Shoal and out alone into the vast Pacific.

She thought she should watch its passage from the beach—a level more fitting for a salute to a cortege—and hurried into gumboots and called Blenkinsop to bring the olive-green-and-yellow tarpaulin she used as a raincape, and fumbled down to the trail below. When she emerged onto the beach the setting was cathedral in its solemnity, and although from this low angle she couldn't see the corpse, she was filled with a sense of occasion.

But as she watched, the creak of rowlocks invaded her mood, and she made out a rowboat, the rower stroking slowly, pausing, stroking again, finally leaning forward as if to examine something. The rower was about to commit a desecration, and Mary Evens climbed onto a log and waved and shouted, "Stop it! Stop it!" but Justin, not even seeing Mary against the dark shore and hearing only what seemed a morning salutation, waved cheerily in reply.

"Damn you!" shouted Mary, and sat down on a log in helpless anger, while Justin, peering at the shape coming into his imperfect vision, realized he'd found a human floater. He'd had his share of them, and didn't want to start the day seeing something with brains over its face and guts trailing down out of sight. He would make sure of it, and then row back and phone Constable Ymenko, poor bugger, and let him do the honours.

As he drew nearer, narrowing his eyes to focus, he saw it was a young woman, her bright hair a great fan spread out from her head, her pale perfect body festooned like a demure Botticelli in seaweed, Her open eyes were an unbelievable green. Her arms were crossed at the wrists and her legs were together symmetrically, as if on a bier. He could make out no rings nor jewelry, nor thread of clothing on her.

She was too perfect to leave floating. Reverently—the feeling surprised him—and despite his dislike of touching dead flesh, he got a line around her ankles and began rowing very slowly toward the beach. The fog, he noticed, was coming up the dark inlet from the sea.

He beached the boat and hauled the body gently up the gravel by the rope, rotating the legs until the head was farthest from the water. In this process the body rolled slightly to expose—on the left back side just below the rib cage—a horrible bubbling of pink flesh protruding from a gash four inches long. He dropped the body abruptly on its back, not wanting to examine the wound. So she had been killed. He wondered for a moment if bringing her ashore had been the right thing. He was assuring himself there had been nothing where she had been floating that might be evidence, when he realized the dark shape he had noticed absently up near the trees was a human figure hunched on a log. He made out a wide-brimmed straw hat and yellow gumboots, and said, "Good morning," and then, "Ah, Mrs. Evens, isn't it?"

"Mr. Fowles, indeed. We meet at last."

"Not under the happiest circumstances, I'm afraid." He felt a moment's indecision, and said apologetically, "You may not want to look at this, Mrs. Evens. This is a young woman. Dead. A floater. A young female floater."

Mary said, "I have heard so much about you. You run a variety store. Or perhaps a museum. In any event I gather you do not run it very hard. I hear it is seldom open."

"It's something of a sideline," Justin said, wondering at her ignoring the body, at her knowledge of him.

"A man of independent means!"

"Not exactly." He was off balance and needed not just to regain himself but to be sharply alert, it having slipped his mind in the urgency of the moment that this was his first encounter with Ottawa's spying emissary. He said, "There's a lot of us around, active in retirement. It's a good part of the world for active retirement." Her lack of response made him continue despite his better judgment. "Yes, good country for productive but well-earned leisure. Pensioners after a life of dedicated toil and taxes."

"Lucrative toil, in your case, I should think. You're well past sixty-five, are you not?" Her speech was irritatingly crisp and darting.

"Well, yes. I suppose I must admit to some aging."

"Hm-m," said Mary, sounding unconvinced, and stood up, staring down at the corpse. "A young woman. I'd thought it a man." She felt uncomfortable. Her mind had drifted far away, so that she had imagined herself mourning not for the one man she had seen from the cliff but any one of those briefly-known young lovers gone to war so long ago. But now there was something more immediate. She came down the slippery gravel and stood by the young woman's head, savouring an unfamiliar delight. "She is so beautiful. Mr. Fowles. She is untouched. Do please carry her. I have a place for her under the trees."

"I think the drill is to call the police," Justin said warily, wondering if she spoke with naivety or out of some unmanageable eccentricity. Annabel hadn't said she was a nut case.

"Oh no. There is no need for that. We can bury her now under the trees. In the silence. That's what she would wish, you see. It would be natural, having taken her from the water, to let her rest beside the water."

"It really must be reported, Mrs. Evens. I'll go use the pay phone up by the wharf." He waited for Mary's agreement but she said nothing, and he walked a few paces and turned to see she had picked up the line around the dead girl's ankles and was tugging at it. "Mrs. Evens!" He started back, irritated but still tolerant. "We've got to leave her."

"I must take her to her rest under the trees."

"For Christ's sake!" He had to pull the rope from Mrs. Evens' hands and press her away to stop her pulling at the body. "Look, you can get into trouble doing that. You cannot make the dead your own." He had wanted to spare her knowing of the crime, but saw she had to know. "This isn't a simple drowning, Mrs. Evens. The girl died violently; there is a wound in her back. The police have to investigate, and they have custody. Even for your own family, the police'd have custody."

Mary sat down on the beach, and Justin thought he'd got through to her. After a time she said, "I was led to believe you were much younger, Mr. Fowles. I think you and I are of the same generation."

He noticed her change of approach, and was about to say or had perhaps started to say something banal about that being possible when she broke in, "In youth death does not approach; it comes from behind, it trips them up and then devours them like this poor thing, and that is tragic. In age we can see it coming."

"Ah yes," said Justin absently, having seldom bothered with thoughts of age and death.

Mary said, "It is time for me to free myself from my lived life, to return lovingly to my past, my heritage. To draw my past lovingly around me. But I suspect you are different, Mr. Fowles. You stare at her and shift from one foot to another. You convey unrest. You speak of productive retirement, but neglect your retail duties. And you spout nonsense about worthy pensioners and dedicated toil, just like a politician! Oh dear—oh where was I? Yes, I think you are either still pursuing something, or are lying."

Justin was shocked. This was a maiden aunt in a Victorian parlour, purveying moral rigour among wayward nieces and nephews. He said, hoping vigorous delivery would hide his confusion, "I am intensely active, Mrs. Evens, in many varied interests. Of which my store is but one. There is a world of difference between activity and restlessness. And I don't see any conflict between a life of leisure and productivity—"

"Oh do stop, Mr. Fowles! You are as evasive as I was told you were."

"As you were told?" he repeated, aghast at how much Annabel, for surely it was she, had revealed. "I am as forthright—"

"Oh, you must forgive me," she broke in. "I don't mean to chase you round your contradictions. My question is, do you run because your past pursues you, or because you are in pursuit? Of something."

"I have no past, Mrs. Evens!" he proclaimed, seeking to rid himself of this damnable examination. "I'm free of it. It is taken from me!"

"Oh don't be impossible!"

"I live each day as it comes. Is that impossible?"

"But to what end? For what purpose? Do you not feel the need to work toward a closure, to achieve a completeness?" She stared down at the corpse. "We have this amazing opportunity, you and I, to prepare. It is so great a tragedy for her, that it came upon her before she ever had time. And now they will cut open this pure body that the sea has cleansed and rip out the organs and test their contents with corrosive acids and saw open her private parts and study the tissue for signs of sexual penetration. Did you say something about indignity? Who is committing the indignity, Mr. Fowles?"

"I'm only telling you the way it has to be." The encounter was becoming so absurd he had to think for a moment about what he'd been saying. "Now will you promise not to touch the body while I'm gone?"

"Of course not."

He grinned at her implacability. "Alright. Will you promise not to move it while I'm gone?"

"I'll promise nothing."

She amused him. He sat down on a log, resigned, vaguely entertained at his predicament. He hadn't dressed for sitting around on a beach at dawn, and was uncomfortably cold. He looked back toward the village, where a smudge of blue smoke amidst the trees showed that people were getting up. He said, "What you want for the girl is natural enough, Mrs. Evens. But she belongs somewhere. People loved her, and maybe people are searching for her. Even if she'd died accidentally, it would be heartless if they didn't know she'd been found."

"If she had people she loved they would know, if they cared. I have a daughter and it would be a complete waste of my time to look for her. This girl was creating a lovely ceremony for her going, and you have spoiled it." She held her arm out from her sleeve, revealing a bracelet of gold chain. "I had a lover who flew in the war. He went missing over Germany. Eleven years later they sent this back to me, that I'd given him. When they drained the Dutch marshes and found his aeroplane. But he had gone. I knew that. I didn't need to be reminded."

"But you wear the chain. It means something to you."

"No. There were too many. I wear it because it links me to my past."

But Justin's attention was less on the conversation than on the body of the drowned girl, which in its elegant repose had begun to disturb him. He was jaded about this kind of death, which initiated a familiar professional compulsion to banish the mystery, to record the facts, to commence the procedures that would reveal who she was and how she had come to this. But the girl reached to him past his practiced objectivity to touch something either deep in memory or foreshadowing what was to come, an odd sensation that he did not understand.

He clasped his hands around his knees and looked up at the rock wall of the East Ridge. Colour was returning; shades of green among the trees, of slate grey and brown in the rocks. He followed along the East Ridge, to where it should jut out into the Strait, and instead saw the fog. The fog was thick, moving up the inlet. Its advancing feelers were only a hundred or so yards away. They'd soon be hidden from the village. He got awkwardly to his feet, stiff in every joint, the familiar jab of pain in his knee.

"I can't wait any longer, Mrs. Evens. I'm leaving the body in your charge. It's okay where it is, because the tide's as high as it'll get. Actually you can go home if you want; the young lady's not going anywhere. I've got to find some warm clothes. But remember; if it's been moved when I come back with Constable Ymenko it will be very serious for you."

He looked at her, hoping for an acknowledgement, but she kept staring straight ahead, out over the water.

"You do understand," he said.

"Oh do go on your way, Mr. Fowles. Your condescension is quite tiresome."

He shook his head, and began slowly walking toward the wharf, with the fog already drifting silently in behind him. She was too madly eccentric to have been sent to watch him, and so perhaps they had indeed abandoned him. He heard the ominous hollow croak of a raven, and looked up to see the great black bird winging up the fiord to his right, the promising dawn becoming grey overcast, his mind too much aware of the murder of innocents or young whores and of his own uneasy doubts, and it came to him that perhaps she had come not to spy but with some judgmental purpose, to call him to account. It was depressing.

8

Mary Evens watched Justin fade into the fog, waited a good half minute, and then walked down past the body to stand with the water lapping the heels of her gumboots. She breathed in the damp sea air, stared up at the fog swirling, thickening among the high branches, and felt suffused with gratitude and strength.

It was entirely strange to stand alone at the edge of the grey world with the unblemished body of the girl on the cold wet gravel before her. There was everything of grace and human beauty about her, yet life had gone. And it was as if this—she and the dead girl, the ocean, and the forest—were all that existed. An old woman ready to die and a girl cut off from life; it was the essence, it was entirely right and natural. Soon Mr. Fowles would be back with the constable and the brutes from the village in their filthy jeans and plaid shirts, and the stained plastic bag into which so many rotting bodies had been shoveled— No, it wasn't the natural way; she simply couldn't allow it to be done.

She knelt down, gripped by overwhelming tenderness, and brushed the sand gently from the skin, so white and finely veined. The skin's coldness shocked her, and she drew back her hand but very slowly, because this unexpected sensation of tender affection now invoked, as she had sensed as soon as she'd seen her lying on the beach, the presence of her lost Gwendoline.

She whispered, "Oh my dear. Oh my dear child. You have come to me." She didn't yet believe the words, but they expressed so profoundly what was in her heart that tears came to her eyes, and she had to fight the tears because there was so much she had to do.

She tugged off her tarp and lay it flat beside the body and rolled the body tenderly so that it was wrapped as if in a shroud, tying each end with the bits of rope hanging from the eyelets. She tied the rope she wore as a belt to one end of the tarp, and hauled the body up the beach, relieved that it was lighter than she had expected. As soon as she had passed through the huckleberry bushes that screened the trail's entrance, she went back down the beach and kicked the gravel smooth and then swept the sand with a brush of cedar. She could hear no sound of Fowles' return, and no sound at all except the distant squeal and grunt of the foghorn at Point Exception. The sky was very dark above the trees, which suggested rain clouds had come in over the fog.

She hauled the body along the trail for two hundred yards until she came to a great sagging hemlock bough like a curtain beside the trail, and she dragged the body through it and set off at a right angle across the rough forest floor. She came eventually to a treeless patch, from the centre of which the twin spires of the great dead cedar rose into the fog, directly below the Cinnamon Cave.

She left the body at the foot of tree, walked back through the forest to the rotting wooden stairway, and climbed step by careful step over the dark cataract of broken stone onto which the Brigadier had fallen to his death. She was hungry and suspected she had forgotten breakfast, and in any event needed her morning tea.

She had little sense of the passage of time, and when she finally returned to the beach, humming to herself to keep up her courage, she was relieved to see he was alone. She had hidden the shotgun beneath her long skirt, and found him standing beside the boat. He said, "I don't understand why you're doing this."

"I am saving her," she said and then, with amusement, "I see you have changed into a vision of loveliness, Mr. Fowles!"

He had put on a heavy yellow plastic jacket, and a day-glo orange sou'wester he'd bought in a yachting boutique. At least it was dry. He said coolly, "I think you're changing the subject, Mrs. Evens. You can't save her like this."

"Perhaps I do not even know what you're talking about."

He said, "Mrs. Evens I've already reported her. Mae Sullivan said she'd send Constable Ymenko immediately. Just show me where you've put her and we can talk about how to avoid getting you into deeper trouble."

Actually the detachment office wasn't open yet, and he'd spoken to the answering machine. Moreover, yesterday morning at the Starlight Coffee Shop Ymenko had mentioned going up to court in Victoria today, so when Mae got in she'd have to call Sooke, and it might be hours before anyone appeared.

"I do not know what you are talking about."

He came slowly up the beach. "There's no point to that. Corpses rot. They stink. They have to be buried or cremated. It's hard work. We've been through this before, Mrs. Evens."

She said nothing.

He rubbed his face and stared at her. "Well you can't have taken it any distance, and if you're not going to spare me the trouble I guess I'll have to go look."

He worked along the beach far past the entrance to the trail, then back toward her, and then he noticed a spot where the grass seemed to have been pressed down and he pushed into the underbrush and hurled himself flat as the gun went off behind him and he was showered by shredded leaves and broken twigs.

He scrambled back onto the beach shouting, "What the hell are you trying to do? What the hell has got into you, Mrs. Evens?"

"Just stay on the beach, Mr. Fowles. You have as much right to the beach as anyone. But move off the beach and it is my private property."

"Mrs. Evens in this country you do *not* fire guns at trespassers."

"Mr. Fowles, as you have just seen, I *do* fire guns at trespassers."

"You don't seem to be taking this seriously. Shooting at a person is a grave crime. That woman is the victim of foul play, and you are interfering with the course of justice. You are obstructing."

"Of what woman do you speak, Mr. Fowles?"

"For God's sake spare me this idiocy! The—" He leapt from the log, suddenly inspired. "Of course! Oh you cunning old—" He stifled *bitch* as he scrambled to the boat, shouting, "What cometh from the sea shall be returned to the sea, eh? So that's what you did!"

He shoved the boat out, filling a boot with water, swearing, muttering, "I should have bloody well known. A scheming anarchist!" When he had the oars unshipped he stood up and spread his arms, ominous, he imagined, amidst the swirling fog, and shouted again, "This is juvenile, Mrs. Evens. Are you trying to attract attention?" He presented his chest defiantly: "Do you want to try another shot? But you've created no more than a petty annoyance, madam! I know this inlet as if I were born here, and I'll find her in minutes. She won't have gone far. And you'll have to answer to

Constable Ymenko and the law. The full and awesome majesty of the law!"

But the beach was now almost invisible. He rowed slowly toward the ocean to go with the tide, seated looking forward, keeping close to what he sensed was the beach and the dark mass of the forest to his right. The body couldn't have drifted more than fifty feet. He hadn't been away that long. Not more than an hour, perhaps an hour and a half. No longer than needed to change and pick up his glasses and a mickey of rye and make up a thermos of coffee.

He turned the boat and rowed back, edging to the left until he could actually make out the beach, and then, when he figured he was about where he started, he rowed slowly out into the fiord again, and then back on a zig-zag course, to cover the area. It made no sense at all that the body wasn't there. Silly old biddy and her damned tricks. It was agitation, and he cursed under his breath for having to bear agitation at his time of life. His rear was cold from the metal seat, which probably foretold a return of the piles, pain with each hard turd, and poking them back up with vaseline for bleeding weeks. Damn the woman!

When he judged he was about a hundred yards down the bay he turned in toward the shore, listening. There was no sound of scrambling footsteps following him along the gravel. If he landed here and worked carefully back through the forest, he might with luck find her, unsuspecting, with the body. He drifted, listening. All was quiet. He ran the boat ashore silently, and was over half way up the beach, delighted at his cunning, when the drooping bough of a cedar tree ahead of him exploded, and the shot ripped into the water off to his right.

He was too furious to take cover. He stood where he stopped and shouted, "You stupid old woman, put that damned thing away before you hurt yourself! Come on out of that tree; I want to talk some sense into you!" There was no sound from the forest. "Good God! No one else on earth would have such patience with you." He could see nothing but trees.

He was perhaps provoking her too much; she might just be mischievous, but she could be quite mad. "Oh to hell with you, then," he said, turning away. But once he had turned his resolve contracted into a hard fist under his stomach, and he had to fight an urge to run. By the time he had shoved off he was pouring with sweat and shaking, and he rowed savagely into the fog, cursing his lack of control. He rowed energetically for some time, thinking only of getting out of range. Eventually the exertion dissipated his rage, and he stopped, leaning on the oars and gasping. He hadn't kept track of how far he'd come. He couldn't recall on what bearing he had left the beach. He wasn't at all sure he'd rowed a straight course.

9

Justin shipped the oars and stared miserably at the transom of the boat which, though no more than six feet away, was hardly visible through the fog. It was a long half hour since Mary Evens had seen him off her beach. He had rowed four sides of what he thought was a square, searching for land. It had begun to rain. He had lost all sense of direction.

He was calm, but this floundering about the inlet made him feel a fool. He couldn't have gone far; even if he'd headed straight down the inlet he'd be nowhere near the ocean in this short a time. In fact all he needed was the cloud to thin to give him an angle on the sun or the fog to open for a moment to reveal the shore. And although the Point Exception foghorn echoing dully up the sides of the inlet simply confused him, a mere shout or a slamming door from Prospect would orient him instantly.

He poured coffee into the thermos lid, laced it generously with rye, and let the boat drift. There was a baleful enchantment about lying on the calm water immersed in thick fog, a drugged suspension of grey, bereft of all but the most primitive sensations; the cries of distant gulls, the whisper of rain on the water, the lapping of wavelets against the aluminum hull. But no sound from any shore.

He hated the ocean. He didn't very much enjoy small lakes or even swimming pools; the ocean was vast and elemental. Vast, forbidding and cold, though the rye was starting to warm him. Apart from a drunken blowout once or twice a year and a few afternoon beers at the Rib'n'Rye, Justin drank little; hangover had become too painful with age. But after two leisurely thermos-lids of coffee with rye he began feeling a strong sense of well-being, so much so that he put the bottle out of reach behind him, resolved to stay sharp as a sentry.

Time passed. The rain had become a slow drizzle; water dripped from his sou'wester past his face. He examined the boat. Paul Ching had put in a plywood floor, but other amenities were minimal: under the stern-seat a white plastic bottle cut open to be a bailer plus two ovoid cork floats each a foot long, and at the bow the disemboweled remains of an old kapok life-jacket. He stared at the empty seat. The isolation was restful, but the limbo of fog and ocean seemed to threaten the discipline which—save for the odd relapse for instance on the Lower Road this morning—kept his thoughts in submissive order. There was peril in the unoccupied mind, in that it closed off the world and invaded itself, straying along forbidden passages to doors best left closed. Satan findeth mischief still for idle memory. Which was certainly not the situation at the moment, where rationality certainly still prevailed, and he remembered suddenly, quite randomly, lying on the beach on Semaphore Bay in a happier summer, drinking red wine and laughing with a topless Annabel beside him writing an editorial on local witches, or was it fortune tellers?

"No indeed!" he shouted self-confidently into the fog. His recent doubts about the relationship were nowhere in his mind and he declared, reaching to drain the last of the coffee, "There is nothing wrong in loving a younger woman. It isn't a vain pursuit of lost youth. It is an affirmation of life! And I am far from dead! Yes!"

He was jerked to attention, his voice having masked a sound—a dog barking or was it a door slamming—not an instant earlier but an instant too late to take its bearing. He muttered, "Shit," and peered carefully around him. Still silence.

He could even recall with equanimity those more taxing encounters with Annabel, including the memorable time when she'd come to him once very soberly saying, "There are no chief inspectors in the RCMP."

"Ah!" he'd replied noncommittally, knowing he'd finally been caught out. "Oh is that so? Well!"

"You said you were a chief inspector."

"What of it, dear heart?"

"I was talking to Ymenko at the Starlight, about his ambitions and I asked him when he was going to make chief inspector and he said there's no such rank in the mounties."

He said, "Well then, obviously a slip of my tongue. I've quite forgotten it; obviously a trivial incident. I mean to say, every mythology has its inconsistencies. Mine is designed to entertain, which is harmless enough."

"Or to hide whatever you're avoiding—" and before he could reply— "You know I've been thinking about your career, Justin. It can't have all been this trendy upscale espionage you talk about."

He tried quickly to divert her, denying any acquaintance with rectal searches, breathalizers, handcuffs, tear gas—"The elite had a merely symbolic exposure to commonplace police work. A brief tour in the trenches, so to speak. We were destined for higher things."

"You were doing higher things for *forty years?*"

"Well—

"Well *what,* Justin? I mean take your hand; first it was a war wound, and then it was a car accident, and after you'd confessed about the security service it was a bomb. I suppose next it'll be barn burning."

"What do you know about barn burning?"

"Well I can read, Justin. So why not, just for a start, try levelling with me about your hand?"

He muttered, grumpily. "I don't know why you're

coming at me like this. Maybe if you were a little older there'd be things in your life you'd rather not dig up. But okay. Maybe I was romanticizing. There's nothing romantic about a great hairy miner in a picket line coming at you with a length of two by four."

She winced.

He said, "Forget the pity. Someone else clubbed him down and then I stamped his face until it was hamburger." To which he added, although he was now dimly aware that he was possibly not alone in the boat, in that the rear seat which he could hardly see was now occupied by something, a presence— "You don't mess with the Horsemen."

And again, defiantly if a little drunkenly to the inescapable fog, "I said you don't mess with the Horsemen."

But the occupant of the rear seat projected an unsettling accusatory insistence. Confession was apparently expected of him, from deeper in his soul than he had revealed to Annabel. He had no idea what the visitor expected but he felt driven to say loudly, "So you want the whole story, eh? Of toiling in the vast human sewer? Of my unremarkable career in the trenches?"

There was no answer, and he continued angrily, "Okay I paid my dues. I've pulled decapitated teenagers from wrecked cars, and I've seen what big men can do with baseball bats to small wives. And I've beaten up pimps and totally harmless addicts, and one night three whores jumped me outside a Winnipeg hotel and put me in hospital for a week. Is that what you want to hear? Would you like to know about the time I perjured myself under oath to put away a little prick who'd shot one of my mates?"

But if it was keeping him alert, the coffee eventually also made him need to pee, and he was suddenly gripped in fear. The boat, never convincingly stable, lurched like a cockleshell when he moved even slightly, and to be safe he slid carefully to the floor, crawling across it in pain having delayed too long. He reached for the bailer as a pisspot, but the cap was missing and the sides cracked, and he threw it furiously against the hull, where it shattered.

He shouted, "Never mess with a Horseman, eh?"

There was no choice but to raise himself slowly to crouch grimly on the stern seat. It was daunting enough to kneel there, maneuvering his penis with infinite care. But to gaze down into the ocean's depth while he voided was to lean out, absurdly exposed, over infinite space. He recoiled, most of the stream warming his underwear or flowing over his plastic trousers and back into the boat.

Terrified, he clambered shaking from his perch and inched back amidships on the floor. His instinct about the ocean had been all too correct. He was not safely afloat; he was balanced precariously over his own annihilation. To raise himself back onto the seat amidships would only increase the fatal disequilibrium.

He felt behind him for the rye, too fearful of shifting his weight to look, and the smell of warm urine rose from inside his jacket. He was wondering vaguely how much it would be wise to drink, but when he found the bottle took a swig, and then another.

On the floor with his back against the seat was more secure, but the stoical composure on which he prided himself was wearing thin. He was confused about the time; the sky was definitely darker than it should be. He was now disconcertingly aware of the menace of the deep, and his mind was starting to misbehave treacherously. He was confident he suffered less remorse than most men his age, and like most men he had patched together the usual truce with his conscience. But the truce was breaking down, the protocols were being bypassed. It was the horror below.

He shouted, with the urgency of his message. "So I was a great chum of the native people. There was a guy Joe Hummingbird, an easy-going Metis in North Battleford, I liked having coffee with. We went fishing. He used to go ape after a few beers and he needed a few beers every Friday night because he had only grade seven and delivered Pepsi and he was smart enough to be a rocket scientist. He was taking this lounge apart, and he started to take me apart, and I got him hard in the gut with the stick. Back in the cells he was leaping about in perfect drunken health and the next morning he was dead. Of a ruptured spleen as the friendly coroner said, from running into furniture. 'A violent encounter with furniture' he had written in his report. Furniture shit!"

It was getting extraordinarily dark but for a ghastly moment he was sure he knew the presence in the stern, the bulk and the way the shoulders were set, relaxed and amiable as Joe Hummingbird, and he put his hands to his face to hide. Unnerved, he lost his histrionic grandeur and mumbled to himself, crouched over, awareness of the depths below paralyzing his will so that he could not fight off how willingly he'd believed the FBI's homophobic social science, how willingly he'd ingratiated himself with people in External and Defence to confirm their homosexuality long after he knew he was ruining decent people and destroying families.

He started up, shaking off the horror, exclaiming, "And thus society is purified, eh? So tell me, how much is society purified in the last fifty years? Or is that now the task of Major Gulag's Combat Crusaders?" But there in the stern clearly outlined in shining white, a creche, a shrine if he could believe it, more chillingly the white bathtub containing the naked white corpse of Hubbard Jansen a clerk in the Department of External Affairs, called back from Cyprus for three weeks of virtually uninterrupted interrogation by Corporal Fowles of A-3 to finger his homosexual partners, ending when Jansen ripped open his throat to die in a crimson shroud of his own blood, greeting his torturer that humid Ottawa morning with astonished eyes staring fixedly over an obscene red grin. And the corporal spat contemptuously into the bath before phoning the office to report wittily that another fag had sodded himself.

Justin shut his eyes, opened them to find the vision mercifully vanished. He had come rationally to terms with Joe Hummingbird and Hubbard Jensen, but now rationality had nothing to do with it. He was gripped by the murderer's conscience in the solitary confinement of the fog-bound and indeed darkening ocean. He shifted to his right until he could just see the bottle, and then leaned delicately backward to retrieve it. As he swallowed the first mouthful he almost vomited.

He growled, "Never mess with the Horsemen."

The visibility was still zero in every direction in mist and patches of light rain, and now although it was surely only a little past mid-afternoon, the light was that of approaching evening. Whereas he'd been convinced that safety was to stay in one place, he now suspected there was something nearby that he must get away from. Forgetting the need for caution, indulging his left knee which stabbed him whenever he pressed sideways, he regained the seat and began to row slowly, listening, not too sure if he hoped to find a landfall or feared coming upon something he did not want to find.

Time passed. After several more drinks he was rowing quite strongly. There was relief in concentrating on the rowing, feathering the oars smoothly at each stroke, keeping a steady rhythm and pulling evenly. It seemed more pressing to get away from where he was than to go somewhere he wanted to be.

By the time the bottle was three quarters gone, he was pulling furiously on the oars and chanting, "Stroke! . . . Stroke! . . . Stroke!" at the top of his voice. He had forgotten about finding land; he was borne along by the action and the confident knowledge he was making good an escape.

Sometime later he found himself roaring happily—

"Away away with fife and drum,
Here we come, full of rum,
Looking for women to pinch in the bum,
In the North Atlantic Squadron."

He was sweating so much he had to unzip his jacket. He felt strong enough to pull the boat out of the water. "Way to go!" he shouted, "Way to go!"

He must of course look where he was going, and he shoved himself roughly around, making the boat swerve, to compensate for which he heaved on the opposite oar, which slipped from the rowlock and from his hand and as he grabbed for it he fell backward off the seat with water bucketing over him as the boat tipped violently, steadied, sluggishly righted itself.

"Oh my God," he gasped.

The water in the boat was three inches deep, and icy. The essential thing—he was too drunk to think beyond it—was to bail. He grabbed a trowel-shaped remnant of the bailer and frantically scooped water over the side. He scooped mindlessly until the water was down to the plywood floor. When he finished, his fingers were stiff and his teeth were chattering. He was still too drunk to even try to think, but he could could no longer deny that night was now actually falling. The prospect of a night at sea horrified him. It was impossible that time had gone so quickly. And now he only had one oar.

But North Atlantic Squadron or not, it wasn't true he had evaded the real war. Damn it, he was hardly old enough to enlist when his sister Joanne went missing, although his parents looked at him with that look. Saying nothing, and he couldn't tell or bring himself to ask whether it was grief for her or anxiety for him. In their day the men did the fighting, and women did not ferry bombers to Africa. In his last year of high school Bill Morfitt—he still recalled the name—came back from England and told how they hosed what was left of a classmate, one of last year's grads, out of the rear turret of Lancaster. Which might have influenced his eventual choice of the army, although consciously it was a group thing, he and five of his pals with great expectations of invading Europe, and certainly without knowing he'd land up in the Military Police guarding POWs in Ontario while one of the five was killed and two wounded later somewhere between Normandy and Holland. He could hardly have stopped her from flying, could he?

On hands and knees, convinced the ocean was about to devour him but defiant, suddenly needing furiously to justify himself, he looked toward the stern seat and shouted, "But I caught you, you bastard! No one else could lay a finger on you but I got you by your hirsute Yankee balls!" Through the gloom it was unmistakably none other than G. Myron Resnick, carrying the ID of a humble clerk-courier in the Department of the Interior (Federal Parks Division), but plausibly Director General of Special Assignments in the Central Intelligence Agency, or perhaps something in between, depending on whose version of those half-forgotten events were to be believed.

Sergeant LeDésert and Inspector Fowles had taken him one arm apiece as he walked from the evening train at Windsor Station, really too conspicuous at six foot three wearing a fur-collared coat to be sent clandestinely across a national border, kept on walking through the other passengers and smoothly right-wheel into the washroom Symons was guarding. Resnick grinned but refused to speak, and when Justin asked for the briefcase he held it up, the grin disdainfully smug, to show the chain with its inviolable diplomatic seal, his expression changing to rage as Symons cut the chain and Justin pried open the briefcase and brought out the papers inside. Among them was the *Draft proposed memorandum of understanding between Sovereign Governments,* exactly as he'd expected. No incriminating names. No date. No signatures. As Symons began to photograph the pages Justin said, "My orders are to retain none of your papers. For fairly obvious reasons, eh? As soon as Constable Symons has done his business, Sergeant LeDésert will escort you by car to Dorval, where a reservation to New York has been made for you. Come again, Myron, when you can stay longer!"

The recollection revived his muddled spirits, and he shouted with drunken bravado, "Have you come to see me drown, then? Or is this all orchestrated? The CIA's revenge, eh? To punish us for not kissing the Company's institutional ass? But you should have been more careful, Myron old chap. Old buddy boy! You see I don't exist! Did you ever consider that? If you could only say, 'I am pleased to report the elimination of Chief Inspector Justin Fowles, who ruined our promising initiatives with the PQ.' But shit, man, I no longer exist! How can you exact official vengeance when your victim has no official being?"

He peered toward the stern, but although G. Myron Resnick had gone he shouted, "Ha ha!" as much to express triumph as to keep the ghosts at bay, as to fight the need for sleep which was overpowering him. He found he had slipped sideways and was half under the seat amidships, lying uncomfortably on his right side but too befuddled to do anything about it. He had indeed been wise to bring the booze, without which this would be beyond endurance, without which he might be denied the comfort of the illusion that now lulled him, of seeing someone very like himself on the far horizon, a tiny mounted figure in scarlet advancing toward the distant snowbound Rockies, and who following reluctantly far behind but Corporal Milton Milton. Justin, muttering obscenities, closed his eyes to shut out the approach of appalling night.

His sleep was troubled. He was either beset by dreams, or wrenched up to the ragged surface of semi-consciousness by chills or sharp protruding metal, or left in limbo too uncomfortable to sleep, too tired to force himself awake. At one point, for no discernable cause, he suddenly came to the surface stiff, wet, cramped, colder than misery and in utter confusion about his whereabouts. He couldn't move his fingers from cold, and still half-conscious he lashed out with one arm against a sudden threat to his balance just as it came back to him he was in the boat, that any quick move was death, and he caught himself, held on until his senses cleared so that he knew his balance wasn't threatened. The boat was riding a swell. He had drifted out onto the long Pacific swell. He was out into the Strait of Juan de Fuca.

He was too cold to care. He put his head cautiously above the gunwale, grateful the sea was relatively calm and the wind light, grateful the rain and fog had gone. Far to the north west he could make out the Point Exception Light, white pulses in a bank of mist that was like a wall of ice.

He grunted, "Oh Christ sweet Christ," because he

couldn't stand the cold. He hammered the metal seat and screamed to warn it away. The cold was unlike his other demons, who were particular and individual and even, at times, whimsical. They were satisfied to harass him, to hit and run, to set small ambushes, make swift unexpected forays and become childishly happy over small tactical victories. The cold was huge, monolithic, and remorseless. It didn't deal in petty irritations, and could be satisfied only by death. It was intent on penetrating his mind, infinitely more sensitive to temperature than flesh, forcing the unspeakable upon him. Stephanie rose from the depths of his soul, Stephanie betrayed and abandoned. Stephanie embalmed in ice.

As she went out the door she said she was staying overnight with her mother in Kanata. He didn't try to stop her; in the past year her moodiness, her sudden departures and unexpected arrivals had become routine despite his appeals for an explanation. The next morning he had an early shift, and sitting in the office he heard a car calling in about a young female sitting naked beside the Rideau River. Frozen. Dead. The man on the radio was yelling as if in shock, "It's an injun. A girl! It's an injun without a bloody stitch on!" and Justin knew it was Steph. When he got there it was a still, cold, cloudless Ottawa dawn, and he ran in dread into a snow-covered landscape, steel grey before the sun made it white, each footstep crunching in the frozen stubble. He ran toward a little shape on a knoll above the ice-bound river. And just then the rim of the sun came over the horizon, and she was incandescent! She was covered in hoar frost, which the sun ignited in a coat of blazing ice, like a billion diamonds.

"I carried her back to the road in my arms," he whispered toward the back of the boat. "She was ice, sculptured ice. Rigid, and so light, and Justine was inside her. We used to say we'd call a little girl Justine if we had one, but Stephanie didn't want to get pregnant. She was full of drugs, and I never even knew. I was no use to her. Or maybe it was more. We just didn't connect."

And suddenly the name came to him again and he shouted in pain into the night sky filled amazingly with pitiless stars, "Justine!"

The shock of the name threw him out of the nightmare to discover himself lying on the floor, staring upward, ready to surrender to cold and despair. But there was deep continuous thunder somewhere, and he lifted his head to listen. He looked up groggily for the lights of an aeroplane, but none of the stars moved—although by God the fog had gone and there were stars! He rose achingly to his knees, the sound becoming more localized, and searched at sea level for light from a boat, but all was black. As the thunder grew he became alarmed, because it was rushing nearer without lights and he had nothing to signal his presence; the only comfort was that anything powerful enough to make such thunder, would have radar.

He crouched with one hand firmly on the seat, convinced it was bearing straight toward him. He shouted, only half aware how absurd it was, but the mere act of shouting rocked the boat and he crouched back quickly.

The sound grew to deafening, and a huge shape blacker than the night loomed not fifty feet away, at which moment a glow illuminated a high bridge or cockpit on which he saw or thought he saw human shapes above which stood out a giant figure clothed in white, its head concealed by a huge white carapace bearing a gleaming crimson sword. Then suddenly, as the thing thundered past in a roar of engines and the unmistakable pulsing of heavy acid rock, he was struck by an intense spotlight.

There was a fraction of a second before the light blinded him, before he hit the floor to ride out the wake, in which he saw a naval landing craft, darkly camouflaged, and the giant in white peering down, gesturing enigmatically with one outstretched arm as the monstrous machine hurtled off into the black night.

"Sweet shit!" he gasped, and just then his boat suddenly reared and plunged, and he slumped back onto the floor and shut his eyes, "Bastards!" he shouted, gripping the edges of the plywood floor. "Bastards! Bastards! Bastards!"

But the thunder faded. He was surprisingly alert. He looked up at the stars and followed the edge of the Dipper to the Pole Star. The machine, the landing craft, had been heading north. Toward Canada, to the beach they called Ganges, the *Beachhead* on Gulag's map he recalled dimly from many months ago, connected by a dotted white line up through the clearcut to the Combat College. He had a passing mad vision of the ice-bound sea bearing a caravan of emissaries from the Seven Priestly Eunuchs of San Francisco, perhaps one of the Priestly Ones himself, come north to consult secretly with Mandril Gulag, Commandant of Mercenaries and American Militias, crossing one of Gulag's non-existent borders to do what G. Myron Resnick failed to do because the Force stopped him, now that no one was watching, and no one cared.

Sometime later he became aware of being awake and of feeling unusually peaceful. The stars, the fact of his survival, quieted his mind. Apart from just having missed instant reduction to a splatter of fishfood, he had drifted all night in fog and rain and survived. He had almost swamped the boat, and lost an oar, and had remained afloat. All the monsters of endless night had swarmed in a vast whirlpool beneath his insubstantial shell of a boat, and it was as if for hours he had crouched in supplication, praying not to be sucked down. It was odd, he thought wryly, pushing against the gunwales, that so small a boat had become so stable.

But he was weak and he must have lost consciousness, because after a time he became aware of pain and terrible cold and drifting visions of horror;

images of huge waves, and fanged chimera, and black ships plunging out of the night that advanced and receded over an undefined margin between reality and nightmare, from which emerged a sensation of spacious calm in which the murdered girl floated in her aura of golden hair, her face eerily flushed as if returning to life, her green eyes staring at him as if striving to convey some message beyond his comprehension. When the visions faded he saw the sky was almost imperceptibly lighter. He was conscious of a great emptiness, as if the entangling guilt and anger of his life had been washed away in the great ocean, as if his soul were purged.

It was later still that something of a morning consciousness returned and it came to him suddenly that the floating corpse of the murdered young woman, and Mary Evens' belligerence were still immediate and with him. It was shocking that the incidents of just yesterday afternoon had dropped so completely from his mind, but returning now entangled with the nightmare night and that awful black ship—he tensed at the memory— intent to devour him. There were things he must face, things he must do, but an immense fatigue burdened his impulse to action. He thought he heard distant cries, and tried to raise his arm, and had to force himself against the paralysis of cold and age to raise himself to see the approaching fishing boat.

10

All through the next day or perhaps the next two days, Mary Evens became increasingly unsure of her perception of events. She had initially been convinced there would be callers the next morning, and in anticipation she had put coffee in the percolator ready to plug in and had checked that the fire in the sitting room was ready to light. She had gone about her household routine half-listening for the footfalls of men on the gravel path, Constable Ymenko come—as Mr. Fowles had so pompously intoned—in his full and awful majesty to repossess her Gwendoline.

But there was nothing that morning, nor that afternoon (although she had Blenkinsop re-arrange the sitting room for tea, and found sandwiches and two crumpets at the back of the refrigerator), and by the following morning she wasn't at all sure, coming across the unused tea service in the empty house before dawn, what she had had in mind.

She was not very good, she knew, with matters of sequence. She could cope quite well with the immediate; her difficulty came in relating the immediate to the before and after. She had heard others speak of time as a roadway, moving past people and events one could choose to meet or to ignore, but for Mary time was the opening and closing of unrelated scenes in no particular order, in which the events were far less important than her feelings. The songs of robins before dawn or the setting sun slanting through her casement windows could make her giddy with contentment, but she did not relate them to evening or morning, or whatever came last or first.

She had for instance the happiest recollection that Annabel's children had called on her, but only the vaguest idea of when, or even how often. It might even be about to happen in the future. She had seated them in the kitchen and asked what she could do for them and Marc had grinned self-consciously and said, "We came because you are old and you are, well, mysteriously endowed."

Mary laughed, but Susan said gravely, "We need some advice about Mummy."

"Good heavens my dears, your mother has always struck me as more than capable of looking after herself."

"In most things, yes. But you know she and Mr. Fowles are lovers, don't you?"

Mary nodded warily. She adored their worldliness.

"Well he must be twice her age. I mean he could be dead before she's forty."

Mary said reassuringly, "That can happen to anyone."

Susan said carefully, "Yes, but in that case—"

But Marc interrupted: "The thing is, we need a father."

Mary said, "I'm sure that would be very nice, but really dears your mother's choice of friends is her business."

"That's not logical," Susan said. "What she does affects us. We get teased at school because of Justin. Even if they lived together it would affect Marc and me enormously. I mean on our whole development."

Marc said, "I could be twisted horribly out of shape."

"And we know what we want. The problem is how to get it. We want Mummy to marry Dirk Plantagenet. He's a businessman and fabulously rich," said Susan.

Marc said, grinning, "He drives a V12 Jag and he's a whoremaster."

"Marc!" Susan shouted disapprovingly.

"Well that's what Justin said."

"It's the kind of thing Justin would say."

Mary was caught up in wonder. They were children out of some fantasy, asking her to join them in wonderland. She said soothingly, "Children. This is a very important step. It may be difficult to reverse. You are sure it is what you want?"

They both nodded emphatically. "It's a matter of intuition," said Susan casually. "I mean right now mummy hates Mr. Plantagenet, but we know he'd be okay."

"Also he's very nice to us," Marc said. "He bought us ice cream, and he's going to take me fishing on his private lake. So will you do it for us?"

Susan said with rather forced formality, "Oh of course, we do understand. I mean if it's against the rules, or anything."

Mary said, "Oh come on, children, what is all this about? This is not being fair to an old woman."

"A spell!" announced Marc grandly. "We want you to cast a spell on them."

Susan was blushing slightly. She said, "We know you can't admit to being a witch, but that's what we want you to do."

Mary was enchanted, instantly tempted by the illusion. She said carefully, "Oh dear. That is so mature of you to understand my position." She stared at the ground, rotating her open hands before her, delighted at the children's silent awe.

"Yes. Yes, I think something can be done."

"You mean you will?" whispered Marc. Susan shushed him angrily.

"It is coming into focus," said Mary, intoning softly so that the children craned to hear:

> "If this spell is to be done,
> you two children, one by one,
> must bring to me within the week

these magic things for which I seek:
of each a tiny living bit
of hair or slimy snot or spit,
guck from navel, jam from toe—

The spell is getting a little out of hand," said Mary breathlessly, unable to find the next rhyme: "But that gives you the general idea. Actually I will settle for anything even vaguely suggestive of the ah, principals."

"Must it be exactly what the spell calls for?" asked Susan.

"Oh not at all," said Mary; "I am a very powerful witch. A Puissant Witch, as they used to say. I can work a spell with practically anything, but I am not fond of messing with bodily wastes. Of course there has to be a Witch's Brew, and this is very important: you must at least catch me a live frog. To boil."

Susan frowned. "A frog?"

"This is not make-believe," Mary said sternly. "I do not see how you can fuss about a little frog."

"To *boil* it?"

"Alive," said Mary emphatically. The children were pale and still. "How else can you make a witch's brew? Witchcraft is disgusting, you know. Not like Mr. Disney would have you think. You cannot imagine what I have to go through."

Susan said meekly, "Well perhaps you shouldn't."

"Even the cat," said Mary smugly, noticing under the stove the scabrous rat-like thing that had recently appeared in the house.

"That's not even yours," exclaimed Susan. "That's Idris, malevolent Egyptian goddess of something crazy."

"It belongs to Justin," said Marc.

"Which certainly explains its temperament," said Mary. "Oh definitely, into the pot!"

Then Susan had said hesitantly, "Well, perhaps you shouldn't," and Mary remembered clearly the giddy sense of triumph she felt as she proclaimed, "There is nothing, nothing more important than your future! You want a father? Damn it, you shall have a father!"

But now she knew there was a more iminent crisis. And it was much later, or was it yesterday? (as she set out the coffee mugs, cursing Blenkinsop for disappearing at yet another critical moment), still expecting the jack-booted constable and his slovenly minions, that she heard a ripple of light sharp footsteps approaching across the verandah, followed by a forceful crash of the front door knocker.

It was Annabel McKinley, smiling sweetly. "Dear, dear Annabel," said Mary, almost too effusively in her relief. "How nice to see you again, and how nicely timed! I have just put on some coffee. The air is chilly this morning. Now come on and we'll have a nice fire."

"Oh I musn't, dear. I can't!" Annabel protested. "This is, well, a professional visit and I have to—"

But Mary had already disappeared toward the kitchen, singing tunelessly to herself, leaving Annabel alone in the hallway and suddenly conscious of how everything had changed since her last visit. She had checked out the dates; Maggie Sunflower was sure the brigadier died at 85 in 1942, and the Indian Mutiny was in 1857, the year he would have been born. Which made that story a lie, just as Dirk's discovery of Mogador's provenance made Mary's ancestry a lie, made Mogador less a crumbling repository of faded dreams than a charnel house. She no longer felt uneasy about Dirk's plans .

She wanted to get to the point of her visit because her day had already been turned to chaos with the discover of Justin's mad adventure. She had been awake at seven so full of such delight at a fresh new day that she was momentarily free of nagging conscience about Prospect Palisades. She felt well-disposed toward her children and toward Justin, whom she was to meet for their scheduled coffee at ten o'clock. She was feeling particularly merry about Justin, the mischievous old bugger, because she decided she had kept him in the dark long enough about Dirk's roses. She was in the midst of planning how best to confront the old trickster when Tommy Laidlaw, an ambulance attendant she knew, called to say Justin had been rescued at sea and was at the Sleepytyme Infirmary. The news was so improbable that she screamed in disbelief, and had to reassure the distraught Tommy that no, he'd not sent her into hysterical shock.

As soon as she'd got the children off to school, and just as she was about to phone the Infirmary, Justin himself was on the phone. He sounded so awful she didn't even think of teasing him about getting lost. He mumbled some quite mad story about searching all night for a murder victim which Mary Evens had stolen.

She asked, "Why on earth would you want to spend all night in a rowboat? You hate boats."

"Damn it Annabel, I didn't *want* to! I retreated under a hail of bullets! I was pressed beyond all limits. The first thing I knew, I didn't know where I was."

Annabel emitted the faintest gurgle, and Justin shouted hoarsely, "Mock me if you will! It could have had the most tragic consequences! Even now Nurse Karlsrue says I am in grave straits!"

She promised to visit him, but decided to check first if Ymenko had heard anything. Ymenko had no record of any call reporting the body. "You're going to have to put that boy on a leash, Annabel. He was just on to me. He wants Mrs. Evens behind bars, can you believe it? I mean what would old Mrs. Evens want with a dead body? Was he drinking? He sure sounded high as a kite."

Justin hadn't mentioned his night at sea, and Ymenko was highly amused to hear of it. She said, "He could make up a story about finding a dead body, but it's not like him to lie about reporting it to the police."

"Ever the inspector."

"You're not supposed to mention that, Ymenko. Do you want the sky to fall?"

"I'm sorry," Ymenko said. "No I don't think he'd make it up. It was probably the answering machine. Mae says it's been acting up."

Annabel was pleased with herself for thinking to get Mary's story before seeing Justin. It would help her check his more extreme flights of fancy. She had her first question ready when Mary emerged from the kitchen with a teapot muffled in a huge stained cosy (the promised coffee apparently having been forgotten, just as the lovely fire had been forgotten) and said, "I do not want to seem inquisitive, my dear, but I assume you and that unusual Mr. Fowles are still, well, on friendly terms."

"Oh yes," said Annabel. "The relationship is still going on."

"I really do not know how to put this. I had this extraordinary encounter with Mr. Fowles the day before yesterday. Or was it the day before? It will be a great relief to talk about it. You see I walk every day. It is important at my age. Walking and calcium. One can ignore these things whilst one is young, but not after middle age. Walking and calcium. So I often scramble down to the inlet, the fiord I think it is called, and yesterday, it was early afternoon, I came out of the woods and there was your Mr. Fowles standing in the rain and fog beside his boat looking quite miserable. And soaking wet, poor man. It was very odd indeed, Annabel my dear. I was quite cheery but he cut me off most rudely. Does he drink intemperately, dear?"

"No—oh no; Justin sometimes goes on a bit of a —" It didn't sound like Justin at all.

"No, I am sure. But he accused me of hiding a corpse. Yes! It was unbelievable! He was really quite loud and, well, I hate to say this—offensive. Loud and offensive. Yes. He accused me of violating a body and threatened me with dire consequences. I was shocked. I had thought Mr. Fowles a gentleman."

Annabel frowned, and Mary gestured sympathetically and said, "I thought of you immediately. I hoped I had not been shown something of his treatment of you."

"No. Oh no," Annabel said quickly, trying to retain her line of questioning. "That— That was the first time you saw him? Yesterday? Afternoon? At the beach?"

"Oh yes. Oh yes. I seldom go into the village you see. The store has lists—"

"No. I mean did you see him earlier? On the beach."

"Oh no." Mary's stared uncomprehendingly. "I am sorry I do not understand. How could I—"

"Justin says you were there with the body, and that he left it with you while he went for the police."

"Oh no!" Mary shook her head slowly, staring sadly at the floor. "What has got into the man? Oh why do men have to do these things to us? What kind of body does Mr. Fowles believe he found?"

"I understand it was a young woman, but I've only talked to Justin on the phone, and his mind isn't very clear yet. He spent the night on the water." She sensed evasion in Mary's denial; things were no longer straightforward. "He says when he came back the body was gone—"

"What a worry he must be for you."

Annabel shrugged. She decided not to press Mary about the shooting until she talked to Justin.

Mary said, "I do think you have cause for concern, dear, with that kind of hallucination. Driving him to such irrational action. When he set off into the fog like that I thought he had lost all judgement."

Annabel moved to get up, and Mary said lightly, "But I am sure everything will turn out all right. The illusion of a young woman's body. A pale virginal corpse. It can be a dangerous attraction for an aging man."

They came out onto the verandah. The Olympic Mountains were clear, across the Straits. Annabel said, "I guess you realize, the police will probably want to talk to you."

Mary laid her hand reassuringly on Annabel's arm. "You must be strong. I suppose they might think of charging him with public mischief. That is the usual thing I think for false alarms."

"Mary, there is another possibility. They may believe Justin. They may want to charge you."

Mary chuckled good-naturedly. "That would be rather a lark, would it not! That would give you something to write about!" She started to talk about the garden and, just touching Annabel's arm, steered her gently along the verandah—minding the rotting floor—to the south west corner, nearest the fiord, where there was a large telescope mounted on a massive metal stand, all encrusted in old grey paint.

Mary paused to peer through the eyepiece toward the Straits. "Ah, a sailboat! I can remember as a child watching the Empress boats from here. They were painted white, with three beige funnels. They had such exquisite lines."

She motioned Annabel to the eyepiece and Annabel, having noticed the tiny boat far out on the water, was shocked at the magnification. "Goodness," she said, "What a powerful telescope."

"There is a family legend that it was used at Jutland. Oh yes —" She swung the telescope toward the East Ridge directly across the inlet. "Can you see that stonework, concrete or whatever it is over there?"

Annabel saw a suggestion of grey amidst the foliage, but through the telescope the grey became a low concrete wall so sharply focussed she could see individual pebbles and patches of rust. The old lookout.

"Annabel dear I do not want to add to your burden but I think I should tell you. About Mr. Fowles. Because you may think I have been too inquisitive about him. You see twice recently I have seen Mr. Fowles watching me through binoculars from that old fortification."

"Justin?" cried Annabel. "Oh no it couldn't be! He promised—!"

"You see how powerful the glass is, dear. I would have to swear it was he. In a court of law, I mean. But perhaps he was bird-watching. It was like—what do they say in the spy stories?—surveillance. But more likely bird-watching."

"I can't understand it," said Annabel, unable to think. They embraced, and she smiled fixedly to herself as she departed. She was sure the old hag had diddled her, without knowing quite how. Somehow she'd botched the interview completely.

It was deception and senile idiocy and they were both doing it and she didn't trust either of them, and on top of it all, Justin was still playing his damned hide and seek with the old woman. But for all her bumbling, Mary was making one thing menacingly clear, and Justin had to know about it before he made an even greater fool of himself.

11

The G. Randall Prowling Memorial Infirmary had been built in the late seventies as a "generous initiative to advance greater community understanding" by Prowloc, the multinational company, to placate local opposition to the massive clearcut they were about to undertake. It was a low cedar-shingled building of some twenty rooms, visible from the highway through a screen of evergreens. Passing motorists assumed it was a motel, and indeed its architect had secretly been ordered to anticipate its conversion to that purpose when the logging was done. There was even a concrete footing near the entrance, supporting a rusting pole to which pieces of an extruded aluminum framework still hung, rattling in the wind. This was all that remained of a dazzling flourescent-white plastic column with SLEEPYTYME MOTEL in scarlet letters, whose appearance the day after logging ended shocked the locals into realizing they'd been had.

Fortunately one of the locals, Findlay Moore, QC, a BC Supreme Court judge who had retired to live in a boat in the woods above Prospect, remembered the original agreement had set no time limit. On the contrary, the agreement extolled the permanancy of Prowloc's commitment, and was so sparse of precautionary escape-clauses as to suggest the company's lawyers had been blindsided by their own PR staff.

Thus the infirmary stayed put, and until the motel sign fell to pieces the resident nurse spent much of every Friday and Saturday night assuring tired or lustful motorists that it was not a motel. This was more a nuisance than an imposition, because the infirmary hardly ever housed more than two patients at a time, although the records, had anyone examined them, showed their stays to be of unusual length.

By the time Annabel reached the infirmary, Mary's report of Justin's continued spying dominated her mind. She was in a rage, near to boundless, and rushed past the reception desk and the sign asking visitors to check in. She saw his name on a door and punched it open and shouted, "You asshole. You unmitigated asshole!" She was too furious to interpret his glazed expression as anything but feigned fatigue. The elaborate winking chrome and glass machinery beside the bed only confirmed that even the medical profession was an easy mark for him.

"Good God, the hero of the deep himself, and what the hell—"

She was interrupted by a female voice behind her, warbling cheerfully, "Miss, will you come and check in please?"

"Oh fuck off," yelled Annabel without turning round, and then in a spasm of regret, clutching her fists before her face in frustration; "Oh I'm sorry. That's no way to talk to anyone. Whoever you are."

"I'm Pegggy Karlsrue, R.N., with three g's, the duty nurse. You're Ms. McKinley. You're the newspaper publisher. We met in the Empowerment Seminar. Don't worry about blowing your stack. It's a common result of impacting bureaucracy in the stressed healthcare environment. The Empowerment Seminar taught me to analyse situations creatively."

"No it's not you Pegggy, really. I'm terribly sorry. I'm truly just out of control with rage at this stupid insensate hulking idiot. The seminar. Of course." Annabel, sick with chagrin, forced herself to meet Pegggy's eyes and extend her hand. "People call me Annabel."

"It's all right, honey. Annabel! Yeah! It's great for me to meet up with you again. You gave such a wonderful lecture at the seminar. You're a real role model for so many of us."

Increasingly abashed, Annnabelle muttered, "Oh please, no — "

"Annabel I'll give you a tip. I heard you expressing hostility toward your dad here—"

Annabel clenched her teeth.

"—and I want you to know that's entirely normal. When a love-receiver is hospitalized the love-giver often experiences a strong sense of betrayal. The basis of this betrayal is that the provider of strength and stability suddenly proves weak and unreliable. Actually anger is the healthiest outlet possible, so you're really doing the right thing."

"Thank you for sharing that with me," said Annabel, smiling sweetly to hide her amusement at the idea of Justin providing strength and stability.

Pegggy said, "So don't go home and cry because you were mad at him, eh? Give him real hell!"

"You're wonderful! You're truly wonderful! Did anyone tell you what a wonderful person you are?"

Pegggy grinned, skeptically. "Of course, honey. All the time. You drop by the desk before you go, eh?"

But the few moments with Pegggy had calmed her, or perhaps restored her self-control. Her original impulse—to tear the covers from the bed and reveal Justin twitching like a moist pulpy sea thing just out of its shell—had gone. Instead, she sat down near the head of the bed with elaborate calm, staring contemptuously at the mound of blankets and green sheets under which Justin was huddled in deep retreat.

"Are you not able to hear me, daddy dear? Are you still suffering from your ordeal, or is this a relapse?"

The noise of a great fart rumbled deep in the mound, and Annabel said, "I'm not here with flowers,

Justin. We have to talk. You have been a fool and are in serious trouble."

Justin's head suddenly thrust up from the covers, gasping dramatically as one hand fannned the fetid air.

"Why do you have to play every scene sophomoric?" asked Annabel, moving her chair away from the smell. "There's nothing more tedious than an old man playing anal tricks. Did you hear what I said about serious trouble?"

Justin struggled onto one elbow, and stared solemnly at her from what could have passed as the ravaged face of a recently deposed prophet, eyes darkly rimmed. His suffering was exquisitely convincing. He said huskily, "Did I phone you?"

"Yes dear heart. Early this morning."

"I am still quite weak. My memory is clouded."

"Of course," said Annabel.

"The doctors have marveled at my resilience. My physiological tone. As tough as a horny thirty-year old, one of them said to me."

"This is the Sleepytyme Infirmary, Justin. It's not a hospital. Sleepytyme doesn't have doctors. It has Pegggy Karlsrue, R.N. The man who spoke to you was Tommy Laidlaw, a para-medic. A nice guy. He called me when he brought you in. He told me maybe an eighty-year old. He said nothing about horny."

Justin waved a limp hand in her direction. "You always puncture my dreams," he said. "I want to sleep now." He dropped to the pillow and pulled the covers over himself. "You may return at normal visiting hours."

She leapt up and yanked the covers from his face. "No you *cannot* sleep, dammit. Listen! I saw Mary Evens this morning. She never saw a body, she never saw you with a body. She saw you only once yesterday, standing by a boat near one of her footpaths. Preparing, she implied, to do trespass." Justin gradually adjusted himself onto his elbow again, staring at her blankly. "She said you accused her of abusing a corpse, and uttered threats of criminal prosecution and were thoroughly rotten to the dear old thing."

Justin jerked up, almost sitting, suddenly animated. "The old bitch. I'm calling Ymenko again. I'll swear an information! Don't you realize she tried to blow me away? Twice? We'll get the old slattern now! Ha!" He crabbed furiously across the bed, reaching for the phone. Annabel beat him to it.

She said calmly, "You're not going to phone Ymenko, because very fortunately you have me around to protect you from yourself. You promised me three weeks ago to stop tracking Mary Evens. So at least twice since then you've been slithering around Fuck Point with your binoculars trained on her cottage. You bloody idiot, Justin."

Justin shrugged. "That's an absurd story. A journalistic fabrication, of which you commit so many. What are your sources?"

"The Queen of Intrigue herself, dear. Little old stooped half-blind Mary Evens. Tell me something; has this gone farther than paranoia? Are you lusting after her dusty little grey muff?"

Justin, cruelly scored upon, snarled, "Even if I were observing her she couldn't have detected me, for Christsake. I am professionally a master of intrigue and surveillance. Did I tell you Nixon wanted me for Watergate? Fuck Point is what, half a mile from the Evens place. The cottage is surrounded by trees, completely screened by trees. Get the facts straight, isn't that the reporter's first rule? Or is this one of your fables?"

Annabel, sensing his confidence was bruised, sat back comfortably in the chair. "One straight fact is that she has a naval telescope strong enough at that range to count your liverspots. I looked through it. Just before she told me about seeing you spying on her. And that was pointedly *after* she'd given me her detailed account of how you'd accused her of making off with a corpse."

Justin mumbled something about its never standing up in court and then blurted, "I had good and sufficient reasons. I have well-found suspicions. No, this cannot deter me. Please—the phone."

"Damn you Justin," she shouted, "Stop the silly game!"

"The shotgun!" he shouted.

"Justifiable self-defence," she shouted back, "Or your bloody fiction. Look I'm trying to tell you that if you keep insisting she made off with a body, Mary Evens will throw the book at you. She'll mention your spying from Fuck Point, and she'll say you came by boat to sneak onto her property to spy some more. I'll bet she'll say you invented the body as a cover for being caught red-handed."

"That's utterly silly. She didn't say anything like that."

"Exactly. She's too smart to spell it out in so many words. Her conversation this morning was all bits and pieces and then just as I was leaving it all came together as coherently as if she'd scripted it."

"She couldn't prove a thing. No one would believe her."

"Tell me who's going to believe you. And think if they ask me under oath about your behaviour toward her."

"You wouldn't—"

"Under oath I'd have to. Not to mention your confessions the Jazz Hall Lady Jane might be asked about. Not to mention your natural propensity to lie and deceive, which the whole village would attest to. And ignoring how a jury would weigh the testimony of a sweet old lady against a pigtailed slob."

Justin subsided slowly to the bed and stared at the ceiling. She said, "I'm not putting you down dear. But your problem isn't how to deal with Mrs. Evens. Your problem is to retract what you said to Ymenko this morning, to stop him coming onto Mary Evens. I suggest you plead mental aberration induced by exposure."

"Fun-*ny*."

"I'm serious. She's not going to roll over and purr for anyone. Ymenko having no record of that call is the best thing that could have happened; now you can tell him you imagined it all, last night out on the water."

Justin continued to stare at the ceiling. Annabel returned the telephone to the bedside table. Justin said toward the ceiling, "There was a body there and she knows it. She must have it somewhere on her property. She must be strong like ox. She can't have put it back in the chuck. I would have found it."

"Don't worry about that. Worry about your next interview with Ymenko."

"He's got a murder on his hands."

"Oh sure; a murder without a victim. Got any ideas of how I should write that up?"

"Just don't write it up. Just forget it. I don't want to read another mangled report of your reality."

Annabel reached affectionately for his hand. "Please, Justin, trust me."

"Trust you?" He pulled away to the other side of the bed. "After you've just returned from consorting with the enemy? After your paper savaged my attempt to lead Prospect to a retail renaissance?"

"*Retail renaissance?* Aren't you the guy who has an odd-job, pardon me *maintenance* business without a phone number? Justin, come to earth! You talked from

February to July about your retail renaissance. You put up an enormous billboard where nobody would see it. You don't advertise. The other day all you had in your window was a box of fake cedar carvings you hadn't even put on the shelves. Summer's almost over, Justin, and there are no tourists in Prospect. There have never been any tourists in Prospect!"

"Shit on you, friend. I'm not giving an interview. I have no comment on anything from this time forward."

"You know you'll be trumpeting your adventures all over the village as soon as you're out of here. Just be damn careful what you say about Mary Evens."

Justin pulled the bedding over himself again. He muttered, "No comment," and turned on his face, hunching his back in the air as if he were in a tent.

"Oh Justin," she said despairingly.

The voice from the tent said, "You must call the nurse. I feel a serious relapse approaching. Caused by stress."

She was exasperated and tired, as if she'd been dealing with the children all day. She said, "Justin I have the most affectionate regard for you. Why do you do these things to me? I'm your friend. We're lovers. Why must I put up with these impossible antics?"

Justin's head emerged like an irate turtle's, shouting, "You believe Mary Evens. You've swallowed her lies as if I never existed. If that's not an assault on me, what is?"

"For Christ's sake, Justin, I never said your story was a lie. I never said Mary's story was true. You *have* lied to me in the past, but Mary lies too. So I just don't know. I just don't know. Oh I really do give up on you!" Annabel regarded the silent mound of bedding thoughtfully, wondering where the truth was, and if it mattered all that much where the truth was.

Nurse Karlsrue swirled into the silence with rustling of efficiency. "I can tell you've shared a cathartic experience, and that's nice. I know because I can feel the calm between you. It's a matter of experience."

Annabel suggested unenthusiastically that she should take Justin home, but Pegggy reacted with horror; "Good heavens no! We must keep him under observation, Annabel. He's no young chicken to venture out on the wild Pacific like that in an open boat. Exposure is subtle. We must be sure of his electrolytes. Oh several days yet. Several days!"

On the drive back to Prospect, Annabel tried to imagine Justin standing yesterday on the government wharf. If he'd had an impulse to spy on Mary, a boat would be the silliest possible way to go. The forest afforded cover, whereas by boat he'd be visible from Mogador the moment he shoved off. Besides, only something far more urgent than watching Mary would have got him into a boat. Once two months ago she'd talked him into renting a boat to picnic on Schooner Shoal. She was looking forward to the fun of sunbathing nude and seducing him. But he was tense from the moment they left the dock, and later she was amused to find him impotent. It was only then he'd confessed his phobia about the water. He couldn't even swim.

Obviously he'd seen something out in the bay unusual enough to demand immediate investigation. It fitted together and, as she'd told Ymenko, it would have been out of his constabulary character to invent reporting a crime. So if he had found a body, which seemed entirely possible, and if it had disappeared, then Mary Evens' denial of its existence was proof she had made it disappear. There was also that odd turn of phrase Mary had used—what had she said?—"young, pale, virginal"? Surely words she'd only use if she'd seen the dead girl or woman. Why Mary needed a corpse was beyond Annabel's understanding.

She would keep her conclusions to herself. They could only encourage Justin to press charges against Mary Evens, and then Mary would crucify him in court for harassment. A bloody mess. In the mean time, she would let Justin stew a bit, the lying bastard.

The road curved around a bare ridge of stone littered with broken lumber and then opened to a view to the south. She saw the flags flying over the Mercenary Combat College down to her right (why did Justin always insist there was only the Stars and Stripes when the Canadian and provincial flags were just as visible?) and far beyond that the rock of Mary Even's

Mogador rising against the sea, and ahead the smoke haze drifting above the forest that sheltered the village. Suddenly, astonishingly, she was gripped by the most powerful aversion.

What the hell was the old woman trying to do? Sitting there amidst the second-hand wreckage of foreign history, inventing lies, pretending concern for Justin's mental health and making counterfeit chatter about birdwatching while she threatened Justin with jail. And somewhere at the edge of her thoughts was the question of Susan and Marc's continued association with—what had Susan called her two nights ago?— " . . our sweet mysterious benefactor . . "?

"*Your* sweet benefactor? What do you mean benefactor? Or sweet?"

"That's what she is. She provides us with benefits in mysterious ways."

"Susan I don't particularly like enigmatic smartass answers to straighforward questions which I as a parent am entitled to ask."

"She will benefit you too," Marc said.

Whoever she might be. Wholesome company indeed for a couple of precocious pre-adolescents. And Justin was no better, stupidly getting conned by Mary over the body, behaving like a spoilt child in the infirmary, breaking his promise about spying on Mary, not to mention his endless habitual boring protestations and exaggerations and obscure allusions to the past—good God the list was virtually endless—

Why were they fighting over a corpse, for heaven's sake?

It came to her with shocking force *that they were old.* She had failed to acknowledge their oldness. She said to herself, admitting it for the first time, "Justin is an old man." It sounded ghastly. It was the man in the infirmary bed, an old bearded man! It hadn't occurred to her that oldness had substance or that it mattered. There was, what?—five or ten years' difference between Justin and Mary, and twenty-five years' difference between Justin and her—and yet she had taken Justin as a contemporary and Mary as a generation older. She drew over onto the shoulder, where it formed a lookout over the shattered landscape, and stopped the engine. This revelation about age had caught her off-guard.

A camouflaged jeep roared by, its horn blaring, the driver gesturing vigorously with one finger raised. Probably Mandril.

It wasn't that Mary and Justin were the same, but that they shared this quality, this oldness. Their words and actions were no longer direct expressions of themselves, but were always for some secret and probably unconscious redemptive purpose. They manipulated instinctively, from a lifetime of practice. Their most constant efforts were to re-arrange the present to provide what the past had denied them. They were weighed down by their personal histories, which they eagerly dumped on anyone who came close. She'd had too much of it. She'd had far, far too much of it.

What had she said to him?—something about really giving up on him, meant affectionately but returning to her now as deliverance. Giving up on both of them and their silliness. There was so much more for today and the future. Prospect Palisades was the future; it was the kind of grand business scheme she had been so good at and she was drawn to it powerfully. It was also in Dirk's clumsy hands a godawful travesty, an environmental disaster floating on financial quicksand, undoubtedly in the wrong place at the wrong time, and yet it fascinated her. He was absolutely right in seeing Mogador as the key to the development, but her initial anger at learning Mogador's and Mary's planned fate had faded sometime this morning, standing in Mary's crumbling urine-scented front hall and realizing the old bitch was playing games with her.

The children were off to Edmonton in the morning to spend a month with their father, but despite the distraction of getting them ready she kept thinking all evening of the Palisades project, and how to move Mary out of the way.

Many of Annabel's best ideas had come as sudden inspiration. Her famous MorningWare jingle had arrived fully formed around midnight. It was in fact in bed and well past midnight, with the children finally asleep, that she sat up alert, and reached for the phone. "Dirk, I've got it," she announced to the bewildered grunt at the other end of the line. "This is what you have to do."

He was to assure Mary dramatically that her house was about to collapse, and show a desire to help. He was to go through the house pointing out the damage. He should emphasize the leaks in the roof, the rotting wood and fallen plaster. She'd say she couldn't afford repairs; he should hint at a deal that would cost her nothing. He would leave her for a few days in suspense, saying he would have to write up a proposal. Then he would return with an agreement of sale giving him title in exchange for the bungalow's complete restoration and an agreement permitting her to live rent-free for life.

"You're mad," he said. "No lawyer would let her sign. It's robbery."

"She won't go near a lawyer. Even if she did, saving that house is too important to her. For you it's the land you want, and she'll be dead and out of your way in five years."

12

Annabel lost track of when Justin might return to town. She had suddenly to start scrambling for more advertising, because Sandy Kelvin quit without warning to go to Europe with her boyfriend, leaving half the accounts untouched. The day after she told Dirk how to deal with Mary Evens one of her steady clients, Highway Foods in Sooke—as if by a divine punitive hand—withdrew their ad for the summer and then another client, Lenny Marshall of Lenny's Hot Tub & Patio died of a heart attack.

She also had startling news by way of Hank Lang of Smith Lang Osborne, who in the midst of a chat about the project she was working on dropped his voice to a whisper to tell her the great Orlando Smith himself was about to offer her a job. "A great job," he said. "So big you wouldn't believe, baby!"

It wasn't as though she'd never thought of returning south, but she was distracted by the prospect of something big and soon, and the suspense of waiting for the details. Also it was agony to find a way of writing the report on Justin's drowned woman.

In the background there was Prospect Palisades and her ambiguous involvement with it. Of course Prospect Palisades was outrageous. It was an insult to nature as massive as the clearcut; her readers would be horrified to know she was connected with it. But the project's excitement fuelled the insidious attraction she felt toward Dirk, a physically repellent man, as she told herself, with far more ambition than ability, misogynistic, humourless, condescending, self-centred and representative of much that she held venal and beneath contempt. Despite which she couldn't get him out of her mind. One night she imagined herself lying beneath him, so powerful a sensation that she had to relieve herself, crying out for him as she came.

She felt pulled in all directions but also very much alive. The paper's problems were a drag but Smith Lang Osborne's attention was stimulating and as the days went by she became eager to know how Dirk had managed with Mary. He was to have seen Mary the day after Annabel had briefed him, and it was about a week later, on a rainy afternoon, that he called again excitedly asking her to the secret office. As soon as she opened the door he shouted, "I did it! She signed!" and they rushed into a furious embrace, laughing triumphantly.

He was still in his rainjacket, soaking wet, but he was trembling, clutching her as she clutched him, opening her mouth to him without thinking. His strength and ardour shocked her, recalling the forgotten delight of aroused male vigour. They began moving against each other, losing balance to fall to the floor, caressing and clutching, Annabel increasingly distracted by his clammy clothes and the hard floor.

"This is impossible," she gasped as soon as she could pull her mouth from his. "Let's go somewhere."

"Go somewhere? What you mean?"

"Somewhere comfortable, for God's sake Dirk."

"But I gotta have you. A man can't stop. I gotta!" He scrambled to his feet and pulled the thin mattress from the cot onto the floor and ran to turn off the lights before she could say she wanted to see him nude. She could hear his wet clothes slapping to the floor but had just found the mattress in the dark and was only half out of her slacks when he was on her.

"Dirk!" she protested, giggling, wanting at least half of what was promising to be a solo performance. He picked her up and she locked her legs around his waist as he carried her around the room, and she cried out, "Oh yes!" and exuberantly opened her blouse for him. When they regained the mattress she was aching for him, and reached down to guide him, whispering, "Oh give it to me, Dirk darling, oh give it to me!" gasping as he drove up into her twice and three times before he gave a shuddering gasp and fell away onto the floor as if clubbed.

After half a minute or so of silence, during which her mind regained a remarkable clarity, she said, "Have you died?"

"Oh hell. Oh my God. Are you ever something." There was another long silence. He said, "What a great fuck, eh?"

The word chilled her. "No."

"What'ya mean?"

"I mean it wasn't. I mean it wasn't anything." She was taut with unfulfilment, furious at his selfishness.

"Oh shit I thought you were with me. I thought—oh Jeeze Annabel I'm sorry." He fumbled around the mattress and grabbed her arm. "I just had to have it, I didn't think."

"Of course you didn't fucking think," she said. "You don't know how to fucking think." She was jarringly unsettled. It was unreal, to be naked in the dark in a strange room—on the floor, no less—with Dirk Plantagenet of all the unprepossessing people, discussing botched intercourse, knowing outside it was still daylight, in Prospect on Palgrave Street where people she knew were at this moment walking by. She felt she'd fallen from the ceiling. She was still hot from his hands over her, his weight on her, still groggy from his urgency and strength, and coldly furious.

She muttered, "God damn you, God damn you," cursing herself because in the suddenly cool air this sweaty botched encounter seemed the inevitable climax of having lost all control of her direction, and not only in the last twenty minutes.

Three mornings later a thick envelope from Philadelphia arrived by courier. She glanced at the first page and had to sit down in shocked exuberant dismay before she grabbed the phone to demand the Jazz Hall Lady Jane meet her for coffee in the Rib'n'Rye. As soon as she sat down the Lady Jane said, "What the hell has happened to you?"

"What do you mean? Does something show?"

"You look, how should I put it?—not yourself. As perhaps after a less than satisfactory honeymoon."

"You are as usual so perceptive, dear all-seeing one. I have been laid, but only once. And since you will never guess, by your own Dirkie-boy,"

"Oh my God! No you're right I never would have guessed. But he would have told me; he tells me too damn much. So a one-night stand with the local stud gets you to call for an emergency coffee session? Not like you dear."

"No it's something else entirely. But yes, I'm screwing up in all directions." The news from Philadelphia was suddenly less urgent, and she told the Lady Jane about Sandy's quitting and about Prospect Palisades and her disillusionment with Mary Evens and about helping Dirk buy her out. "I don't really know how I let all this all happen. I feel such a damn fool. If he'd mentioned Prospect Palisades at that meeting two weeks ago I'd have hit him over the head. But he lets me in on the big plan and I get sucked right in. Pie in the entrepreneurial sky. I mean I know it's a bust; his business plan looks lovely but I did the numbers and it's pure BS. He's brainless, for Christ's sake, and here I am lusting for him."

"So it is a honeymoon. How nice for you!"

"There's no need for sarcasm, dear lady. He keeps phoning but honestly, I've sworn off, and really that's no big deal. I just suffered a sudden rush of the hots. What bugs me is I've compromised my values over this ecological disaster. And I've probably committed criminal fraud over Mary Evens. Not to mention my journalistic integrity."

"Lovely big words," said the Lady Jane.

"I shouldn't even be telling you this. Probably I—"

The Lady Jane smiled. "Rest your conscience dear; he told me about it long ago. But keep in mind Dirk is a fountain of impractical dreams. There are no principles involved in dreams, so don't fret yourself. It's not as if you have any financial interest in it."

"It's sweet of you to say."

"It's not sweetness, it's just reality. After all your problem with Prospect Palisades is the same as with the Prospect Advertiser."

"I—?"

"I asked you once early on what kind of work you did, and you said it was creating fantasies. The best thing about the Advertiser was those crazy stories. I'll never forget that one about Ingrid Vandercamp as Ophelia, the woman who buried three husbands with the girl who killed herself for one. It was really quite cruel."

"Her evicting that single mother was pretty cruel too."

"I'm not accusing you of anything. I'm just saying fantasy's your thing! It's what made you big Yankee bucks. It made the Advertiser special too. And so when you came across Prospect Palisades it was your element. You just slipped into it. I'm trying to say don't blame yourself too much."

Annabel frowned. Perhaps she was being too crowded by events; perhaps everything was simpler than she thought.

The Lady Jane said, "But am I to take as significant that you haven't mentioned Justin?"

Annabel made a helpless gesture with her hands.

"He got home today."

"Oh God! I didn't even know." She put both hands to her chest. "You see he's not here any more. I don't really understand it but he's moved off into the distance and I am here and up to my tits in a bloody seething crisis." She paused, thinking. "Maybe it's because I know he needs support and I can't spare anything right now. We had fun, and I never wanted more than that, but whenever I've needed even basic elementary candour, for Christ's sake, all I get is oratory and evasion."

"But you can't ignore him."

"Oh I've got to level with him. Yes I do know. I've got to meet him and level with him. I just don't know right now how to do it. Not only that, but it's been torture trying to write up his adventure with Mary and that body, and I know he'll go ballistic when he reads what I've done."

She searched in her purse and pulled out a fat envelope. "And then this morning this arrived." She passed the letter to the Lady, Jane. "I knew this was coming, but it's the shock of actually having it in one's hands."

"Embossed letterhead," said the Lady Jane. "Impressive. Who is Orlando Smith in Smith Lang Osborners vast multinational universe?"

"The great one. The senior partner, who strides his world like a colossus."

"This doesn't say much except that he urges you to consider the enclosed contract offer and so on. Warmest collegial welcome. Etcetera."

"Collegial sure; he's a damn dictator. No I iust wanted you to see it's the real thing. The contract is for a full partnership in a new office they're opening in San Francisco. A salary well into six figures plus stock options, a car of my choice, a huge low-interest mortgage. The works. They want me."

"Seems to me we decided several weeks ago you're ready to get back into it."

"I wasn't expecting it coming quite as rich as this. But I'm trying to be sure it's what's best, not what's the easiest escape from the mess I'm in here."

"Hell, you loved the work."

"Yes I loved it. And this'll be everything for Susan and Marc."

"Well stand back a bit, darling The so called mess you're in is mostly overheated conscience and damp drawers. You're being offered a big career move. There's no decision. The only obligation you've got is ordinary personal etiquette, to say goodbye nicely to your friends. For one of those friends it's going to be difficult, but you can do it."

13

Justin managed to extend his stay at the Sleepytyme Infirmary for six luxurious days. At first Pegggy Karlsrue was pleased to have him, because his suffering was so conspicuous that she imagined setting a new record for patient-retention. She was even more pleased to see him go, because his demands for magazines, coffee, toast, adjustments to the bed, tea, sedatives, bed pans, Snickers bars, stimulants, arrowroot biscuits, ice water and so on were finally beyond endurance. Her attempts to reduce him to normal clinical subservience failed, and when she was slow to answer his bell he would appear in the corridor, genitalia swinging defiantly below his hospital smock, roaring obscenities about the service.

He didn't tell Annabel immediately when he returned to Prospect. She'd bullied him mercilessly the morning of his rescue and then ignored him. He could admit his behaviour during her visit hadn't been entirely without deceit, but she'd obviously decided the wretched Evens was truthful, that his trivial bird-watching on Fuck Point was unforgivable, and that his night on the ocean was a self-serving prank.

The night on the ocean stayed with him. In his first night in the infirmary he had become half awake climbing the headboard, gasping with sweaty fear as he stared wide-eyed at the swirling covers sucking at his feet. On two later nights he was clutching frantically at the gunwales of a mattress that was Paul Ching's boat lurching in a cauldron of black sea and sky desperate to avoid the devouring maw of a towering landing craft.

He arrived home with such terrors behind him, but uneasily aware of change in himself. He sensed a displacement of perception or attitude—he couldn't describe it more clearly—as if the night adrift had affected him more deeply than he realized. Not that he changed his behaviour; he returned for morning coffee at the Starlight and was boisterously welcomed, dawdled over grocery shopping to gossip with the Pollocks, and on his second evening dropped by the Rib'n'Rye for a beer. He had hoped to talk with the Jazz Hall Lady Jane, but she had gone up to Victoria on business. He even did a J. Fowles Inc. job, felling some cedars blocking a client's view of the inlet, although he was exhausted after only a couple of hour's work. But he was sleeping well; he realized one morning the flickering ghost of Joe Hummingbird no longer haunted his dreams.

But as his life resumed its routine his mind turned more often to the mystery of the floating corpse. He realized there was no sign Ymenko had acted on the tip he had phoned in from the Sleepytyme Infirmary, and decided he must ask why. He found Ymenko at the Starlight and told him about the wound on the body. "It was in the back, under the rib cage, and large. On the right side. It couldn't have been self-inflicted."

Ymenko said, "Okay. But to have a wound you have to have a body, right? So where's the body?"

"The old lady's hidden it. I told you that."

"So where's she hidden it?"

"How the hell do I know where she's hidden it? I tried to find it and she fired a shotgun at me."

Ymenko made a frowning indulgent grin. "That old woman bent double with osteoporosis fired a shotgun at you? Are you kidding me, sir?"

"Of course I'm not kidding you. She fired at me twice, and I can show you where and you will find pellets on the beach. And somewhere on that property, and not too far from where I brought it ashore, you'll find a decaying female corpse with a bloody great hole in her back. Why the hell am I having this trouble convincing you?"

Ymenko leaned forward. "Mr. Fowles, while you were away I had an invitation from Mrs. Evens. She was upset by rumours there was a dead body on her property. Rumours you were allegedly spreading. She wanted me to search her property. She was very insistent. I had a couple of the guys down from Colwood and a dog and we spent four hours looking. Those are experienced guys and that dog is one of the best. I can tell you, sir, there is no corpse on that property."

Justin returned home chastened, furious, and baffled. He had to give the cunning old bitch credit; the search was a brilliant preemptive move. But he knew there was a body, a murdered body. He had towed it ashore. He had pulled it up on the beach. It had lain on the beach as he talked with Mary Evens about it. He cursed Mary's deviousness, Ymenko's indifference.

He would be justified to dismiss the incident as the casual suicide of some rejected vagrant, put the body's disappearance down to an old woman's eccentricity, and forget the matter. Except for the wound. He had seen it for only a fraction of a second, but it was large and had been savagely inflicted. Even if the corpse were nameless, even if the police refused to believe it existed, he could not ignore murder. For all his disdain for the commonplaces of police work, crime unsolved provoked Justin with the force of forgotten years of training and practice.

But he was no less worried over Annabel. The time away from her forced him to face what he'd continued to deny; that they'd not been on very good terms. Her stormy departure at the infirmary could if he were honest about it have been a final goodbye. The possibility of her rejection returned alarmingly. She had put a notice in her handwriting on his front door—"Closed until further notice"—and he had been touched by her thoughtfulness, but the day after his return he had called by her office and she wasn't there, and a day later he had phoned both her home and her office from the Starlight and had left messages, and she'd not replied.

He was not sure what to make of it, because although at first he felt slighted, he soon realized they'd regularly not see or hear from each other for as much as ten days or more. In which case his discomfort was simply about not being welcomed back, which was a little vain.

What grew more ominously in his mind was his prank with the roses. She had still said nothing about the card. By now he suspected, he was almost sure there was something between her and Plantagenet. He'd picked up a fragment of conversation at the Starlight about them, drowned in a roar of laughter at Frank Mewhouse's loud report that Mary Evens had ordered seventy-two dollars worth of toys from Sears. Justin was suddenly stirred by long-forgotten sensations of sexual competition.

The newspaper's arrival helped explain Annabel's failure to contact him; the last stages of production were always hectic. He read the story with mounting consternation:

EVASIVE NUDE IN DAWN CAPER

Two of Prospect's more senior and respected residents were unwittingly drawn into questions of perception, ontology, and truth last week, as Mary Evens and Justin

Fowles disagreed vigorously on the nature of an experience they may or may not have shared.

In the very early hours last Thursday, Mrs. Evens and Mr. Fowles were attracted to the shore of Prospect Inlet. Each was separately taking a usual early morning walk, splendid therapy for those of advanced years, when Mr. Fowles sighted an alleged floating corpse. The alleged object was beached by Mr. Fowles, using Paul Ching's rowboat without Paul's permission, beneath Mrs. Evens' property, Mogador. Thereupon the body, which was nude, almost immediately vanished.

Mr. Fowles claims the body to have been that of a young woman, which he left on the beach in Mrs. Evens' care while he reported his discovery to the police. Mrs. Evens claims she never saw the body, but came upon Mr. Fowles just as he was about to trespass on her land. Constable Ymenko states there is no record in the police log of Mr. Fowles' call. The officer also states there is no outstanding report of a missing person to fit Mr. Fowles' description of the woman, although in policing terminology, "When the subject missing person is an adult, a report may be eventuated only in extended subsequence, and thus entail considerable retroactivity."

Ymenko has decided not to proceed further. "Mr. Fowles is a reliable citizen, but he hasn't been able to produce a body. Mrs. Evens is a reliable citizen, and she denies a body existed. At Mrs. Even's request her property has been searched and no body was found."

An interesting sequel to the affair was that Mr. Fowles, being unable to find the body he allegedly left on the shore, and wisely equipping himself with hard-weather potables, commenced to search the inlet in rain and thick fog. He was picked up at dawn Friday by the seiner "Sweete Virgin-Maide of Sooke", drifting ten miles south of the Pachena Shoal. Although a spokesman from the ambulance service claims Mr. Fowles was suffering from hypothermia and hallucination, Mr. Fowles claims he was deliberately going with the tide the better to find the body, and would deny he'd seen the legendary Junk of the Seven Skeletons.

The Junk of the Seven Skeletons is the most notorious of several Japanese vessels that have drifted across the Pacific on the Japan Current. The first was reported in 1834, a junk wrecked near Cape Flattery carrying three men of a crew of forty who had survived starvation. The Junk of the Seven Skeletons was first sighted off Cape Beale in 1837 by an English fur trader, who left a vivid description of the dismasted derelict looming out of the morning mist, seven human skeletons clearly visible on its listing deck, propelled by an invisible force across a windless sea. There are records of at least six sightings since then, in fair weather and foul, all within fifteen miles of the coast between Prospect and Cape Beale, but several attempts to take the vessels in tow have failed. The last previous sighting was in 1979, by the late Mr. Gilmour Brewer of Prospect.

Good manners restrain us from asking the questions this incident poses. However we are taught that the body is insubstantial, and perhaps this body was unusually so, becoming dust rather more rapidly than Mr. Fowle's expectation or Mrs. Evens' apprehension.

Condescending polysyllabic horseshit! She had made a roaring joke of the whole affair at his expense. The fable-maker run amuck. Not to mention the vicious little pairing— he and Mary Evens in their . . . *therapy for . . . advanced years.* He scanned the words again: . . *would be emphatic in denying he'd seen the legendary Junk of the Seven Skeletons.* A clever dance around libel, but with the smear intact. What the hell was the woman trying to do? He'd never mentioned the Junk of the Seven Skeletons! While she was about it, why didn't she include the Priestly Eunuchs of San Francisco? Had he burbled something about a junk with skeletons in delirious agony? Was he ever in delirious agony? It would only have been to impress her, a fiction of persuasion, a small intimate prank for Christ's sake upon which she'd hoisted him aloft for public ridicule. He'd never seen murder reported so irresponsibly.

This week she had made it the Prospect Poetic Scribe and Larkin. One of her more arcane elitist giggles, to confirm her superiority over the native plebes. She'd been cunning, inventing "hard-weather potables" to link him with old Gil Brewer, so aptly named, the last of the legendary village souses. *Questions of perception, ontology, and truth* be damned. There was only one question, and that was the old woman's stinking lies. Justin paced the creaking linoleum floor behind his store, raging at his fate.

But the truth of the matter was that he needed her. It came upon him suddenly, perhaps as reflexive to his anger, perhaps out of an intimation of mortality the night at sea had given him. He needed her companionship. He needed the assurance her presence gave him that he was fit for human company. He needed her much more than her damned schedule of limited propinquity provided. In all the years of his exile he had never felt such yearning. He had wryly seen himself as the ultimate existentialist man, childless, without past or future, alone. She offered in some obscure way an imperfect hope of comfort against the inevitable depths of the dark ocean.

But just briefly to indulge such thoughts of Annabel brought him up short against the absurdities of his situation. They were decades apart in age, the children she was devoted to disliked him, and there was only the flimsiest evidence—to look at it coolly— that she in any way valued him above mere convenience.

With Annabel and the woman's murder unresolved his mind, nagged by unwelcome questions about the landing barge's destination, he was caught in a depressed limbo of inaction, accusing himself of dithering, and longing for simplicity, clarity, certainty. As he drifted toward troubled sleep he became aware again of the essence of the dead young woman, but in a form elevated into a serene presence, emerging from some familiar legend that he could not at the moment recall as the Drowned Maiden, whose green eyes now conveyed a promise of refuge, not simply of calm but of renewal, of refreshment of the soul as well as relief from the bodily frailties of age.

The Drowned Maiden. Her presence was stronger but he remained skeptical, and applied himself to business. He was conscious of a returning energy and a new acuity of perception, and attributed them to his night on the ocean. The cultural artifacts in the storefront window were not moving, but people needed doors re-hung and appliances repaired. Demand was so good that he thought of increasing it, abandoning his long-standing boycott of the telephone which he'd imposed long before Prospect out of conviction his line would be tapped. He ordered one installed immediately, ignoring the fact that he was already turning away half the requests for his services, and never admitting to himself that hope for easier contact with Annabel had anything to do with it.

It wasn't the only change. There was a mirror hanging lopsided above his washbasin and looking at it one morning, scissors poised to trim his beard, he discovered an unusual affection for himself, to which the beard suddenly seemed incongruous. When he had finished removing the beard, wondering how the crowd at the Starlight would react, he was delighted. He looked reassuringly younger. Impressively wise. And certainly milder. He observed his face from varying angles, and chuckled contentedly.

It was a day later that Justin, lying under a car in his back yard doing an oil change for a client, heard the jangle of bells from the front door. Annabel always came the back way; it was a customer!

It took him less than fifteen seconds to reach the spyhole in the wall, to see a slight man of medium height, bald on top and white at the temples. Wearing jeans and a T-shirt bearing on its back a large grinning Mickey Mouse in stetson and day-glo orange tunic. Sergeant Mouse of the Mounted. When the man's face became visible, Justin drew in his breath. A large nose, with a wen of Cromwellian prominence on his left nostril. It was of all people the veteran Horseman, the Force's own legend of ineptitude, Corporal Milton Milton.

It was unbelievable! They were stupid enough to set Milton Milton onto him! His spirits rose; he had not been passed by; the Force still had him under surveillance! Ah Milton Milton, he thought giddily, unwelcome Sancho Panza in my less than convincing visions of the national dream! Milton Milton whom he'd fired from the Quebec office for erasing the only useful tape out of the one hundred and two reels of wiretap collected over four boring months in a cold rooming house in Quebec City! Oh Milton! It was typical that having been sent secretly to observe a man he'd worked for, Milton was making no attempt to conceal himself.

Justin, chuckling silently, decided on a frontal assault, and marched briskly into the store shouting, "Milton! Tell me plainly. What are doing here?"

"I'm a modest collector of aboriginal artifacts. I'm looking for some choice item to take home to Saskatchewan," said Milton as if by rote, and then with convincing surprise, "You know my name?" and then joyously, "Inspector! Inspector Fowles! My God! I'll be damned. How we lose touch, eh?"

"Yes, Milton. But what are you *doing* here? I know a cover story when I hear one, especially when Milton Milton starts talking aboriginal art."

Milton laughed, but waved a hand in warning and peered cautiously around room. He said mutedly, "I'm not in the Force, sir. Retired years ago. I've set myself up in business. Making use of my career skills, as they advise in retirement counseling. I'm a private eye, as they say on TV. Right now I'm on a case."

"Hah," said Fowles skeptically.

"As a matter of fact you may be able to help me. It's a strange case, as we used to say. Remember when we used to say that?"

"Hah," said Fowles.

"There's a business executive says his lady friend's honour was tainted by a guy who sent her an obscene note. Not quite the kind of thing we used to run into in E Special, eh Inspector?"

Justin looked at Milton solemnly over the tops of his glasses. "Milton I must tell you one thing, to keep you out of trouble. When I left the Force, I was declared classified under the terms of the Official Secrets Act. Neither I nor my career exists. You call me inspector once more, and you risk the dungeon."

"Oh. Oh I'm very sorry."

"The other point is, your story is ridiculous. People haven't talked about a lady's honour since about 1910, and the concept of taint died even earlier. So you tell me you've retired from the Force, but you're not admitting you transferred to CSIS, is that it? I understand CSIS welcomes people like you. Your cover is the kind of thing those little vestal English Lit BAs would dream up. Tainted Victorian womanhood indeed."

Milton looked aggrieved, but continued, "The executive in question ordered these flowers for a woman in this village, and included an amorous note. But when the woman opened the box, the original note had been replaced by the said obscene card."

"Very interesting," Justin said non-committaly, concealing his shock at this turn of events.

Milton said, "The question is, how could the obscene card be substituted for the note."

"Indeed," said Justin, leaning languidly againt the counter in an intended Holmesian pose. "Milton, assuming I can help, perhaps you can tell me if I'm getting the feel of this case. Now if this note were amorous, the flowers were those conventional to such sentiment. Thus I deduce these flowers were roses.

Furthermore if they were imported from Victoria, it must have been for some attribute not commonly available in the rustic stores nearer to Prospect, the attribute of long stems. If I add from common knowledge that such roses are usually sold by the dozen, I can deduce we are dealing with a dozen long-stemmed roses."

Milton was grinning broadly. "Capital!" he said. "You haven't lost your touch sir."

"Moreover," continued Justin, "And this point is also elementary. There is only one person in this area who might be considered, or more accurately would consider himself to be, an executive. Thus I deduce your client is one Dirk Plantagenet."

Milton chuckled admiringly. "I'll be damned! Of course I'm not supposed to reveal who I work for, but you're amazing, sir. You certainly are. I remember in Q we used to say you were the smartest—"

"No more! No mention of the Force!"

"Oh. Sorry, sir. But now you're going to wrap up the case for me, right?"

"Oh hardly, Milton, hardly. But I will say it's not too difficult to identify the second party in your case. You see Prospect is a name touched with irony. It was once a town of dreams. There was lumber and fish, and rumours of gold and coal in the hills. A few miles west, by the old Indian village of Clo-oose, an entity called the West Coast Development Company was building the biggest resort in the Pacific Northwest. People from

England and Germany bought lots sight-unseen. Prospect boomed. There were drunken loggers in the taverns and fights in the bordellos and plans for an opera house. But it's all gone, eh? And now Prospect is just a community of geriatrics hoping Canada Post won't close down their post office. But the exception is a woman of divine attraction, Milton, the only one in miles. A mousy journalist by day, but at night, wow! Certainly the only one to catch the lecherous eye of this self-styled executive. So I can deduce the lady in question is one Annabel McKinley."

"Right on!" cried Milton happily. "But you know this Plantagenet fellow eh? He seems pretty keen on this lady."

"He's an animal, that one," said Justin. "A human stoat."

"I'm figuring," said Milton modestly, "That the bottom line here is sex. Mr. Plantagenet's note possibly had sexual overtones, if you know what I mean, and—" Milton held out a smudged photocopy of the Brighton postcard "—the offending substitute is sexual."

"Disgusting," said Justin, waving it away. It was a shock to realize Annabel had shown Plantagenet the card.

"Do you think so sir?"

"Ah?"

"The naughty card. Did you say disgusting? I thought it was just an ordinary crude joke. In bad taste, but I'm not sure I grasp its connection to the lady's honour."

"Well, yes," Justin said, "I suppose so." Milton's liberality surprised him.

"So what I think is, it's rivalry," Milton was saying. "Either it's a woman competing for Mr. Plantagenet against Ms. McKinley, or vicery-verso. So it's got to be good old police slogging. List the people, eliminate them one by one. Shouldn't be hard, but I'm handicapped because I can't talk to Ms. McKinley. Mr. Plantagenet insists she be protected from such sordid business."

"That bloody hypocrite! Dirk Plantagenet is one of the great local satyrs. He prowls the corridors of his resort by night to service women disappointed by their partners. An insatiable stud. And as for Ms. McKinley, she is the one piece of nubile tasty within miles! Incredibly popular, a worldly divorcee from the lewd city of Toronto. You're going to have a list of suspects a mile long. I hope you're working a fat hourly rate, because this job is good for six months."

Milton stared soberly at Justin. "Six months?"

"Oh yes. Oh six months. Yes. But tell me, Milton, what do you suppose this Plantagenet intends to do with this defiler of Ms. McKinley's purity?"

"He said he was going to beat the living shit out of him."

Justin braced himself, hoping he hadn't betrayed his delight. "Hah! Well you're certainly lucky to have come to an old mentor, an old comrade in arms."

Milton, grinning warmly and mumbling some kind of gratitude, suddenly gaped as Justin shouted, "Milton you silly little prick, don't you see what you're getting yourself into? If this lumbering sexual athlete beats the shit out of some snivelling pornographer it's assault, right? It may be worse, like aggravated assault. And what if the victim dies? If you know his intent, and finger his victim for him, it's game over for you. Accessory before the fact, conspiracy to commit an assault, conspiracy to murder."

Milton was oddly calm, displaying a confident smile. "What if it turns out to be someone who's more than a match for Mr. Plantagenet?"

"Well," said Justin, a little flustered, "I suppose he could hire an enforcer, a hit man." He didn't like the direction in which the conversation was moving. His recollection of Milton was of placid obedience, and this new Milton was too cool, and almost frisky with confidence. He suspected, just too late, that things were out of hand. Milton was saying, "I appreciate your warning, sir. Mind you, I had thought of that. But I was thinking of it more as a matter of protecting an old and respected comrade. Although—" and here Milton observed Justin with a wan smile, "—when he treats me like a blundering idiot I wonder if it's worth it."

Justin, his defiance crumbling, croaked, "What do you mean by that?" But he knew too well what Milton meant, and was already feeling slightly ill. And then, because he had to get there before Milton, he blurted, "The delivery boy told you where he left the bloody box!"

Milton shook his head sadly. "It was much simpler than that, sir. You see it was a joke. The guilty party had this inspiration, and rushed to the nearest store. No one with serious intent, specially one with a brilliant record in counter espionage, would have been as careless. The key is that this isn't a florist's card, and there's not much traffic in naughty British cards in Prospect, and Mr. Newhouse—"

"Mewhouse," said Justin lamely, aghast at Milton's insight.

"Yes. Well he remembered very clearly the guilty party making the purchase. When I made that discovery I thought you might like to hear that your old anathema (isn't that what you used to call me, sir?) isn't such a fool after all. But I must tell you you've been very hurtful. You don't need to act superior, just because you're a very bright man."

Justin was choked with chagrin. "I'm sorry, Milton. I'm afraid I was carried away. I know how it must come across but I don't *feel* the way—"

"I rather doubt that, but it doesn't matter. There was always some doubt in our minds that you had any feelings. You were always with that crowd, the suits, you know?—the superintendents and the FBI chiefs and the crowns—with the foreign cars and the expense accounts. We figured having a heart'd be a liability."

"That's a little unfair. It was a brief phase. I was—"

"I'm not saying fair or unfair, sir. It's just the way we saw you." Milton smiled shyly as he moved to the door. "But we also thought you were the best."

Justin, in agony, struggled hopelessly to emit some note of grace.

Milton turned at the door. "I've got to get back to town. Mr. Plantagenet paid his fee, up front. Very generous. By the way I've already reported the case to be insoluble. It wasn't just loyalty, sir. If the guilty party was an ex-mountie, which he officially isn't, he could have beaten a lot more than the living shit out of my client." He paused, smiling almost affectionately, and gave the old open-handed salute. "Goodbye, sir."

Justin staggered to the window to see Milton Milton drive off in a huge cream Cadillac. He stood for a long time in the middle of the floor, staring at the door, and then, with the weight of mortification heavy through his whole body, he shuffled into the back room and collapsed on the bed in embarrassment and shame.

He stared at the sagging ceiling and knew he had never felt so small. He had been inexcusably rude, loutish, condescendingly arrogant, and Milton had borne it with angelic forbearance. And when he'd run out of blustering insults and sarcastic asides, Milton had quietly demolished him.

But it was so much more than that. The disdainful Inspector Fowles, seen by his subordinates as cold and unfeeling, caustic in his criticisms and incapable of praise. Was this why the Force had dumped him? Was this why Annabel had fled perhaps even to the grungy mattresses of the Sensuous Rendezvous? He had a disconcerting sensation of moving through warped and tinted lenses between time present and time past, to meet a man he didn't recognize; himself.

As he continued dredging the murkier depths of his self-esteem, one small tentative fact emerged, grew, finally dominated his mind; Milton had endured insults and ridicule and had never wavered in his quiet, touching loyalty. And Justin had betrayed that simple human loyalty.

14

It was the following afternoon before Justin reached Annabel, by phone at her home. By then his determination to confront her, to state his new-found need for her, had become mired in the doubts that Milton Milton's visit had provoked. He had been reasonably confident of their past relationship but the prospect of asking her for more, of giving more, which he had vaguely considered from time to time, was thoroughly daunting as an imminent act. His anxiety was sharpened by the lack of enthusiasm in her voice over the phone, but she agreed to meet him at the Starlight the next morning, at 9:30 before the coffee crowd arrived.

As soon as he saw her he was struck by the meeting's unreality as a reunion of dear friends or desultory lovers. She was not a stranger, but no longer familiar. Or perhaps the unreality was in what he had expected or at least hoped for, a hint of warmth.

Annabel was dreading the meeting. It had to be done but she knew she could not handle it. At first sight of him she screamed in surprise; for a poignant instant the disappearance of his beard recalled his refreshing unpredictability, and she put her hand over her mouth and stood for several moments with her eyes closed to contain her tears before saying brightly, "Oh my dear. Oh my dear the beard. I hardly recognized you."

He said it was a mark of his rejuvenated soul cleansed by the ocean, a protest against going gentle into the dark night, noticing she slipped into the booth opposite him before they could embrace. She said he looked younger and cleaner and, jokingly, more moral, although actually it confirmed her recent feelings toward him in making him seem ten years older. He wanted her to say she liked it but she did not use the words.

He felt awkward himself but she seemed even more uneasy. He had driven up the highway and bought a posy at the fruit stand just past the Far Pacific, instructing the attendant fussily about the difference between a posy and a bouquet, and he handed it to her and said, guardedly, "Nice to see you again."

She said, "Oh you dear boy," but her teeth were clenched under her smile. His anger over her newspaper report still persisted, but in the tension he sensed between them he could think only of avoiding anything that might make things worse. Her failure to mention the roses came suddenly to mind and he suppressed it. Finally he said lightly, "Well I've found you at last! I've been home over a week with no word from you and so I was worried. I have regained my manly vigour, but you are ignoring the—"

She interrupted, smiling archly, teasing him, "Manly so soon? Come on, Justin. What has Fraulein Karlsrue been up to?"

He told her something of Pegggy's behaviour, ending by saying. "Well, in any event, I have missed you. Even though we haven't resumed our, ahem, schedule." He knew instantly he'd blundered, and added a clumsy chuckle. "Not that I'm complaining."

"Has it really been a week? God, I didn't mean to ignore you, but it's been so hectic." She couldn't bring herself to be more direct, to bring everything to a head for instance by saying flatly that they were no longer lovers.

He asked after the paper and after Susan and Marc, expecting her usual stream of anecdotes and complaints, but she was cursory and brief. He sensed her preoccupation and said, "You okay, dearie?"

"Oh marvelous!" And after a pause, knowing she had to at least approach the truth, "I don't know how to put this. I guess. No. I think I haven't got over your stay in a hospital."

Justin snorted ironically. "*You* haven't got—"

She said abruptly, "Justin dear please be calm." And before he could protest he was completely calm she added, "I'm trying to explain something and it isn't easy. The essence I think is that I need a little space."

"Whatever that means."

She made small circles with a finger on the table top, avoiding looking at him. "I'm not too sure what it means myself but I really— Oh shit, Justin, the hospital— I just haven't come to terms with that. I used to be comfortable with you and now I'm not. I don't want to go any further than that because that's all I'm sure of. I mean it's easy to be carried away into abstractions about basic incompatibility of temperament or the unbridgeable chasm of age but that would—" She paused, frowning.

"Would—? "

"Well it would be more than I feel. I can't promise I won't come to that, but I'm not there right now. I mean it would be dishonest to say— anything more."

"Oh," Justin said dubiously. He felt suspended over a void, as if the earth had opened and gravity had ceased to be. He was aching for the warm companionship they had shared, for her humorous affection, now more than ever, and she had become— unbelievable. More than the rescue at sea, more than his return to Prospect, she had seemed the final affirmation that he had survived the ocean, that he lived, and suddenly she had put a wall between them. He muttered, "I don't understand—"

"But Justin dear you *must* understand— I need this place. Your friendship is part of being here, and it's helped me heal. But I've never felt I belonged dear. Not like you."

"Christ, girl," he said. "I belong nowhere. You know that. This isn't geography, this is you and me. What the hell are you talking about? You are being bloody evasive!"

She put her hands to her head, feeling cornered. "How can I explain? God Justin you're making this difficult." Which she knew was totally unfair, the difficulty being her own stupid mismanagement of things and her lack of candour with him. It was Prospect Palisades and screwing Dirk and swindling Mary Evens and leaving for San Francisco and it was all too complicated to explain even if Justin had been still close and contemporary. She simply could not face him any longer. She was feeling faint, and it was an effort to slide to the edge of the booth. She lied in desperation, "I'm sorry. I have to be in Victoria at noon. The printer is fucking up on me and it's absolutely vital. This is the worst time to walk away but I simply can't be late."

He sat alone, amazed. She was gone. No kiss, no brief touch to his arm. The posy lay on the seat where she had been, and he left it there. At least he now knew the truth—and what else could it be?—that Plantagenet had won. The sense of defeat surprised him in its intensity. For all his verminous qualities the hateful man had youth and vigour, and could satisfy her like a satyr possessed. And despite her reassurances he knew his sexual powers were faded. It was the shits, but he had to accept it. He set about convincing himself it was over, stamping out small sparks of hope that persisted in rising from the past.

Toward bedtime, still depressed by the complexity Annabel presented, his mood was momentarily lightened by thoughts of the Drowned Maiden, who had seemed to offer some tentative promise of balm from his discomfort of heart but seemed now to manifest a perplexing duality. She appeared in sharper focus, clearly a beckoning, seductive image of youthful certainty and of dreams fulfilled, of ease amidst what vaguely recalled the Lady Jane's Elysian Fields, with the nation secure from sea to shining sea. But there was also the butchered corpse of a murdered girl, demanding her crime be pursued in the cause of justice, stirring a conflict in his mind between the harsh call of present duty and this nagging illusion, a fanlike swirl of golden hair about a beckoning smile confused with what would by now be a stinking corpse, drawing flies.

He needed relief. Such sensations were ephemera, fleeting mists in a stressed imagination and actually sick in suggesting even faintly the attraction of a cadaver. He sought out the Lady Jane, who had sent a note demanding he report personally on his night at sea and dispel the rumours that Mary Evens had peppered his butt with duckshot. He told her about discovering the floating woman and about Mary's intervention and about becoming lost in the fog, but didn't include the visions of his past that had afflicted him or his close brush with the landing craft. He'd intended to stick to a bare narrative until the Lady Jane said the story was much more restrained than she'd expected from him.

"But it was transforming!" he protested. "As I was saying to Annabel was it yesterday or perhaps earlier. Yes. I have undergone some kind of spiritual enema. I am cleansed."

He could not bring himself to admit his difficulties with Annabel or that he was conceding defeat to Plantagenet; he had come to escape his burdens in her company rather than to unburden himself. But after three beers he said, "I am wondering about idealized womanhood. Do men by nature idealize women?"

"Well both men and women idealize each other. In love—"

"Oh sure. Sorry, a silly question. I meant can a woman *represent* some ideal notion. Say of youth, of renewal, of great purpose achieved, that kind of thing."

The Lady Jane smiled quizzically. "This is not like you, Justin."

"I said I was transformed."

"Of course. But *represent?* I'd say yes, symbolically. Like the Statue of Liberty?"

"I was thinking of something with more flesh on her," said Justin. "A real person. Maybe *embody* rather than represent."

"The feminists would call that objectification. Which mind you is cant. But I'd be more inclined to call it illusion, a common enough frailty."

"Or a dead person."

The Lady Jane chuckled. "Yuck! But then we'd be nudging necrophilia. But what are you getting at, dear boy? Are you troubled?"

"Heavens no," said Justin. "It was a passing thought. It is the kind of question that arises as I try to accostom myself to an altered lifestyle, My post-Pacific period. I want to be sure I avoid illusion."

"Or delusion," said the Lady Jane.

By the time he returned to the store the Drowned Maiden had again subsumed the murdered woman, and he was soberly aware of the path of duty. It had come to him that he'd once heard old Piper Herdman, who lived in the attic of his otherwise deserted farmhouse up near the highway, mentioning a boathouse far past the Coulthurst property facing the open Straight.

Ymenko's search of Mary's property had undoubtedly been thorough, so if the body was not on the property Mary had either put it back in the water or hidden it somewhere else. She hadn't refloated it during his brief absence that morning; there was no tide at the time, and he would have come across it despite the fog while rowing along the shore. And it would have been fairly easy even for the stooped osteoporotic old woman, as Ymenko had her, to tow a body around by the shore.

The next morning, his heart heavy at Annabel's loss, he set out at daybreak. He put sandwiches, fruit, coffee, and a half-bottle of wine in his knapsack and took the well-worn trail down to Semaphore Bay and then headed west. He could have followed the beach, but knew the sand eventually became coarse gravel and tiring to walk on and there were rocky promontories to climb around. He took the trail above the beach that was inside the trees and almost overgrown, but more secure than on the exposed beach. He was soon in Gulag's broad definition of Combat College territory, which made him wary of paintball attack.

The coast at that point described a crescent a good mile wide, and every hundred yards or so he would stop and examine the shoreline ahead with his binoculars. At one point there was a wide gap in the trees which gave him a view of shocking beauty to the south over Point Perez, with Schooner Shoal awash in white breakers and the whitecapped sea a deep blue, and above the far Olympic Mountains a tumult of white cumulus rising majestic into a clear sky. He realized suddenly that these, utterly transformed, were the bleak and fogbound waters on which he'd drifted into his resurrecting night.

But there was no sign of a boathouse, or where one might have been. About an hour along the trail, however, looking west, he made out a puzzlingly unnatural regularity where the trees met a sandy beach which seemed, from his distance, to be oddly furrowed. He advanced along the trail cautiously, remembering now this was the beach they called Ganges, where Riordon had once reported the *Liberty Belle* to be anchored, the beach Justin had thought or perhaps hallucinated to be the destination of the landing craft.

He noticed the sentry just as he was about to make a noisy descent to a ledge about thirty feet below the trail. He froze, catching his breath. The sentry was barely visible a hundred yards away, sitting in the shade of a row of tall firs at the far edge of a level area roughly cleared above the tide-line. In the middle of the clearing was a jeep and closer, where the clearing ended about fifty feet from where Justin stood, there was a building the size of a double garage, with plywood walls and roof painted in a blotchy camouflage of black, brown and dark green.

Justin focused his binoculars on the sentry and frowned. The man was reading. He wore the red armlet with the white S of a staff-member, and there was a rifle leaning against the chair. A paid staff member with a real rifle. Justin crouched to ensure he was concealed. He had stumbled on something too important to be guarded by a trainee commando with a paintball gun.

His attention was so concentrated on the sentry that it was several seconds before he became aware there was an unusual regularity of shape behind the trees in the background. Within the shade there were indistinct angles of grey, a dull glint of metal, and then a strangely meshed texture which resolved itself into camouflage netting draped over a landing barge hidden under the cliff.

The landing barge was smaller than it had seemed in the night, but large enough to carry perhaps a couple of small trucks or a good crowd of passengers, and it had the same high bridge on which he had glimpsed that towering figure marked with the flaming sword. But Justin couldn't see how the boat itself, well concealed, high above the tide-line and undoubtedly requiring machinery to launch, could justify an armed sentry. Thus whatever was important must be in the shed, and he couldn't reach the front of the shed, the entrance, without being seen.

Obviously he'd gone as far as the day allowed in seeking the murdered woman. But now he was gripped by renewed curiosity about the Combat College, about its true nature and who it was training and its finances and its connections south across the Strait, everything that he had resolutely put behind him months ago as beyond his energy and resources, as the fragments of a campaign which he had long ago abandoned. He retreated carefully back down the trail. He must dismiss the Combat College from his mind; he was too old for the high path of international intrigue. Best he limit himself to simple police work; to find the body of a murder victim.

When he estimated he'd travelled about half a mile he stopped for coffee and a muffin. The trail was hard going and he was tired. Pegggy Karlsrue had told him to take it easy for a month and perhaps she was right. He lay back on the bank beside the trail and closed his eyes, and although thoughts of Annabel haunted him for a moment he must have dozed, because when he next looked at his watch it was two o'clock. He guessed he was still two hours from home the way he had come, and although he wasn't familiar with the terrain west of Prospect he'd heard people talk of ways directly down to the shore west of Semaphore Bay. Soon after he'd resumed the trail, he came to a branch off to the left and heading east, a reassuringly open trail, and he decided to follow it.

It was reassuringly open for about half an hour. Over the next twenty minutes it became increasingly difficult, and some fifteen minutes later he realized it had disappeared altogether. But it was a sunny day and he was confident of handling rough country and so pushed on. And then, fighting through a patch of thick undergrowth, the ground gave way shockingly beneath him.

He fell rolling and tumbling, bouncing off stumps and crashing through bushes in a cloud of earth and shale to fetch up on a mercifully soft bank of moss. The cliff edge, when he opened his eyes to see, was a good hundred feet above him. When he moved himself, testing one limb at a time and then his neck and back, he realized he was uninjured.

There were still a hundred feet of slope below him, and he worked himself down carefully, mostly in short controlled slides on the broken shale. He descended slowly past the canopy of evergreen foliage and down past huge columnar trunks of fir and cedar, and down finally onto the floor of a forested ravine. It was an older, primeval forest whose floor was a heaving sea of moss, and the giant trees emerged from this turbulence on massive knuckled roots like mountainous foothills, so that the effect was of a single organic entity in which the invisible earth and rock supported a luxuriant green sea solidifying into these enormous trees, rising to a dense interlaced ceiling of foliage. There were ferns and a scattering of delicate bushes, but the great trees had long ago cut off the sunlight in which their own progeny might thrive. Spanish moss hung abundantly from the bark of the tree trunks and the branches, and there seemed to be an unusual number of dead trees and great broken limbs, windfalls, lying at awkward angles to the ground. A boundless gothic cathedral, falling in upon itself. There were no cut-off stumps; the place must have been inaccessible to logging.

He judged the ravine lay roughly north to south, so there might be a better way out to the south, where he was headed. The silence, the sense of isolation, made the atmosphere sepulchral, though here and there sunlight dappled the mossy floor.

The terrain became less hospitable as he advanced. He had to avoid crumbling grey-brown boulders four and six feet high that broke out from the carpet of moss, and climb over and under windfalls forming a massive obstructing lattice. This wasn't the high serene and melancholy cathedral he had first encountered, but a jagged and unsettling place in which the moss-covered outlines were harsh and irregular. The trees were just as impressive, and he wondered if it were his mood, or if with the advancing afternoon the light was falling at a different angle.

He needed to rest and sat down on a log, which crumbled so that he descended about six inches into rotted wood. He shifted to a firmer base on the moss carpet and poured some coffee. Shafts of sunlight sloped from the canopy above. It was good to rest. He breathed on the lenses of his glasses and wiped them clear. Ahead there were two trees leaning apart to form a V at ground level, and beyond them a pale green bush, and a little beyond the bush a short upright stake standing in a shaft of sunlight, holding a brown human skull.

15

He whispered, "My God!" and got slowly to his feet. He walked toward it and stopped. It was unmistakably a human skull, brown, old, a piece missing from the left temple. He was within six feet of it when a voice to his left called out, "Ah! Mr. Fowles! An expected caller!"

It was Mary Evens. She was standing within a ring of whitewashed stones, in front of a small tent.

He said, mystified but wary, "Mrs. Evens, I presume. Did you say expected?"

"Ah we all come to this, do we not?"

It was her usual cryptic nonsense and he ignored it. "I didn't know you had a second home. Very nice." There was a smoke-stained kettle hanging over the ashes of a fire, and near the tent's entrance a green garbage bag disgorging clothing and food boxes.

"You are limping. Did you hurt yourself?"

"Well I fell down a bloody great cliff twenty minutes ago but got away with it. The limp is my left knee, where I was wounded at the sea wall at Dieppe."

"It does not seem to handicap you. It is observable that you walk alone a great deal, Mr. Fowles, in the early morning if not in the evening. Evening is the time of sexual longing, so perhaps that is in your favour, but they say early morning is the time of troubled conscience."

"I'm past the time of sexual longing, ma'am, and have come to terms with my conscience." He wondered if this were simply chit-chat or a prelude to reviving their encounter surely three weeks ago over the drowned woman. He suppressed an instant's impulse to declare that since his night at sea his conscience had indeed been less burdensome. Instead of which he said, "But you camp here?"

"It is fulfillment for me, Mr. Fowles. A shrine. I sleep among my dead and death, you must understand, lifts my soul. I yearn to see beyond it." She made a sweeping motion with her left arm. "Do you not see?"

He looked toward where she had indicated, to his right, but there was nothing but the trees and bushes over the undulating moss. Mrs. Evens was staring past him, smiling as if enjoying his puzzlement.

"Go on! You must look carefully."

He tried to make out what she was staring at but still saw nothing. He glanced at her, irritated, and she said, "It is revelation! You must look hard!"

And then suddenly, amidst the featureless maze and mix of green there fused a configuration so astonishing that his hand jerked involuntarily to his face.

A great moss-covered snag rose at a forty-five degree angle from the ground, and attached to it and resting on the ground, now that he saw it, was a bulbous moss-covered mass from which two bent moss-draped sticks extended at an incongruously precise angle of one hundred and twenty degrees, behind which a green embankment, half-concealed in shrubbery, now revealed an impossible symmetry.

"A wing. An engine nacelle," recited Justin slowly. "A propeller. And the fuselage."

They stood for a time in silence, and then Mary, behind him, said, "It is from the war. Our war. I come here to be with them. I want them for myself but it troubles me because perhaps it should be reported."

He thought the answer obvious. "Oh there's no need for that. In a place like this they'd just take out the bodies; they wouldn't bother moving the wreck. If the news got out today the gawkers would be here in swarms, dropping beer cans and condoms—" And then he remembered the skull. "You mean they're still here?"

"Why should I lie, Mr. Fowles?" He turned and saw she was smiling, a little challengingly. The question opened some left-over store of exasperation and he exclaimed, "God knows why you should lie. God knows why you *do* lie. To mislead me? To mislead yourself? To prove old age inconstant? I can't answer that, poor bewildered male that I am."

She chuckled as she extended her wrist, with the gold chain on it.

"Ah yes," he said. "Your boy friend's, from the mud of Holland."

"Another lie, I am afraid, Mr. Fowles. It was from here. This one was thrown clear. That is his skull I freed from the earth, poor lamb, because he was taken from the bright sun and the warm air too soon. I have not looked, but yes, I think the others are still in there."

She walked toward the wreck, handing him the gold bracelet as she passed, saying, "Come. Come." He glanced at the gold disk with its small enameled air force badge and the engraving:

P/O L. R. Campbell R.C.A.F.
For Dearest Bobby My Eternal Love
Helen.

She went off to the side of the overgrown fuselage and he followed to where she stopped by a clump of dwarfed birch and said, pointing to the ground, "This is Bobby's place, poor dear. I was walking by, an important walk I think it was although I had not seen the bishop, and this metallic glint caught my eye. I had not noticed the aeroplane. I stooped to pull at this odd little loop of exposed root and there was an eruption of bits of cloth and bone and in the midst of it the bracelet."

There was a smooth declivity in the earth where she had taken the skull, and he knelt and pushed aside the moss to reveal more brown bone; teeth in a piece of jaw and the missing fragment of the skull. When he picked up the fragment, it crumbled through his fingers.

"You see, the tree grew from him! He endowed the tree with life. The tree perpetuated his life!"

"Of course," he said, unimpressed.

Mary was staring thoughtfully at the embankment that hid the fuselage. He said, "You shouldn't have disturbed anything. Technically taking the bracelet is looting. We must leave everything undisturbed for the investigators. And we'll have to report it. These men have been listed missing all these years. Their families have never known what happened to them."

She said, "I wish I could be so sure. The families know by now they are dead. So I have wondered if after fifty years they will welcome hearing their boys were killed to no purpose by a pilot stupid enough to fly into a forest. Pro patria mori."

"Some people keep hoping. But feelings are beside the point, because it's the law; it must be reported." He had had this argument with her before, but this time he felt little conviction.

"Whatever feelings are provoked."

"I don't think we can assume anything about that. I always found—" he checked, about to reveal too much "—well, I imagine it often helps to know how someone close died. I think the fashionable term is closure"

He walked up to where he supposed the cockpit was, on the left side, and pulled away a handful of moss to reveal greenish brown paint. It was indeed military, probably some kind of twin-engined bomber. He pulled off more of the moss, uncovering a cracked perspex window. He peered in, and recoiled.

"Shit."

Crammed into the near corner of the window was a mess of mildewed leather and bone, from which a single eye socket peered out, the pilot's leather-helmeted head smashed against the perspex. Beyond, Justin could just make out the control wheel, still clutched in the pilot's gloved right hand. The seat on the far side of the cockpit contained a crumpled bundle; what was left of the co-pilot.

What he saw next shocked him into rubbing violently on the window to clear his view, spitting on the window and rubbing again. The nearer pilot's gloved right hand was certainly still on the wheel, but there was a band of rusted metal around the wrist joined by a chain to another band of rusted metal on the wheel itself. The pilot was handcuffed to the wheel.

He stared at the handcuff for several seconds. It was inconceivable: the pilot of a military aeroplane, sitting in the left hand seat and thus almost certainly in command, handcuffed to the controls. He retreated a couple of steps, then turned back to peer inside. He hadn't been mistaken; it was a handcuff.

"You seem unsettled, Mr. Fowles."

He hadn't noticed her approach. He said, "There's something unsettling in the cockpit, Mrs. Evens." He told her about the handcuff, and made a stirrup with his hands so that she could look in.

When she got down and dusted herself she said, "Well I am not sure what that means. If it means anything. Oh it is all so futile. So futile. Do you think we had kamikaze squadrons we have never admitted to?"

"I'm sure we didn't."

Justin walked slowly around the wreckage, baffled. Mary sat down on a little mound, absently playing with the bracelet, dimly conscious of those slim pale bodies that had slept beside her so many years ago. She tried to remember why Justin Fowles had come. There must after all be a reason, but perhaps Blenkinsop had forgotten to tell her. But looting, of all the ridiculous things! And his fussing about this silly handcuff. Above all she resented his intrusion into her cherished communion with her dead. At least he had touched the dilemma that nagged her, and might help resolve it. It was all a muddle. She had claimed these dear dead her own because they were woven into the context of her existence but that in truth was an abstraction. In those occasional moments of either lucidity or fearful vertigo—she was never sure which—she knew none of her own transient Calgary loves lay beneath the moss. Which meant their deaths were only meaningful in the context of those who loved them, to whom they must be restored. Unless she claimed dominion over them. But it was not at all clear.

She noticed Justin had returned and said, "We would have been all the same age. Them. You and me."

"And a few million others," he said. He had, suddenly, become deeply troubled. He produced the thermos, and his hand shook slightly as he poured for them both. The wreckage had caught him off guard. It stirred vague echoes of the pity and revulsion he'd felt amidst the bloody carnage of the one big airline crash he'd attended, although in comparison a fifty-year-old wreckage was mere archaeology. But what shocked him was to be confronted in his mind, unaware, by a recreation of Joanne's death, in a twin-engined bomber, a Martin Marauder if he remembered the type, crashing somewhere north-east of Lagos, where undoubtedly she still lay lost and uncounted as these men were lying. The war he hadn't gone to, reaching from the past to make his facetious exploits with the 41st Acadians almost blasphemous. It revived too vividly the envy and remorse, the suspicion of flawed courage he suppressed each Armistice Day standing resolute in glorious full-dress scarlet, the worm of reproach gnawing inside his skull. He was sitting drinking coffee beside Joanne's plane, with the dust of Joanne's skull still on his fingers.

After a time Mary said, "It is unusual to see you so silent, Mr. Fowles. I was sure you were unaffected by these things."

Her words jarred him into the present. He said, "Well yes and no. I would have thought so, too." It was difficult to move away from Joannne. "I'm at something of a loss."

"To see these dead young men."

"Well, no. No not exactly." And to avoid confessing all he felt, "It's totally inexplicable. "

"Oh hardly. There was a war. Young men were killed. I slept with young men because I could not bear the thought of their dying. When I found this I wept. I wept. It is ghastly. But it is explicable."

"I don't mean that. It's the handcuff."

She said impatiently, "The handcuff makes no difference. These are boys, these were boys of our own age, Mr. Fowles. Cut down! Cut down in their youth! Does that mean nothing to you?"

"Doesn't it mean anything to you that the pilot is chained to his controls? Don't you see something grotesque in that? There's no explanation for it."

"What is there to explain? One had a gold bracelet, one had a handcuff, God knows what the others had. The overwhelming fact is that they were locked in the machine of war and are dead. Unless one is completely dehumanized, everything else is trivial."

He grinned at the ground. "Mrs. Evens, I think we are completely incompatible."

She laughed heartily. "Oh I agree completely! Oh completely! But there is nothing to be done now, is there, but to report this to Constable Ymenko."

He said, "So you've made up you mind, about reporting this."

"Heavenly days, Mr. Fowles, surely you agree? Isn't that what you said a moment ago? As I seem to recall your saying once, civil order is not to be denied?"

"It's very difficult," he said testily. "The handcuff puts a different slant on it. It's humane to report those who were missing are dead, that the book is closed. Wives, lovers—I guess then they were called sweethearts—children. But—"

"You are absolutely right," she broke in. "You see there are the women, most of them I am sure married to others, who are also of our age. You see it is so important at this stage of life to gather everything together, to achieve completion. It has been so important for me to do that. To have all my old things around me. I have found such strength in it."

Justin said, "What I am trying to say is that the handcuff changes the scenario. You are saying reporting this will be a comfort to—"

"No no!" she interrupted loudly. "I am talking of something *much* more profound than mere comfort, Mr. Fowles, I am talking of life's fulfillment!"

"Oh all right, Mrs. Evens. The point I am making is that something very unpleasant was going on here. The original casualty reports would have hidden it; the services were good at that. But to make it public now could cause a lot of pain. That handcuff implies crime, disloyalty, betrayal, confinement, guilt, punishment; take your pick. Do you want to let that out? And after all that time there won't be any clear cut answer, so there'll be suspicion and uncertainty about all of them. Is that going to fulfill any lives?"

She was clutching her knees, embracing them, staring at the ground in thought. He walked back to the aeroplane, because it all came too near him, that these crumbling pieces of bone were of his age, of his contemporaries, of Joanne's comrades-in-arms. He looked at his fingers, which had held Dearest Bobby's skull, and moved them. The sight of his fingers moving ran a little perverse trill through his heart.

He looked for broken trees which might mark the aeroplane's final plunge, but it was too long ago. The ravine's direction made it almost certain it came in from the south, from the sea, lost or with a faulty altimeter, but the presence of the handcuffed man added the bleak possibility of suicide, murder, God knew what.

When he walked back to her she had tears in her eyes and she said, speaking with obvious control, "I see what you mean. The handcuff. You are a wordly man, Mr. Fowles, and in those terms what you say about the handcuff is true. I might argue the handcuff is a universal truth, that everyone in a war knows—how did you put it?—betrayal, guilt, punishment. These men are great voids torn from the lives of so many women, who need them for their own *completion.* And there are ceremonies of dying to be performed. I *know* how important they can be; I could not live easily now without my Gwendoline." She wiped her eyes. "But you are right Mr. Fowles. It is best they lie undisturbed."

He shrugged. "I don't like the idea. But the alternative bothers me more."

She said, "I told you about my young men going off to war. The aircrew trainees at Number 3 Service School I think it was called. There were so many, just boys. Most did not know what bed was for." She chuckled, and went on in a soft sing-song. "I tried to have babies by them, I insisted on having their semen. I wanted so much to cancel out their deaths. And *every* boy I slept with was killed, did you know that? Isn't that strange? And I know that one of those very boys is there, under the moss. " She grinned up at him, almost triumphantly. "One of those very boys!"

He wanted to lighten her mood. He said, "Annabel mentioned you had a theory wars were a good thing because they got rid of men. She gave me a hard time over that—"

"Oh but not until they have inseminated their women! How else would the race go on?" She moved to stand and held out her hand and he grasped it, helping her up. She smelt strongly of mold. She said, "It must occur when both sexes are young and lecherous—" and then breaking off, "But you do realize there is something quite urgent we must consider."

He frowned. "I can't say I—"

"The time, Mr. Fowles, the time."

He glanced up, and was astonished. The sun was slanting across the tops of the trees; the forest around them was settling into dusk, and he had been too absorbed to notice. He had no idea how to get out of the ravine, let alone how to find a trail back to Prospect, far less in the dark. Mary said it was impossible; he would have to stay the night. She said, "It will be a splendid test of our civility, Mr. Fowles! I do look forward to it!"

Justin looked forward to it not at all. Only two weeks ago she had shot at him, and he was uneasy about trusting her through the night. Possibly he might pick up a hint of where she'd hidden the body, but apart from it's being a poor time and place to confront her, he had no damning new fact to force her beyond a useless exchange of accusations and denials. If she brought up his spying on her he was defenceless. Moreover this darkening ravine chilled him; it was a gothic cemetery filled with ghosts. He was relieved to see the tent was too small for two.

Mary set about preparing food, using the sandwiches, apples, and wine from his knapsack and cooking some kind of blotchy egg concoction over the fire, for which he gathered the wood. She was conscious—beset as usual by shifting moods and sudden alarms—that Fowles was a threat to her. She couldn't remember the details but he would have taken Gwendoline from her. She glanced at him approaching with an armful of branches, and was suddenly suspicious of his uncharacteristic acquiescence and charm.

The meal had been the first break in Justin's day. He was tired, and the pain of Annabel's defection had returned. He felt relaxed enough but was edgy at Mary's unpredictability. She muttered to herself constantly, but gave away nothing about the dead woman. Once when she was telling him how she had inherited Mogador she stopped, stared upward with the semblance of an ecstatic smile and cried out, "Oh it will be so lovely, my terraced lawns and new kitchen!" It seemed to be a compulsive spasm because before he could ask her what she meant she was talking about her grandfather, a British admiral who had built the property.

Eventually, when the fire had died, she said it was time for her to sleep. "I am content now. I am sure we are doing the right thing. To restore the dead to those who loved them. To tuck her in at night. Ah the closing, the closing!"

He was sure she had agreed earlier to quite the opposite, but it was too late to argue. The disposition of the wreck and its cargo no longer seemed important; he was too damn tired. She had given him a groundsheet and he laid it in a mossy depression about a hundred feet from the tent. He lay on the groundsheet and pulled his jacket around him. It was amusing that she'd not remarked on the absence of his beard.

Lying on his back, he could see the occasional star through the forest roof. The last thing he could have imagined this morning was that he'd spend the night with Mrs. Evens. And maybe someone called Blenkinsop, who had come into the conversation several times. And Gwendoline, and Mary's cryptic remark came back to him—what was it?— about *being with* her Gwendoline. Which surely suggested the corpse was still around. Somewhere. Somewhere and thus findable. If the babbling old bumbletit was to be believed.

He was too tired. He drifted toward sleep filled with melancholy intimations of Annabel, which devolved to a calm hopefulness emanating from the dim image of a pale face with green eyes, which some time later merged into a more substantial dream of warm skin against his skin, of stroking the soft skin of curving back and buttocks. The sensation faded, dreamlike, renewed, faded again so that he groped for its return. And then soft hands were on his back, on his hips, and he opened his eyes out of the dream and gasped, "Oh Christ!"

The face starkly before him was that face of horror, grotesquely deformed, looming from the mist and darkness that morning on the Lower Road, and he tried to push the ghastly apparition away.

An apparition, but it was Mary Evens. He thought immediately of moonlight because her naked body glowed with a cold flourescence as she crouched over him, beside him, her free right hand on his genitals. She was wrinkled, her breasts pendulous over a vast belly, her head disproportionately huge and her face a glowing pale grey with protruding eyes and her mouth a dark crimson grin. She smelt of rotting meat and he gagged, swallowing bile. Writhing in her grasp and furious, he yelled, "For Christ's sake Mrs. Evens! What the hell goes on?"

"It is our time, dear man. We must leave together."

"Will you get your fucking hand off my cock? Come on! This is ridiculous."

"Death is no harlot, darling. A mistress maybe, but a faithful one. Each to his very own. And I am yours, come for you."

But there was no moon. He had perhaps escaped from dream into nightmare, and must now fight back to sanity, to which end he grasped the luminous arm that supported her over him and shoved. The arm held solid, and she began screaming curses close to his ear. He found himself pressing with all his strength against the arm, astonished by its resistance, deafened by her screams, and trying to reach her head, kicking up with his left leg. He was gasping with the effort before she finally fell away from him, holding him long enough to give him an instant's wrenching pain in the groin, and he scrambled to his feet. Mary was up too, standing grotesquely ten feet away, shouting, "I am offering you the completion you came for! Among your comrades my sweet loves of yesterday! It is fitting! It is your time!"

"Horseshit! My problem is that it isn't my time!

"Did you know I shall live in the halls of paradise?"

"For Christ's sake Mrs. Evens go back to your tent."

"We will meet you know! We must come to end this!"

She was backing away from him, fading into the darkness toward her tent, screeching inanities. He stood for some time, tucking in his shirt and doing up his fly and refastening his belt. The actions reassured him it hadn't been a dream.

He sat down on the groundsheet. He must already have slept for some time because he was no longer tired. He couldn't completely grasp it had happened. And yet he was in fact unusually calm and yes, refreshed. Which was further reassurance it had been no nightmare; nightmares left a wake of troubled emotions. It was real and vivid and yet it lacked the impact he expected; he was relaxed rather than agitated or fearful or in any way upset, conscious of a wonderful sense of relief, as if it had been a virtual experience perhaps, a spiritual experience. He did not believe in spiritual experience.

And yet one rain-drenched night fifty years ago that huge metal coffin burst down through the trees shedding huge fragments—an engine, a wing—to slam violently to earth in an explosion of mud and metal and smashed branches and five, six, seven men his own age were instantly cut off. They knew deafening sound, vibration, terror, then instantly nothing. To be dust, crumbled between his fingers.

It was right to leave the airmen undisturbed. But in reassuring himself he heard Mary's words which in the heat of argument he'd failed to notice: *I could not live easily now without my Gwendoline.* And suddenly the mystery began to fall away, her odd solicitude to the corpse that bleak morning, the nagging illogic of her kidnapping it. Suddenly he had what his training demanded; a crazy deluded motive but nonetheless a motive, to have her long lost daughter with her. And not only that, the clear message that his Drowned Maiden was not gone with the tides out into the unreachable Pacific but was still on the property.

He lay for some time simply savouring the revelation and eventually dozed. He woke with an anxious glance toward Mary's tent where dim shapes were forming out of the darkness where the aircraft lay. There was the pale sky of a new dawn above the arching filigree of the forest ceiling, and he lay back on his elbows and watched the sky grow brighter. There was soft birdsong that he hadn't noticed. He was suffused with unusual delight at the prospect of the new day.

Perhaps in no more than a corner of his heart, as a whisper, as a faint prayer, he sensed the beginning of wonder. It was out of place, and he frowned in uncertainty. There was no reasonable source of such feeling. It was inappropriate to a cemetery, a ravine of death. It was much too early in the morning. And yet his heart was filling with yes—improbable as it seemed—astonishment, a joyous astonishment that he existed, that he could taste the freshness of the air breathed into his lungs, hear birdsong, feel his sore behind against the ground.

He stood up, shakily because the knee was acutely painful, and hobbled behind a tree and peed. He was floating on a strange tide of the deepest gratitude, for simply being alive. He had escaped Grandmother Death! He breathed! He was trying to define this unfamiliar mood, trying to adjust himself to it. He had never—never since childhood—felt such quiet exhilaration in the mere sensations of existence. He made his way cautiously toward Mary's tent, a pale blur beside the dark mounds that concealed the aircraft. The air was a thin mist, with the scent of ash. The tent was empty. Mary Evens, her cape, her garbage bag, had gone. He clenched his fists and shouted, "Yes!" with relief.

It was euphoria, a sense of power, as if in fighting off death he had risen above his muddled past. To be alive, to possess human consciousness was the ultimate blessing, and in this reinvention of youth his immediate anxieties were subsumed in the radiant vision of the floating dead, perfect in form, elegant of youthful feature framed in that immense fan of golden hair. Botticelli had occurred to him on the dark inlet, a

Venus emergent from the waves, and now his own Drowned Maiden was within his reach. He recalled again, and chuckled, *I could not live easily now without my Gwendoline.* The mad old bitch had given the game away.

16

After their ghastly meeting at the Starlight Annabel needed three days to steady her resolve to confront Justin again. She was too busy and preoccupied to plan any kind of approach, but knew she was behaving unconscionably toward him and it couldn't go on. She had to tell him about both Dirk and leaving Prospect, even if she fell to pieces in the process. It would be easier at his place, and she phoned to tell him she was coming over, and even then found it difficult to speak with the reserved cordiality she thought right. The weather was cool and there had been showers, and walking to Justin's would help clear her mind for the encounter.

It had been so much easier with Dirk. She told him immediately after their tumble on the floor that there was to be no affair, and the last time he'd called he accepted her final good-humoured rejection with a nonchalance that somewhat disappointed her.

Dirk's attention had in fact for several days been elsewhere, fixed on the secret marketing plan he had hinted at to Annabel, an unlikely collaboration with

Mandril Gulag set by coincidence to take place the same evening she had arranged to meet Justin. An hour before she left her house, Dirk began phoning newspapers and radio and TV stations in Victoria, after which he left the Sensual Rendezvous and headed excitedly down the highway to the Combat College. As he was waved past the gate into the camp he could see the convoy standing beside the road, three camouflaged canvas-covered trucks and a grey truck carrying the hydraulic cherry-picker. It had started to rain heavily and the commandos in their rain capes crowded together climbing into the trucks. He checked his watch; his brilliant scheme to increase the Rendezvous' cash flow by the three point two percent needed to finance Prospect Palisades was under way.

Mandril in battle camouflage greeted him in the operations room. Dirk said, "Your troops are loading, eh? Right on time."

"Of course," said Mandril curtly. "This is military now."

"Where's Doctor Pete?"

"He's with the Strike Force. He wants to be in the front lines. To motivate the troops in their Christian task. Shit, what a fucking windbag! You contacted the media?"

"The press releases were delivered by courier this afternoon. And I phoned everyone again tonight. Don't worry; they'll be there."

"Yeah. Well I appreciate this," Mandril said. Dirk had convinced him tonight's operation was specifically designed to attract college enrolment. The College was in no need of money, but Dirk had shown him the tabletop model of Prospect Palisades with its huge College campus and had pitched the need, as Dirk put it, ". . . to maximize present demand for future market growth potential, man!"

However Dirk's sole aim was really to publicize his Sensuous Rendezvous. He'd started with a vague idea of a collaborative stunt between the resort and the college, but within a short time, and inspired by the College's current Priest-in-Residence, the Reverend Doctor G.K. "Pete" Urban of Tacoma, Washington, the idea had become "The Strike Against Sin" in which—with full media coverage—the commandos would run through the Resort's grounds shouting scripted condemnations of sin. The angry sinners would be flushed from their rooms and cabins, whereupon Doctor Pete, spotlighted in the heavens aboard the cherry picker would describe through a bullhorn the horrors of Satan's pit. Dirk had set the publicity in motion, but unknown to Mandril, because he didn't trust the commandos not to go berserk, he had also ordered his secretary to call the police as soon as the attack began.

The College curriculum featured several films and lectures on fundamentalist Christian themes, and in preparation for the Strike Doctor Pete gave one of his favourite sermons, "Satan and the Hospitality Industry", which featured graphs showing how the number of rooms in motels, hotels and resorts in the United States had grown since 1960, demonstrating to the statistically naive, startling correlations with increases in divorce, drug use, illegitimate births, teenage pregnancy, and AIDS.

Doctor Pete ended with a booming peroration: "Friends, I am not speaking of a biblical Sodom and Gomorrah. I am not speaking of far-off San Francisco or distant New Orleans. Satan the Dark Angel is multinational! He roams the global village! Satan reigns in all his bestial glory not three miles from where we sit! At this very moment lewd bodies are straining in rut, frenzied animals devoid of human love, bereft of Christ's glorious and sanctifying blessing!

"I speak of the Sensuous Rendezvous Resort, my friends, just down the highway! A house of carnal orgy, of the prurient worship of the foulest human organs, thirty bedrooms fully furnished in rich gold and chrome, in easeful silks and satins, with all the perfumed accoutrements of profligate self-indulgence! Yea, lechery! Yea, harlotry! Yea, I look up to the stars and see the tears of bright clouds of golden angels falling in despair!"

By the time Dirk and Mandril left the camp, with Mandril waving to the convoy to follow, the rain was torrential. The plan was for the trucks to proceed down the highway at twenty miles an hour, while Mandril sped ahead in the jeep to set up his command post in the Rendezvous parking lot and to return Dirk to his office. So it was that the trucks drove slowly through the drenching night, the commandos in back happily sharing marijuana and Southern Comfort, the drivers conferring anxiously with their front-seat companions over maps and schedules, checking watches, peering past thrashing wipers into a black confusion of forest until they slowed, crept ahead cautiously, and then turned right off the highway down an even darker, more thickly forested road.

About three quarters of an hour later, as about the same time every Saturday, the Rib'n'Rye Room became unfit for human habitation, the cigarette smoke having reached a concentration so corrosive that the bar attendants' eyes were inflamed nearly to blindness. They wore earplugs against a percussive thunder battling a chorus of guitars and the amplified self-pity of a nasal tenor. A straggling procession of men and women began lurching up the exit stairways to stand gasping in the parking lot or to vomit or urinate into the shrubbery until the rain, or dreams of prurient high-jinks, drove them again below.

The Fabled Jazz Hall Lady Jane sat as usual half-hidden at the end of the bar, immunized against smoke and noise by generations of exposure, able to scan the whole room with the slightest move of her head, ruminating on her lost loves and praying that the doormen were keeping a good count.

Her intuition, which was seldom wrong, told her the place would be swarming with cops and firemen before the night was out, itching to enforce the fire marshal's occupancy limits. It would be the ultimate humiliation to be closed down through the ineptitude of the likes of Mandril Gulag and Dirk Plantagenet, but she sensed fate was thundering toward her on the leaden wings of country rock. She wished Dirk would stop bringing her every mad idea he cobbled together.

She knew all too well what they had planned for tonight, but thought it was already underway. Thus she was surprised to see Dirk and Mandril pushing their way through the tables toward her. Mandril was peering angrily around the room, and from Dirk's hangdog look she knew the worst was upon her.

They were both in soaking-wet camouflage coveralls, and Mandril had a tiny forest of bracken tied on his hat. His face was distorted by running black makeup that emphasized his forbidding features. He stared at the Lady Jane accusingly and shouted above the noise, "You got my troops in here? My troops have fuckin' vanished." He leaned forward to survey the heady depths of the Fabled One's cleavage.

She looked at them questioningly. "We've screwed up," shouted Dirk. "Mandril's commandos have deserted. We waited half an hour for them at the resort, and they never showed."

"What a surprise!" She shouted sarcastically. "Why are you bringing me into this? I'm monitoring a basement throbbing with primal lust."

"You helped us plan the thing—"

"Like hell buster! All I did was buy you a coffee! I said it was the looniest thing I'd ever heard. I said it was doomed." Her phone began to ring, and she waved them away. "Be gone! Be gone! I'm too busy."

Dirk and Mandril pushed back toward an exit. Half way there was an empty table; they conferred briefly, then sat down. About ten minutes later the Lady Jane came and leant over the table, interrupting a loud argument about VHF radio contact and radio silence. She said, "The radio isn't your problem. Your troops are your problem, and I'm telling you you'd better be damn sure they don't try to crash here."

"You don't understand," shouted Dirk. "The real problem is media. Half dozen media—*at least* a half dozen—and maybe a TV crew maybe two TV crews, lights, cameras, coming to cover—"—he stretched his arms wide—"CHRISTIAN COMMANDOS RAID SEX HAVEN! Ten thousand dollars worth of publicity, and if they don't find action I'm dead." He cried out in despair, almost in tears, "This is a disaster!"

"Don't count on it," shouted the Lady Jane. "You really think they'd rush down 14 in a night like this on an anonymous tip about some crazy commando raid? Do you think they don't know a scam when they see it?" She threw her hands in the air despairingly just as screams came from a far corner of the reverberating room. There was a sound of breaking glass, and suddenly the Lady Jane's face lost its tenseness, and she smiled at Dirk with pure and dazzling tenderness. Her body straightened, assuming energy and vital form, and she turned to the sound like a soul recalled to its element, her feet a good inch above the pounding floor. She touched Dirks cheek as she moved away. "There's nothing like a good barroom brawl, dear lad. They are my life's blood, and food of my heart."

17

Annabel's walk through the rain failed to refresh her mind as she had hoped, and she arrived at the store drained of the wit and ready energy she needed. When she entered the back room where Justin was standing, the memories came suddenly to them both, creating an awful distance. They exchanged conventional hellos while avoiding each others eyes, and she attempted to behave heartily while disposing of raincoat, hat and umbrella by the back door. When finally she saw him in the brighter light without the beard she realized her first impression—that he had aged— was wrong. It made him a stranger. She lied companionably, tilting her head, "Yes, it is an improvement. It really is. And distinguished. Youthfully distinguished. But why this revolutionary step, Justin? I mean, after all—"

He forced himself to vivacity but without confidence or true feeling. "I think I am undergoing profound change, which you will notice I am bearing stoically as usual. Your word 'revolutionary' is dead on. I have had two experiences recently, signal experiences, epiphanies possibly, and although the effects of such things aren't instant, it may be that I am being transformed! Amazing, eh, at my age? But it's too early to tell. When I am become my new self I'll let you know!"

He had welcomed her phone call before realizing it was pointless; the meeting at the Starlight had told him everything. He had no idea why she wanted to see him again, and her coolness on the phone had been troubling. He had moved beyond her desertion to Plantagenet, if only so far as to abandon the idea of a direct and immediate approach.

His thoughts since the morning in the ravine had been wholly on how best to evade Mary Evens while searching her property. He knew she was mad, but his need to find the Drowned Maiden erased his previous faith in Ymenko's search. He would need only to watch the lower level, because there was no way Mary could carry the corpse up the rock and into the house. And perhaps because of its warm intimacy amidst an outpouring of nonsense, the phrase she'd used in the ravine, *to tuck her in at night* had stayed in his mind. From Fuck Point he would be able to see a flashlight moving under the trees on the lower level, or detect her with the infra-red scope if, as rumour had it, she could move through the forest without light. The surveillance would probably take several nights and he was anxious to begin, but when Annabel phoned the rain had already made him cancel the night's expedition.

He made coffee with unnecessary care, and Annabel circled the room nervously, unable to concentrate on what he was saying. The silences were made the more melancholy by the sound of the rain on the roof. She said stiltedly, "So apart from this exercise of rediscovery, are you keeping occupied?"

"Well for one thing I am dismantling the apparatus of my cold war period, when my paranoia was most rampant. If you care to look in the alcove by the entrance to the store you will see the monitor and the VCR and the camera are all disconnected."

"Oh God, Justin," she said, hearing his old self, laughing, "You never cease to entertain." She recalled discovering the TV camera could be trained at the bed, recalled his shocked denials of recording their intercourse. "But if you lose your paranoia what on earth are you going to do with yourself?"

"Well," he said, "With all that equipment on my hands I'm attracted to the idea of producing TV movies of local myths. *Grandmother Death*—wasn't that your name for her?—*the Monster of Mogador,* or *Mandril Gulag*—with Ks instead of Cs as in—*Kommandant of the Kristian Kombat Kollege.* What do you think? For the Yankee dollar?"

"No, Justin." She had to chuckle. "I think not!"

"Also I must become more zealously entrepreneural. Greater emphasis on repairs, maintenance, landscaping. J. Fowles Inc. Now that I have a phone. Perhaps a new logo on the truck." It was all evasion and he so longed to be candid with her although there had been no candour between them for months. He couldn't imagine how she'd react to the story of the dead airmen and Mary Evens in the ravine, or to hearing that he now knew where the Drowned Maiden was hidden. He ruffled through the papers at the end of table. "Can't find it. I received official notice yesterday to take down my beloved billboard on the Lower Road. First they force me to move it, now they want me to destroy it! The reactionaries have won, but only temporarily! Yes! So the fight must go on, this time in the court of public opinion! I trust I can rely on the support of the Prospect Anguish and Sympathizer, my dear."

It was so long since she had heard his antic conversation, and it struck her how sadly poor Dirk compared with this articulate, civilized, self-deprecating man, just as Justin's satirical commercial fantasies cast so ludicrous a light on Dirk's flawed and cumbersome visions. But she was tense, needing to grasp the fleeting moment just right for her speak with tact and sensitivity.

It was about then that they both began to hear unidentifiable noises toward the village centre, and later, a few moments after they had started the coffee, with both uneasily aware that small talk had run out, there was a bright flash outside and instantly the sullen crunch of a nearby explosion. The windows rattled, and voices from the street cried out.

Justin said, "What the hell?" and started to the door.

There were shouts and a frantic hammering, and Justin opened the door to reveal a drenched and frightened Riordon Pollock, and behind him Kitchener Street transformed into a crowded scene of gothic battle and revenge. Three large trucks were parked a hundred yards up the street, and beyond the trucks, in the middle of the road, a large fire was burning. Through the rain and smoke the fire reflected deep orange on the trees and the buildings beyond, and on the people milling around on the wet street.

Riordon shouted, "They've smashed a window in the Starlight, and I saw one of the bastards peeing in the street. I tried to get through to Ymenko but they must have cut the wires. Has anyone got a cellphone? This is a bloody riot, a *real* riot. They're going to burn us down!"

"Who the hell are *they?*" said Justin, feeling immensely steady. He had moved out into the furious rain.

A woman shouted, "They're from the Combat College."

Justin said, "They can't be. Gulag controls his troops. This is a mob."

A ripple of sharp reports sounded somewhere beyond the fire, and a great laughing shout went up.

Annabel said, "And fireworks, too!"

"That is an automatic rifle, sweet child," said Justin calmly.

"Justin I've got to tell you it's out of control!" shouted Riordon, and at that moment Jennie Harbison hurried up sheltering Janice, the waitress from the Starlight, under a rain cape. Jennie whined, "They smashed the glass in the door and when Janice came down to find what had happened they tried to carry her away. It was rape, I tell you. Poor lamb, she's awful upset."

Riordon was almost right; it was near out of control, and Justin knew what he had to do. It wasn't a time for oratory, though perhaps the weary mud-soaked 41st Acadians might benefit from exhortation. The stern imperatives rose from deep in his memory of the Force, of his years in the trenches. He said briskly, "All of you, get inside."

They scrambled into the store, spilling back into the all-purpose room. Irene, Frank Mewhouse's wife whined, "They're all drunk, and I know they're going to start looting. Frank's staying to protect the mail. He's got a rifle and he's going to blow away the first little bugger who comes in. Frank was in the mail when it was Royal and a sacred trust, but it's a worry because a few envelopes aren't worth that."

Justin was grateful that Annabel was putting on the kettle; tea or coffee would calm them. On a night like this, with accidents along the highway, it would be an hour before they could expect Ymenko. Justin moved unnoticed behind the screen by the clothes closet. He knew the trousers no longer fitted, but he forced himself into the scarlet tunic and the boots and spurs, and when he added the Sam Browne belt and the stetson, not to mention the empty holster, it made so powerful a statement that the soiled blue jeans were hardly noticeable. He picked up the riding crop and gloves as he turned back into the room, and Betty Flegg gasped. He called out, "Riordon, have your coffee but get up to the phone at the hotel and try for the police. I'll play for time. This may not work, but someone's going to get hurt if we don't do something."

As he stepped down into the street Annabel came to the door. "Justin what are you doing? The tunic!"

"It doesn't matter any more, dear heart. I am, you remember, in metamorphosis. There was a siege, remember? This is the occupation!"

"But it's a bloody mob, Justin! For Christ's sake, *don't!*"

He dismissed her with a grin and a flick of the riding crop and strode with measured pace down the centre of the road, staring disapprovingly at the fire, wondering who in the name of hell they were and what they were up to. Steady in the ranks. Indeed. Hah! he shouted. Or did he? The tunic was suffocating; he undid a button. Steady. The clouds of steam and smoke glowed from the pyre below, rising into the rain to merge with the low rolling scud, moving east. He slapped the riding crop against his thigh.

He was indeed charged with frightful potency, an appalling figure in scarlet, high as the clouds or at least the store-fronts, his wide-brimmed stetson half-hidden in the mist, and the rock of Mogador glowering above. A timeless national legend, the scarlet and the gold. Glowering down. Upon. Albeit with greying beard—good heavens, for an instant he forgot!—that refuge shaved away and his bifocals increasingly smeared with rain. Whatever— Whereon—

A bullet whined by. "Shit," Justin muttered to himself, striding on unflinching.

But it was no great conflagration, a bonfire made of an old garage door, a couple of oil drums, the rusted Hillman from Graham Tuck's alley, bits of crating and scrap lumber creating a stench only relieved by the soft perfume of marijuana. But surprisingly bright as he perceived. More than just sizzling in the rain and thus evidently chemically augmented. Which might account for that first explosion. Yes.

In the empty lot behind the bonfire he made out the sagging Stars and Stripes, surrounded by murky figures drinking, toking, shouting and laughing, and there was a more concentrated group, a noisy crowd, in front of the apartment building at the corner of Kitchener and Wellington. A summer at Wasaga Beach Ontario, he seemed to remember. Mass hippie exuberance requiring the presence of authority. Indeed. At this moment something hit him on the head and his hat flew off; people shrieked joyfully and when he picked the hat up it was covered in oily muck. Of course, a paintball. Luckily brown; yellow would have invited mockery. He wasn't sure if this was a scene from his personal inferno, or perhaps his salvation, but despite the paintball, people drew back as he strode up. Luck was still with him.

"Who the hell lit this fire?" he shouted, thwacking the riding-crop once more against his thigh.

A voice cried from the darkness beyond the flames,"It is the Lord's!" and another voice cried, "The angels have lit a beacon for their sheep!"

"If the angels light a beacon on the main street the sheep are going to end up in the clanger," barked Fowles in his best ringing voice of command. The night air, or perhaps the fumes from the Lord's beacon, were clearing his mind, and he could make out the Combat College logo on the trucks, their tailgates down. Not what he expected, but perhaps it confirmed his suspicions of Mandril's philosophy. Further along the street a cherry-picker, of all improbable things, seemed to be rising unsteadily from the intersection of Kitchener and Wellington, bearing a figure in white coveralls he had seen somewhere before. Three men in camouflage approached him and he asked angrily, "What's going on here?"

"We're about the Lord's work, friend," said one of the camouflaged figures. "We'd welcome your help in scourging these souls of sin—"

"Praise the Lord," wailed someone in the rain-soaked night.

"You'd best help yourselves by getting the hell out of here," snapped Justin. He turned back to the crowd around the fire and struck what he thought was a posture of intimidating authority—booted legs apart, riding crop in both gloved hands—and shouted, "Quiet! Listen to me! Quiet everyone!" There was, hearteningly, less noise. "What you are doing is against the law. This is vandalism and disturbance of the peace and you are liable to arrest and imprisonment. Do you understand? A heavily-armed emergency response team of the Royal Canadian Mounted Police is on its way here. I am warning you to disperse. You must put out the fire and clear out immediately."

There was a resentful but encouragingly subdued mutter from the crowd, but Justin had just concluded the lecture had worked when another paintball splattered across his shoulder, evoking more applause and laughter. At that moment Maggie Pollock ran up in flopping slippers with a dressing gown wrapped around her shouting, "Justin! Justin! I called Ymenko ten minutes ago."

"For God's sake, Maggie, I'm dead if anyone hears that. What do you mean you were talking to him? Riordon's over at my place. He just said the line was down."

"Oh Riordon always panics. I had to finish my bath. That's where he is, eh? Well—" Maggie broke off with a delighted grin. She put one hand to her face and said, "Oh Justin, what a cute outfit! And the lovely colour accents—ooh, sticky! You've come out of the closet! I thought your past was supposed to be deep dark secret!"

"It was absolutely secret!" he snapped impatiently, its being the worst possible time for all that. "You got through to Ymenko?"

"I told Ymenko there was an invasion. He said if it was an invasion to phone the army. You know what those two are like when they get in bed. If this isn't an invasion what is it?"

"Mandril's animals are out of their cages. Phone Ymenko back and tell him to get off the nest and get over here. Fast. This disguise won't work much longer."

The crowd around the fire was becoming rambunctious again, but he thought he should go across the street to the Post Office to warn Frank to put his rifle away. He sensed the three camouflaged men who'd approached him earlier were uncomfortably close beside him. One of them said, "We truly beseech you to assist us in our mission of purifying this den of iniquity, which has been revealed to us as a cesspool of bodily lust."

"You're out of your mind," said Justin. "There's been no bodily lust in Prospect for decades. There isn't an active hormone in the place. Now look, douse the fire and clear out. Get out fast before the law arrives, or Constable Ymenko and his riot squad will demonstrate the true meaning of the Wrath of God."

"We obey a law higher than the law of man," said the second man, and then the third, bigger than his two companions, said belligerently, "We can deal with any cop who stands in the way of the Lord. Do I make myself clear, little old man in drag? I got some good advice for you to avoid pain. My advice is to totter back to your nursing home. Real quick."

At that moment Justin detected the slightest sound behind him and jerked round to see a man hurling himself forward. Justin feinted, bent his knees, turned as he grasped the man's arm and twisted, sending his assailant somersaulting with flailing arms and legs to crash into the ditch, howling, holding his crotch.

Justin stood up, forcing self-control as he recovered the riding crop and stetson and dusted his jacket, relieved at the respectful hush that had fallen around him but suspecting he'd injured his shoulder. He could have shouted in triumph; he'd got the move right—the one he'd screwed up with Gulag!

He turned to proceed on down Kitchener when the heavens opened in acoustically augmented thunder: "Brethren I see Satan in his scarlet dress roaming freely in the streets of the Sensuous Rendezvous! I see Satan striking down one of our crusaders! Satan, I defy thee! Satan, I renounce thee!"

Justin looked up to see the gondola of the cherry-picker high above him in the smoke, bearing—he recalled now vividly—the same ominous figure he'd seen on the bridge of the landing craft, its head hooded in a white helmet bearing a crimson sword. He was struck with huge relief because it had not been hallucination, because everything came together—the shed by the shore, the landing craft crossing the strait at night, the College's dubious finances—and all power was suddenly delivered into his hands.

"Yeah, oh Satan, I defy thee," boomed the loud-hailer. "And I summon all the soldiers of the New Age to bring forth the sinners flushed from their sweat-soaked beds of passion." There was a confused chorus of replies: "We can't find anyone, Doctor Pete," and a tiny voice, like a child's, "The fuckin' maps don't fit, Doctor Pete," and another, "We got the wrong place, man." The cherry picker made a clicking, mewing sound, and Doctor Pete began majestically to descend.

"What's your name, sir?" shouted Justin, cupping his hands, smiling to himself.

"I do the Lord's work under the name of Doctor Pete. And who, sir, are you that you disrupt our sacred mission, our Strike against Sin?"

"I am Justin Fowles, a Chief Superintendent in the Royal Canadian Mounted Police," Justin said loudly for all to hear. "I have warned your people to put out the fire and leave peaceably. An armed detachment of my men, a riot squad with truncheons and pepper spray, will be here within minutes."

Doctor Pete had scrambled out of the gondola and Justin went forward to meet him. Doctor Pete peered down at Justin from under his enormous helmet and said quietly, his public smile unchanged, "Listen, little brother, I've seen a lot of policemen in my time and I never seen one like you. Pink coat that don't fit, and a ponytail and bifocals and spurs? Spurs? You guys still use horses up here? If you're a cop I'm Billy Graham. We are doing God's work here, so clear out peaceful or I'll throw you to Mandril's goons."

Justin, unflinching, slowly raised the riding crop to touch Doctor Pete's chest just under his chin. He tapped it twice and said calmly, "If you don't order your goons to get their asses out of here within fifteen minutes, trucks and all, you personally will be charged with entering this country illegally and the Combat College will be charged with smuggling its students into the country illegally by boat at night and that pre-fab down on the beach at Ganges will be searched for prohibited substances to be smuggled into the United States. The major may even find himself the centre of a big political storm about CIA outsourcing." He stepped back briskly, glancing at his watch, which had stopped, and barked, "You have fifteen minutes."

"That's a god damn lie," whispered Doctor Pete, his eyes betraying his alarm. "The place is clean."

"Dream on," said Justin quietly, and added, "And remind Gulag that borders still have meaning." He turned, a splendid parade-ground about-turn, and paced away toward the crowd, which opened before him. He permitted himself another tight smile, thinking grimly *never mess with a Horseman.* Behind him he heard

Doctor Pete blaring orders through the bullhorn, sounding the retreat. He passed the fire, where men were peeing into the embers. About a hundred feet from the Variety Store he stumbled, recovered, and suddenly realized that each footstep was incredibly heavy. The pain in his shoulder was severe.

The people he'd left at the store were outside in the road. He heard Riordon saying Ymenko was on his way, and several voices congratulating him, and there was scattered clapping. Annabel took his arm and said, "Justin you could have got killed."

"Hardly, my love. It was the normal line of duty."

Back in the store he pulled off the scarlet tunic, heavy and stiffened with rain, reeking of smoke. There were three or four paintball hits he hadn't noticed. An amazing experience! The uniform, give or take a few sixteenths, fitted perfectly, although one of the buttons seemed to have gone. He was in superb condition, whatever they said. Fighting fit, as that fat bugger had found out. Ha! He had life in him yet, by God, and to hell with Mrs. Evens. The old reflexes were as sharp as a boy's, his timing precise as a frightened astronaut's. He heard the thin wail of distant sirens. Blucher was on his way.

"Well!" he said enthusiastically, rubbing his hands together, looking around the general purpose room where half a dozen villagers still remained. And Janice whatever-her-name, from the coffee shop, sitting on his bed. "I was if I say so myself, magnificent! Inspector

Walsh at the border, defying the massed might of the United States Army eager to avenge Little Big Horn! Inspector Walsh with but one hundred and fifty of the Force! Standing between the US Seventh Cavalry Division and four thousand battle-hardened warriors! To hold the line! Maintiens le Droit!"

"You could have got yourself killed," said Annabel, said again if he remembered correctly. He proclaimed to no one in particular, "Do you know the story of Inspector Walsh of the North West Mounted? Defender of the 49th Parallel, saviour of the Sioux, one of the true founders of the nation?"

Annabel, a pained expression on her face, said quietly, "You were very brave, dear, but I don't think we should get into what happened to the Sioux."

Harold Mealy of Harold's Tonsure Parlour was standing with a few other near the kitchen sink. He said, "You didn't rough those guys up too much out there, did you Justin? They send us trade you know. I shave a few heads every course."

Justin frowned, thinking he'd misheard. "What do you mean, trade? This was an organized attack. We weren't the target but it was an attack."

"Sure," said Elgin Rock, who did shoe repairs in back of Pollock's. "But it doesn't matter who the target was. If Prospect gets a bad image for hospitality, we lose money."

It was so bizarre that he laughed in a quick bark that brought a jab of pain sharp enough to force him into a chair. "Hospitality?" he yelled. "Are you nuts? There was fire out there. There was looting. There's broken glass from your stores all down the road. Get fucking real. Another half hour and this bloody village wouldn't exist."

There was a moment's quiet and then a voice said, "Don't be a cunt, Elgin." There were shouts of agreement and calls of "Great work, Justin," and "Thanks, man," and as people started leaving the voices were farther away and mixing with the sound of trucks grinding by, heading back up to the highway.

Annabel, looking extraordinarily tense, said, "Those assholes. Are you anywhere near all right?"

"Yeah, I'm okay. It's the shoulder. Taking that guy down. I still have the moves, but the hinges are rusty." He didn't want to talk, even to Annabel. He wanted to sleep; even the ingratitude didn't bother him. He said, "I'm out of it. Age is upon me. Do me a favour and take that waif off my bed when you go." Blue and red lights flashed across the ceiling as Ymenko went by. He said to the girl, sitting down beside her, "It's safe in the village now, Janice. The Force has arrived."

He lowered himself carefully onto the bed as Annabel led Janice to the door. He was exhausted, and he closed his eyes to shut himself off from everything, from everyone. Some time later he felt Annabel slide a heating pad under his shoulder, and felt her gently wiping the soot and oily paint from his face and neck with a warm cloth.

After she had covered him with a blanket, Annabel made herself a cup of coffee and sat relaxed, watching him, believing he slept. She felt at peace, despite her failure to tell him about Dirk. That would come, but for the moment it was good to end it this way, together in the familiar room. She was filled with the deepest tender regard for the figure on the bed, because for all that he was screwed up and eccentric and untruthful and crazily obsessed, he was decent. Tonight he'd had nothing to gain, but he did the basically decent thing, and without thanks.

It was a disarmingly filial regard, a sense of deep affection but wonderfully free of encumbrances, as if she were standing alone for the first time but fully appreciative of his past dearness. It was a feeling of strength which she thought quite strange, and she wondered if the coffee had been too strong or the night too full of stress, and suddenly it came to her that it wasn't strange at all. He had done what had to be done, decisively and quietly, and had shown her the way. She had found herself again.

She tiptoed over to Justin. He felt her kiss his head and heard her murmur "Oh Justin, Justin," with so penitent a tone that he mumbled, "There's no need. All is well." He heard her breathe in sharply, and heard her footsteps receding, and the door closing. Drowsily, without opening his eyes, he pulled off his trousers and snuggled back under the blanket. Everything smelt of oil and sweat and smoke; wood smoke, oil smoke, marijuana smoke. He was bruised and battered; it had certainly been a night of jostling, drunken stinking humanity. The kind of thing over which the Fabled Jazz Hall Lady Jane, strange woman, so fondly presided in her eternal Rib'n'Rye Room.

He thought he'd perhaps accomplished something tonight, which was satisfying. He had almost forgotten what satisfaction felt like. It lulled and fulfilled, promising untroubled sleep. With the uproar and clamour all slipped away, he drifted toward a dim vision the Drowned Maiden, now so near.

18

It was three nights after he had repelled the commandos from the village, and Justin stood in the darkness below the verandah steps at Mogador. The night was heavily overcast, and he could hear Mary shrilling tunelessly inside the house, a clatter of kitchen pans, a silence, the sound of a chair pushed across a floor, a longer silence. She was safely in the house for the night, and he could proceed. He moved carefully away from the verandah and through the overgrown garden, sheltering the beam of the small flashlight with his hand as he picked his way to the south edge.

His shoulder remained tender, but he had treated it carefully and it was strong enough for what he had planned. He had been out of the store only twice since the raid, the first to apologize to the Lady Jane for having contributed to her misfortune. Gulag's thugs had retreated from the village to the Rib'n'Rye Room, where their frayed tempers and rebel yells had provoked chaos. Ymenko's police reinforcements were still in the village or nearby on the highway, and five carloads of irritated Horsemen responded to the Lady

Jane's 911 call. Seven commandos and fifteen of the Lady Jane's regular patrons were in jail, and the Rib'n'Rye was shut down for being near double its legal capacity.

The second time he left the store was to find his way to Fuck Point under cover of night, there finally to begin his nighttime surveillance of Mary Evens' property. With the night-vision scope at the ready, he spent an uncomfortable two hours peering down into the forest across the inlet, hoping for some flickering indication of her passage beneath the trees. There was no light from the bungalow, and he was ready to give up for the night, but before he packed the scope he swept toward the bungalow and quickly stopped at a dim blurred image. He raised his eyes excitedly from the scope to check the location, and it wasn't the bungalow; it was below the bungalow. There was warmth in the Cinnamon Cave! And then, by astonishing good luck, an indistinct moving shape formed in the cave's entrance, undoubtedly Mary Evens come to peer out into the pitch black night, to reveal without question where she had hidden his Drowned Maiden!

He spent the next twenty-four hours in a rapture of anticipation. He could guess how she'd done it, because the mythical brigadier was said to have installed a capstan to haul up supplies in case of a Russian or an American siege. But how she could have regular access to the cave was another matter, although one day some weeks ago he'd made out a slight discontinuous ledge leading from a declivity in the garden across the rock face to the cave. Possibly Mary was using it—she had unsuspected strengths as he'd discovered—but the mere thought of edging along such a toehold at night above a sheer hundred and fifty foot drop made him queasy. He had decided to rappel down to the opening from a solid-looking pine tree directly above it.

When he reached the edge of the cliff he secured a line to the tree and let himself slowly down the twenty feet to the cave opening. Once inside he could see dim angular shapes to his right that could be machinery; there were stories in the village of the general having mounted an old cannon to command the entrance to the fiord. The cave was about twenty feet wide and in places as much as seven feet high. He touched the ceiling with his hand, and brought down a small shower of sand. He saw no cannon, but there was a cast iron winch and a tangled pile of rope surrounded by a clutter of empty wooden packing boxes, broken chairs, a couple of old iron bedsprings, a rolled-up hammock, a cricket bat, all covered in the undisturbed dust of years.

The winch confirmed how she had brought up the body; the floor around it showed footprints and marks where the rope had been moved. But he wondered why anyone would haul broken chairs and bedsprings up from the forest below, let alone carry them over that suicidal path across the rock face.

He was in some kind of outer chamber; the cave narrowed to become a passage back into the rock, back surely to where she lay. He was tense; he had come to the end of his search, perhaps more accurately—in his present state of mind— a quest that stretched back beyond the past few weeks to include his lifetime. Off to his right he saw what he mistook at first for an empty sack flung against the wall, except half was in some striped material and the other half black, with what was definitely a skeletal hand protruding from what might be a sleeve. He gave it only a sidelong glance; the cave and his presence in it were already too unreal, his final goal too overwhelmingly near, to make the object remarkable. The flashlight in his hand was shaking; he turned it off.

He reached out to the nearby wall, breathing heavily. To be in control. To move with deliberate caution. He was moments away from a revelation of enormous profundity, the more consuming because he had no idea of its nature, nor how it would affect him. He moved forward determinedly and then checked; there was a sound in the darkness ahead. It was very faint, from a distance, gradually growing clearer but muffled in its confinement, until it became a voice, a tuneless sing-song, without question the voice of Mary Evens, her advance marked by a dim wavering light from deep in the cave.

He had been bloody stupid not to think of it before. The brigadier had been an engineer, a sapper; he had tunneled down from the bungalow to the cave. But Justin's attention remained fixed on the sing-song voice which—he'd pushed himself into a niche to be undetected—was now just around the corner from him. The voice had assumed a conversational earnestness, snatches of which he caught: " . . I had to come tonight, to tell you specially . . . . and they came today, just this afternoon, the dreadful little upstart Mr. Plantagenet, and his lawyer . . . . make it all official. They insisted I have a lawyer look over the documents but I told them I already had a lawyer living here who had given me the best of legal advice!"

So this was where Gwendoline had been brought, ready to be tucked in for the night. And now all was confirmed. Justin edged toward the voice, so conscious of the Drowned Maiden's closeness that Mary's conversation hardly registered, and the mention of Plantagenet—it sounded like Plantagenet—was so unlikely he was sure he'd misheard.

"I have been terribly clever," she was saying, "To renovate Mogador will cost him hundreds of thousands, and to maintain it and me forever will cost more, and all he is getting is acres of useless rock!"

She had trailed off into nonsense and Justin, increasingly impatient to see at long last his beloved Drowned Maiden, ignored the words and peered cautiously around the corner. Mary was about fifteen feet away, sitting in a wicker chair beside a wicker table, facing half away from him and holding a book.

There was an old kerosene lamp on the table casting deep shadows and silhouetting Mary against a strange glow mostly hidden by a bend in the passage.

She was saying, "Last time you remember it was chapter four, which is called 'In which Eeyore loses a tail and Pooh finds one', and I was where—wait a moment—was where Pooh has gone to Owl's house to ask Owl—he is the wise one, remember—how to go about finding Eeyore's tail. Now Owl asks Pooh if he saw the notices that Christopher Robin had made for Owl's front door, and you remember Pooh doesn't really hear what Owl is saying so he says no, and Owl takes him outside. Here we go then—"

She started reading, slowly and hesitantly, some children's story weirdly out of place in the shadowy cave about a conversation between an owl and someone called pooh, and Justin peered around the corner to see Mary bent over to the lamp holding a book close to her face. He grimaced in frustration, unable to move, wondering how long the story would go on and what his next move should be. A minute or two later, concentrating again on listening, he realized she had switched to the story of the three pigs; when he looked the wolf had just huffed and puffed to blow the straw house down and Mary exclaimed "Oh dear me, oh dear me!" as the lantern guttered.

Finally she yawned, stood up, put the book on the table, and then unexpectedly sat down as if to say more. He wanted her gone! If she would only go! This mad charade was irrelevant to his desperate need, which now possessed him so strongly that Mary Evens' presence seemed trivial. He was gripped by a trancelike urgency, and stepped from behind the rock into the lamplight.

He was unaware of making a noise, but she rose and turned, seeing him immediately. She said sharply, "What are you doing here? How did you get here? This is no place for you."

He hardly heard her, his attention consumed by what he could see lay beyond her, a dim refulgence, pale, marmoreal, an elegant, magnetic presence. It was the moment of revelation; Mary was a mere aggravation. He blurted, "I'm sorry, I didn't get that," shocked at his own apologetic tone, at how his goal's nearness was confusing him.

"I said get out!" Mary shouted suddenly. "Get out of this sacred place! You profane it, Mr. Fowles! You profane wherever I go."

He was transfixed by the small shrouded figure beyond her, which lay beneath a strange glowing mist sparkling with countless shimmering points of light. It made no sense. He had rehearsed a ringing peremptory demand for access to the victim of a murder but the resolve vanished in a mood of hesitant, almost pious expectation and he said quietly, "I intend no harm, Mrs. Evens. Ignore me. I'm not here to take her away. This is a personal thing. I'm not even sure what kind of personal thing. I'm sorry I can't explain any better. I simply have to see her again."

"Go!" she shouted, "Go! Go!" and then, changing her tone, "You surely notice the power of my love? It is my love, you see, that prevented her decay."

"Good God," Justin murmured, because there was indeed no stench of putrefaction, and that also made no sense, and he hadn't even noticed.

"I have saved her from being cut off in youth. It is something you reject, Mr. Fowles. But you persist in your claim on her. As an agent, I suppose, of the civil power? I cannot allow that. No! No! Here you must respect *my* authority."

He kept staring at the back of the cave, trying to understand what seemed to be an aura, a flickering mist of light around what he was almost sure was the bier. He said absently, "I'm making no claim on her, Mrs. Evens. And I'm nobody's agent. I suppose I'm searching for something. Have been searching. I'm not sure." He turned back to find her pointing the shotgun at him. He said impatiently, "Oh put that damn thing away!""

"I have the authority of death, Mr. Fowles."

"That's what you were saying in the ravine, wasn't it? Well to hell with your authority. Your idea of completion is crap, lady; it just means quitting. You want me to believe my life was rich and meaningful and above all cozy. And finished— " He glanced at the table, at the book. "I am experiencing a measure of decrepitude appropriate for my age, Mrs. Evens, but I'm not terminal. Perhaps that's why I'm here. Perhaps I am hoping she will make sense of it."

The gunshot in the confines of the cave was deafening. Stunned, his ears ringing, he automatically threw himself sideways onto the floor, and suddenly she was onto him, beating him about the head with such surprising force that he had to back away, using his arms to shield his head, shocked by her raw physical fury. He had a glimpse of her raging face—surely not faintly luminescent—and when for a moment he grasped her she wrenched herself away with astonishing quick strength.

She kept grunting, gasping, "Out you go. Out you go. Out. Out and down. Down into the pit! Yes down!" He tripped and fell backward, vaguely aware they were nearing the entrance. He was scrambling to his hands and knees when she leapt savagely onto him again, knocking him sideways to the floor. This time he managed to grasp the gun and shove the barrel away from them both, but she used it as a pivot to leap around him and attack from the other side, so that he had to grapple the gun in the opposite direction, kicking out with both feet against her, yanking the gun toward him just as it offered no resistance so that he was hurled backward smashing his injured shoulder against ragged stone as his finger caught the trigger and the second barrel fired deafeningly into the roof in a shower of dusty sand. He yelled at the pain but scrambled to his feet, tense for her next attack, peering through the dust and the shadows until he heard—what was it?—a groan, a gasp and turned to see at the cave's edge an indistinct movement of scaled clutching tentacles, to which he reacted compulsively as if to a huge insect in the act of some gross metamorphosis, smashing down on it with one furious blow of the gun stock.

He stood for nearly half a minute gasping for breath, bent forward with his hands on his knees, staring at the dark night framed in the wide maw of the cave, not believing it had happened, too battered to feel anything but relief. Still breathing heavily, he shuffled cautiously to the edge of the cave and looked down into the abyss. There was nothing to see, and no sound but the wind and the rain now falling heavily in the trees. Down into the pit. A hundred and fifty feet, straight down. His mind was still full of the fight itself; that it was over and that he had killed her seemed less than real.

He walked unsteadily back into the cave. He knew he wasn't thinking clearly, or perhaps thinking at all. He picked up Mary's lamp from the table and searched for his glasses. They lay near a rusting flat tin cigarette box, what used to be called a flat fifty. Miraculously, the lenses were unbroken although the tines were bent.

Now that he could see better, he brought the lamp very slowly and cautiously toward the pale form on the stone slab. The tiny lights that hovered over her were scores of sequins and the reflective eyes of minute but strangely threatening plastic insects suspended in a swathe of spun glass.

Half a dozen votive candles edged the bier, forming a border for a jumble of toy animals; a teddy bear, a Mickey Mouse, a leering raccoon, some My Little Ponies and Barbie Dolls, a vivid orange dinosaur. The toys from Sears that Maggie Pollock had reported. There was a small space creature with huge eyes, grinning up from behind the thigh in guilty surprise as if caught eating dead flesh. Garlands woven of wild flowers, wilted now, lay across the body, and wedged in its fingers a little china or rubber bird or perhaps a fetus. The base of the bier was piled with wilted leaves, as if dumped by the basketful from the summer just passing.

He finally forced himself to look directly down at the body, still braced for some transcending sensation, of youth regained, of ideals affirmed, of reconciliation, but with growing doubts. Despite the dim light he could see her more clearly than on the beach, but her skin was as smooth and pale as he recalled, and the staring eyes as vividly green. There was a faint suggestion of cheap perfume. He grimaced at the awful smear of lipstick across her mouth and the patches of cosmetic colour around the eyes. But there was certainly no decay.

He reached out gingerly and touched the nearest arm above the elbow. The rubbery flesh was firm; it yielded and expanded again when he released his grip. "Shit!" he muttered. He gripped the forearm and pulled it cautiously toward him; it moved with wiry reluctance, and he thought he heard a metallic click at the shoulder; when he let go it remained rigidly suspended. He bent close to the hand and pinched; it was so elegantly like human skin that he couldn't tell the difference.

He stepped back several paces and stared at the thing. Nothing was to be as expected, nothing was as it seemed. He was still in shock from the fight, but this abomination made his confusion absolute. He suddenly found himself laughing, at the bizarre absurdity of it, at his own witlessness, but the humour drained away even as he continued laughing, leaving him with a terrible emptiness, at everything having come to nothing, at whatever he had sought, whatever pursued, come to this ridiculous, cunningly-contrived plastic monstrosity.

Dazed, half-unbelieving, he approached the bier again, bent over and touched the rigid arm again, grasping it, letting go. And he had of course believed, let himself believe or perhaps refused in his gullible subconscious to disbelieve that in some metaphysical way the Drowned Maiden embodied all things possible, the fulfillment of all that never was or could be except in a man's dying heart.

He turned away, baffled. He started to walk unsteadily around the vault in pain and distraction, covering his face with his hands, not thinking where he was going so that he collided violently with the rock wall just as he discovered his left hand was slippery with blood. He stared at the rock, trying to collect himself, absently tracing the blood to a gash above his ear, then turned slowly back to the bier.

A thing of plastic, and he'd never twigged. He noticed the tiny stuffed bird-thing wedged crudely under the plastic hand at her breast, and a fragmentary thought of Justine hovered a moment, faded. Somewhere in that awful night at sea the burdens he'd carried had been swept away, but now there was to be no redemption.

He felt betrayed, even knowing that no one had asked for his trust or his loyalty, even realizing dimly that it was he who had betrayed himself. Or more realistically he'd simply tricked himself in believing there had to be more to redemption than facing down an overweight American evangelist in a clown suit amidst the rape and plunder of a burning city. Allowing of course for his habitual hyperbole. But the betrayal burst upon him in sudden rage at the pile of cheap trash before him. He grabbed the netting with its freight of spangles and tinsel and ripped it away. It was connected with or tucked under the mannequin itself, so that the whole garish display tumbled about his feet, with various pieces tinkling and clattering away over the rocky floor. He grasped the mannequin by its hair in his good hand and brought its staring eyes level with his own and kissed its cold stained mouth before hurling it in self-disgust against the wall.

He was having difficulty breathing. He was straining to both inhale and exhale, and he realized the effort was not to breathe but to hold in check the emotion rising within him, which finally engulfed him in a great wave of the sharpest melancholy, of grief and disappointment and failure. It was of such power that it blotted out all physical sensation, and he was only half aware of being forced to his knees by the weight of agony in his heart, of his knees giving way so that he collapsed to a sitting position on the floor, tears pouring from his eyes, gasping for each breath in a flood of tears, totally bewildered.

The pain in his soul was so acute that it overcame his self-control, and he was without any sense of space or direction or of the passage of time. He lay on the floor weeping, breathless, vaguely aware that his leg was jerking and he couldn't stop it and knowing he was committing other involuntary acts of which he was even less aware, gripping his head in his arms, hammering on the stone floor with his fist, glaring wide-eyed at the blurred roof of the tomb, howling. Strange dim discontinuous images of remorse and infinite loss loomed and dissolved, images of youth, of a white CPR Empress ten days out of Tokyo steaming through a yet-unbridged Lion's Gate, of the smell of spices and fish along Water Street by the docks, of a flight of the first Hawker Hurricanes booming across the sky above Point Grey, of standing in the north Ontario snow talking to a major of the Luftwaffe, of spring mornings so mild, so full of bird-song and so rich in golden promise that his young soul had soared. All lost and gone.

He gradually regained some semblance of equilibrium. His face was drenched in tears, and he was still gasping for breath, but he could pull himself up to a sitting position on the stone floor. He was bewildered by the strength of his emotions, sitting amidst a jumble of sequined netting, dried flowers, assorted toys and wreathes woven of leafless twigs, from beyond which the mannequin seemed to be staring past him in uncomfortable disbelief. A single votive candle remained lit, flung on its side against the wall to his left.

He stood up, slowly, clenching his teeth at the pain of joint and ligament that had invaded his body. He was weak and a little dizzy, and had to steady himself against the wall. Standing there, looking down at the wreckage he had created, he was filled with utmost desolation.

19

He drove at once to Annabel. He drove through the rain, wildly, cursing each lurch and slide, his head in and out the window because the wiper was broken. He had to see her because she was his only human contact. He had no idea what he would say, what claim to advance. He hit a puddle which drenched the windshield and he had to stop. He beat his hands on the wheel, groaning from the pain in his shoulder, in his heart, until he could see the road again. Perhaps the only claim—which wasn't a claim at all—was that he couldn't face the prospect of solitude.

He had to knock three times between long pauses before she came to the door, in her dressing gown. She looked shocked when she saw him. "Justin—what in the—Oh my God Justin! You're bleeding! Don't stand out there!" She led him to the kitchen, repeating, "What happened? Justin dear what—?"

He was incapable of spontaneous reply. It wasn't until he was sitting in the kitchen, with Annabel studying his bloodied head, that he managed to say, "It looks more dramatic than it is. I'm sorry if I woke you. I am not thinking too clearly. I thought you'd still be up. It's much later than I thought."

"Justin you didn't wake me, but come to the point—!"

"I believe I collided with— a hostile rock. You see, she did take the body. It's in the Cinnamon Cave. So I was not hallucinating, as you slanderously proclaimed to the world." He told her he had found Mary Evens reading to a decomposing corpse, unable to admit to the Drowned Maiden, or that she was plastic. He couldn't stop shivering, and his attention kept wandering so that he was not sure that he was being too coherent. He said, "Yes. There was sweet Gwendoline, quietly rotting in the basement apartment."

"I knew she was lying, the poor old thing."

Justin said, "Poor old thing my ass. The poor old idiot tried to blow me away. This time it wasn't a warning shot. She was aiming for my balls."

"Justin!"

The fact that he had killed her seemed not to bear on the present, and to mention it would in any event frustrate what he had dimly in mind. Annabel's dear voice was so sweetly familiar that he could almost forget they'd parted, even though much of him was still back in the cave, and perhaps he should go somewhere and sleep, to clear his mind, to overcome the desolation he was feeling. But it struck him suddenly how monstrously she had put upon him and he shouted,

"So you knew she was lying? And you treated me like shit for gallantly searching the high seas for my immaculate Drowned Maiden—"

"Immaculate *what?*"

"Yes alone on the vast Pacific! And all the time you knew she was lying! You've ignored me for weeks and all the time you knew I was telling the truth."

She shut her eyes wearily for a moment and said in a flat, pleading voice, "Please, dear. It's more than that—"

"I've just had some kind of breakdown. You may take that as one of my normal manipulations, but I am simply stating fact. Something shifted in my head. I bawled for what must have been half an hour. It was truly absurd. I was out of control."

"Justin dear," she said anxiously, impatient at his bluster, "You've been injured. There's a hell of a lot of blood. You've got to have this looked at." She had filled a bowl with water and began to wipe the blood from his head and arm. She said, "This is buckshot for Christ's sake!"

"No you are being sweet but I will see to that later. It isn't important at this stage of the story. Nor is it important that she tried to kill me. Those are matters which will be referred in due course to Constable Ymenko. Indeed. Yes!" He winced as she touched his head. But he knew clearly now his impossible need, what had never occurred to him before and yet was suddenly of desperate urgency and he blurted, unable to plan any preparation, knowing he was being absurd but forced by his desolate heart, "I want us to get married."

She stood up, the bloody washcloth in her hand, watching him with what he thought hopefully was tender concern. Her eyes were filling with tears.

He said, "You react as if you'd caught me in an unnatural act."

She took a deep breath and clasped her dressing gown around her and said, "Justin dear, we've been so open with each other. But a lot has happened. And, well, I haven't been doing too well." She shrugged. "To tell you the truth the last couple of weeks have been quite dreadful. But I've come through it, and to skip the sordid details, I'm leaving Prospect. I'm going back. To work."

He was stunned. He burst out, uncontrolled, a wild shout— "Oh no! No!"

To whatever extent his befuddlement made coherence possible he was ready to advance his suit against the imposter Plantagenet or even her indifference, but her departure was beyond imagining. "No you can't possibly! You're not ready. I have just had this experience—"

"Justin dear the last time we met you'd just had two experiences. You didn't want to talk about them. You said you were working through them. Is this a different experience?"

She seemed vaguely, irritatingly amused. He said, "I am filled with the most awful sense of desolation. This awful feeling. I am turning to you because you are the only one I can turn to. I am *possessed* by this awful feeling—" He was repeating himself, and shook his head "—of, well—"

She took his hand gently and led him into the living room and sat him down on the couch. The room—he hadn't noticed—was piled with cardboard packing boxes. She said, "You poor histrionic dear, you're absolutely beat, aren't you. But it's probably good for you, Justin, to stop pretending you're the invulnerable Horseman. I'll get tea."

"No I don't want tea," he cried petulantly. "It's all very well to be sweet and kind to me, which rekindles hope. When you've decided to leave forever."

She held his wrist and said affectionately, "I want to tell you something, because I'm truly grateful to you. The other night you went out alone into a riot and put it down. You were brave and modest and decent. You were so brave and decent that it suddenly, I don't know, illuminated I guess, the mess I'd got myself into. I knew I wasn't being decent and I wasn't being brave, and you showed me the way."

"How you could run away? How can you sit there—"

"Justin stop it! Don't be a dork. I'm not running anywhere. It's the old tired story, about finding out the only person who could help me was me. Maybe I leaned too much on you in the process, I don't know. But we had fun. And now I know I'm ready to go back. And you gave me the final push to get on my own feet again."

"This is indeed a night of triumph," he said mordantly. "I have restored you to your feet, so you can move on. The Prince of Muck didn't measure up, eh?"

She took her hand off his wrist and put it slowly to her face. "I'm sorry Justin. I didn't have the guts to tell you. I finally got up the nerve, but that was the night of the riot. It's no good now saying sorry, but I am wretched about it. I still feel wretched about it."

"I can imagine," he said sarcastically, angrily. "Sure, wretched. Give me a break. Wretched every time he mounted you, I bet. Is his prong as big as they say? Can he ride all night?" He saw he was hurting her, which was satisfying. "How can you exchange that sweaty monosyllabic embrace for barren Toronto, eh? So is it to be Mrs. Plantagenet, or do you have some more convenient arrangement?"

She broke in, abruptly cold: "Cut it out. We had a very limited commitment and you know it. And we've hardly spoken for over a month. I'm not proud of how I've behaved, but don't take it too—"

He put up a cautionary hand. "Spare me! There's no need." He remained as numb as when he'd arrived, her presence warming only an edge of his consciousness, while all behind was glacial solitude.

"You need to rest dear."

"I undoubtedly need to rest, but on the other hand I have acquired this horror of being alone. I don't want to freeze to death alone beside an Arctic river."

"Justin you are a charming man and dear to me but—"

"I know. But now you are healed. Ha!" He stood up shakily.

"You shouldn't be driving around in the state you're in. Stay here the night. Please. Let me look after you."

She touched his arm with what he could interpret bitterly as fondness, and he said, "Eh, there's irony there, eh? No I must go. I must go search somewhere for my permanent, orthodox, immutable love!"

"Justin, get real dear. There's no such thing."

He chuckled. "At last he found reality, and it was plastic. Shit!" He lurched across the living room, toward the corridor to the front door, and only then noticed the printing on the packing boxes—*San Francisco.*

"San Francisco? San Francisco?" He had been shockingly deceived. "You're going to San Francisco? You never said anything about San Francisco. What the hell—"

"Oh dear," said Annabel. " I didn't mean to mislead you. Honestly. I arrived here from Pittsburgh, if you must know, but the States was part of my trauma. I never wanted to live there again or talk about being there. And then when I learnt how you felt about America, I just didn't want the ranting. And San

Francisco is because they want me to open an office there."

Nothing was as it had seemed. He was truly alone, abandoned in the glacial night. He stared at her, full of rage.

She said, "Justin for God's sake. It's not consorting with an enemy. They're not extra-terrestials. They're people with normal human feelings and needs and—Damn it, why am I on the defensive against your bloody anti-Americanism?"

"Why indeed?" He shouted. "Do you know? It's because—amazing, my politics or your distorted take on them are now as irrelevant as Scrofula. my termagant cat. Because I have passed through the portals of Peggy Karlsrue, keeper of the gates of aging. But Grandmother Death is no more! I can too seldom get it up, and am blurred of vision and various joints and connective tissues are failing to respond with their accustomed speed. And now I have lost you—"

"Justin be realistic. I'm not alone in the world. If you ever had any interest in the children you'd know how important they are to me. This is what I need for them. This is—"

He had to get out the house before he started to scream or break into tears again, or whatever was necessary to express the emptiness in his heart. He shoved the door open and walked out into the rain without any sense of sad parting, without any desire for one last embrace.

He would do anything to escape the aching desolation. There was a place on the East Ridge with a two-hundred foot drop where the dark night would receive him. He drove down the highway in a half-conscious fog, dimly remembered there was a turn off and slowed, thought he saw the painted tree and wrenched the wheel over but he was still going much too fast and the truck crashed into the brush and rolled, wedging itself on its side between two trees, the windshield showering broken glass.

Cursing, too befogged to think, he dragged himself out of the wreckage and pushed through the tangled undergrowth searching in the dark for the trail up the slope. Eventually he found a track that was unfamiliar but led upward and he followed it, his hands in front of him to avoid the branches. He had to stop several times to catch his breath, but finally he came out of the trees and onto the grassy rock. The wind had got up, and he had to press against it as he reached the top of the ridge.

He stood there, breathing hard. Boiling clouds rushed overhead, and to the west streamers of lighter cloud parted to reveal dark avenues twisting into edifices rising and collapsing and obscured again by the rolling streamers, through which he saw for an instant a horseman and a small portly companion hurled across the sky, to pass behind black columns and then to emerge and suddenly—virtually in his face—to explode in a blinding, deafening fork of lightning.

The shock knocked him off his feet. He scrambled up defiantly, overwhelmed by the majestic symbolism of it all. It would be his one last gesture of defiance. To prove his soul unconquerable. He shouted into the storm, "It is time! It is inescapable fate! It had all the promise of an heroic voyage! An epic! But it has come to this!"

He stood at the edge of the cliff and looked down to find the village hidden in the teeming blackness. The isolation was so insupportably heavy that he thought himself stooped. He straightened himself and stretched out his arms to fly. He would rise like Icarus into the receiving night, rise unburdened in a triumphant soaring arc, and then falter, at the trembling nadir, and like a rock be hurled everlastingly—and all unnoticed—down.

Yet he was not sure. He walked back from the edge and sat down. The storm was passing. He sat on the wet grass staring westward until the last fragments of the turbulent clouds past over him, leaving the sky clear. There was the thin crescent of a new moon. He recalled looking up at the night sky as a child. If he looked long enough he became filled with the wonder of his own infinitesimal smallness in a universe of infinite magnitude. But now, as a few lights became visible in the fugitive village below, as the dark battlements of the Olympics loomed dimly to the south, he knew he was nothing. It was all over, and he had accomplished nothing, and the wonder had gone. The wars had meant nothing. The victories had meant nothing. And if he were to jump, it would also mean nothing, one way or the other.

The voice behind him shouted, "Justin!"

He turned, not believing it possible. "Who the hell are you? What the hell are you doing here?"

"Annabel phoned. She guessed you'd come here." It was the Lady Jane's voice.

"Annabel," he said sarcastically. "How solicitous of her. But the plot has become clear. I have sought Annabel's hand in marriage and have been rejected. She's been humping the loathsome Plantagenet and is about to leave for the gilded empire of G. Myron Resnick. The Drowned Maiden, icon of my somewhat questionable salvation, has turned out to be a plastic joke. Mary Evens is dead. Our revels, as someone wrote, are petering out."

" Annabel says you're wounded."

"Mary Evens got in one last shot. It was in the Cinnamon Cave, and she came at me with her shotgun to defend the honour of her Gwendoline. I'm still not sure what happened. It was too dark, but for a moment her tentacles were clinging to the edge, some horror I had to crush before it got a foothold. But I have lost Annabel."

"I'm sorry about you and Annabel. You were good together. But Justin dear be realistic, she's young enough to be your daughter. She has her future to find."

"No I don't blame her." He shook his head because he did blame her. "It's just that tonight I have discovered a great need for companionship. Maybe love. I speak theoretically, being at the moment bereft of such emotions. My current emotions are dread and loss. I had this ill-founded belief that she could rescue me from this desolation She is I am sure capable of many more million-dollar lyrics. I may not look it, but I am utterly fucked. I feel my major arteries have been cut, in my thighs perhaps. The femoral arteries? A terrible sense of life draining away."

"Well actually you do look utterly fucked."

"It is in any case irrelevant. I tell you I'm emptied." He knew he was rambling, but was grateful for her patience. "You see it has been a night of deconstruction. One aspect of which is she has revealed that her true allegiance is to the enemy."

"Don't be ridiculous! You take your nationalism too far."

"It is my life!"

"Oh come on, dear old friend! You really are too much. Such a dramatic flair, the old chap has, even in extremis! Your life was a lot more than a couple of years in Quebec."

"Ha," he snorted caustically. "Then engage me in discourse on the meaning of life. You are ageless, and have seen maybe a thousand generations, and therefore should know—"

"Well I *don't* know. You're being impossible, sweet lad. There are no answers. And besides, as you've possibly noticed, I am only a kind of chorus but quite inadequate in the action because I lack human sensibility. I can't for instance offer you the love you need."

He said, "You see it should be possible now for me to go on, relatively cleansed of guilt, and having overcome death. But I know I can't."

"Justin just go on being yourself. You know how to enjoy life. You are a help to people, and people enjoy your company. What makes it so necessary to botch the whole thing by wanting more? Transcendence is smoke and mirrors, didn't you know? The people who think the essence of life is in death deal in metaphor and sham. By the way, when you came to offer your condolences about the fire marshal the other day, you never said a word about what happened in the village. I hear you were magnificent. I mean you saved the place; could anyone else have done that? And you came out of the closet, tunic and stetson and all! Someone said you quelled them by mere force of will. "

He felt a moment of lightness revived. "Yeah, it was mostly arrogance, I think. The force of hubris."

The Lady Jane smiled and shook her head. "Your little friend Milton Milton still bugs you, eh? You're a bit pompous at times, and more than a bit theatrical, but I don't think of you as arrogant."

"Maybe the word I'm looking for is *hauteur.* Maybe that's what turned off Annabel. Ha! —there's a quality the hairy Plantagenet could hardly boast of! Yes, *hauteur!*" He felt a flicker of animation within him. "It has style."

"Oh Justin, it's time for new beginnings! God, I've never seen you so down. Oh you are just too much! Come on, you old fool. We can be ageless together. Life is good, I tell you. Life is good."

He stood looking down at the ground. There was relief in talking to her, but it was troubling. He said sadly, "I know what you're saying, and it's thoughtful. But my head is utterly fucked. This sensation of draining, or maybe I told you? I had it once when German shrapnel opened—" he checked himself, remembering Joanne dead in Africa—"Terrible sensation of the soul draining away."

"Man, forget your fucking soul and come back to my pub. It's miserable up here, or did you notice? We'll sit and talk a while. Get drunk and see what the morning brings. There's lots of room upstairs. A little sleep can make the world a different place and it'll be a beautiful morning now the front's gone by."

"I know what you're doing. Talking the suicide down. Standard procedure. But you won't win because I know all about it. You are subverting my destiny! It is inescapable fate!" This time the words were empty, but he persisted, "You are denying me an exit on a heroic scale."

"No one would see anything heroic in your corpse at the bottom of the cliff. Justin your trouble is you've always been a cop. The umpire who's got to live a little apart. Isn't that it? Up there in the saddle, the Horseman? It's time to dismount, Justin, and live among the ordinary people."

"I am not pretending to be anything else."

"So you did the right things. You went where you were sent. Didn't I read somewhere you were shot up?"

"Hell, I'd forgotten about that. He was just a kid. He was so upset seeing me bleeding he cried!"

"So?"

"Maybe I just hoped for more."

"More is killing yourself?"

He stared down at the village for a long moment. The lights actually seemed to beckon. He turned back from the cliff and walked to her and she held out her hand and he grasped it. It was as cold as ice, but he supposed she was right.

END

ISBN 141201454-9

9 781412 014540